"*The Red Door Inn* by Liz Johnson took my breath away! The Prince Edward Island setting hooked me from the beginning, and the compelling characters and vivid writing kept me binge reading until the book was finished. These characters are as memorable as the ones in *Anne of Green Gables*. Highly recommended!"

— **Colleen Coble**, author of *The Inn at Ocean's Edge* and the Hope Beach series

"Liz Johnson is a rock-solid writer. Any book by my friend Liz will be creative, well researched, and intriguing. I have worked closely with her for many years and endorse her heartily."

— **Max Lucado**, *New York Times* bestselling author and pastor

"A charming inn in need of restoration, Prince Edward Island, and a love story? Yes, please! In *The Red Door Inn*, Liz Johnson crafts a story about new beginnings and fresh hope. I thoroughly enjoyed this first novel in her new series and the vicarious visit it offered me to the Canadian Maritime Province of Prince Edward Island. I could almost feel the sea breeze!"

— **Becky Wade**, author of the Porter Family series

THE
RED
DOOR
INN

A NOVEL

Liz Johnson

R
Revell
a division of Baker Publishing Group
Grand Rapids, Michigan

Published by Revell
a division of Baker Publishing Group
P.O. Box 6287, Grand Rapids, MI 49516-6287
www.revellbooks.com

Printed in the United States of America

Library of Congress Cataloging-in-Publication Data
Names: Johnson, Liz, 1981– author.
Title: The Red Door Inn : a novel / Liz Johnson.
Description: Grand Rapids, MI : Revell, a division of Baker Publishing Group, 2016.
    | ?2015 | Series: Prince Edward Island dreams ; book 1
Identifiers: LCCN 2015037052 | ISBN 9780800724023 (softcover)
Subjects: LCSH: Bed and breakfast accommodations—Fiction. | Man-woman
    relationships—Fiction. | GSAFD: Christian fiction. | Love stories.
Classification: LCC PS3610.O3633 R43 2016 | DDC 813/.6—dc23 LC record
    available at http://lccn.loc.gov/2015037052

Published in association with Books & Such Literary Management.

17   18   19   20   21   22   7   6   5   4   3   2

For Twila, Hannah, and Julia,
who helped me uncover the hidden
treasures of the Gentle Island.

◆◆◆◆◆

And for the people of PEI,
who so generously share the joy of the
island with visitors like me.

1

The change in Marie Carrington's pocket wouldn't pay for a ferry ride across the Northumberland Strait to Prince Edward Island, let alone a bus ticket to anywhere else in the world. As she cupped the Canadian dollar coins in her shaking hand, they clinked together, drawing the curious gaze of the man in the seat next to her.

Marie shifted on the painful plastic chair, putting her shoulder between all the money she had access to in the world and the gaze shrouded by bushy, white eyebrows.

Two. Four. Five. Six. Seven. Seven twenty-five.

The sign on the café attached to the ferry terminal announced a fish sandwich lunch special for $6.99, but tax would be more than a quarter. Besides, that would completely wipe her out. And then she'd be penniless in a strange town.

"Which color do you like better?" The man with the eyebrows and more wrinkles than she'd ever seen on one face leaned forward, holding out four paint swatches.

Marie rotated farther away from him, shoving her coins back in her pocket, but he didn't seem to notice.

"My wife liked the pale blue, but I think we need something brighter for the shutters of a bed-and-breakfast. Don't you?"

She couldn't fight the urge to survey the swatches, even if just out of the corner of her eye. With one finger she twisted the necklace at her throat, imagining each color on the front of a robust, two-story Maritime home.

He dipped his chin as though waiting for her answer. "Well? Don't you think it's too light?"

Finally she whispered, "Unless the house is a deep blue." Keeping an eye on him, she scooted to the far edge of her seat, the armrest digging into her side as she bent to scoop her backpack into the safety of her lap.

"What?" His eyebrows nearly reached his hairline. Pulling his glasses from his front shirt pocket and planting them on his face, he held the color swatch in question to within an inch of his nose, mumbling her words over and over. "Deep blue. The house could be deep blue."

After several seconds of peace, she decided he'd forgotten all about her until he flipped the same blue color swatch over her shoulder and pointed to the darkest hue on the row. "Is that dark enough?"

"No."

"Then what would be?"

Shoulder still in place, she pointed with her other hand to the blue of his pants. "Maybe with a hint of gray mixed in."

Holding the color card against a handful of jean fabric, he nodded slowly. "That might work. But not too much gray." He scratched his chin, his whiskers rasping beneath aged fingers. "What about the trim? Would you do the same color as the shutters?"

"It depends."

"On what?"

"Lots of things. What do the neighboring houses look like? Do you have other colors around the house?"

"Like what?"

She relaxed her back a fraction of an inch so that she didn't have to strain her neck to watch his reactions. "Maybe a flower garden or water feature. If you already have several other colors, keep the trim and shutters the same color or the house can look disjointed and unappealing."

"Never thought of having a flower garden." He poked his tongue into his cheek, staring at the color cards as though they'd failed him. "Suppose women might like that."

"Men too."

He raised one of his bushy brows at her.

"Really."

"Well, if I have to have flowers and a red door, I suppose the shutters and trim should be one color."

"Why a red door?" Marie hadn't asked a voluntary question in two months, but this one just slipped out before she could clamp her hand over her mouth.

The old man didn't seem to notice her surprise. Instead, lost in the colors in his hands, he cleared his throat. "We visited the island for the first time fifteen years ago, and the red doors captured her imagination. She said we had to have a red door. There was no argument. No discussion, only—"

"The nine thirty ferry will begin boarding shortly." The voice of the announcer echoed over the tinny intercom. "All passengers please make your way to the boarding area and have your ticket in hand."

The old man shuffled his cards and tucked them into his

pocket before slipping one arm into his oversized coat. He reached for and missed the other arm twice before Marie set her bag back on the floor, stood, and held the jacket open for him. "Thank you."

She nodded and slipped back into her seat, fighting the urge to hug her knees to her chest and let the tears roll. She could sit here for hours, but it wouldn't make the money she needed appear. She'd never have enough for the ferry traveling north. She couldn't come up with the sixteen dollars to keep moving.

"Aren't you going on the boat?"

He wasn't from New England or the Canadian Maritimes. Any self-respecting man from that area would know it was a ship or a ferry, not a boat.

"No." Her fingers brushed over her pocket and the outline of her meager funds pressing through the black corduroy.

His eyebrows pulled into a V that looked like a single angry caterpillar. "Have some more ideas to ask you about."

She looked anywhere but into his ice-blue eyes, her gaze finally resting on the posted ferry schedule above the ticket counter. "I'm not going to Prince Edward Island today." If she was honest with herself, she probably wasn't ever going to make it to PEI. More than likely she'd have to call her father back in Boston and face him, no matter how much she hated that.

"Don't you want to go to the island?"

Her laugh was more stinging than humorous, even to her own ears. Of course she wanted to go to the island. Of course she wanted to keep putting more and more distance between her and her past.

She'd grown up reading books set on the island, dreaming of finding a home there. She'd even managed to squeeze one of her favorites by the island's beloved author into her backpack. Of course, the corners were bent and the edges worn, but she'd never loved the book or the dream of the island any more than she did sitting just a few miles away.

Of course she wanted to go to the island.

But wanting wouldn't get her more than a toe in the icy water.

"I don't have a ticket."

"That all? I'll get you a ticket."

She shook her head, swallowing the hint of hope that was quickly coupled with certain disappointment. "Thank you, no. I can't accept."

But he was halfway to the counter already, spreading the mouth of his cracked wallet and pulling a colorful bill from within. He said something to the raven-haired ticket agent, who tipped her head to shoot a curious glance around his arm.

Grabbing her bag, Marie jumped to her feet. If she were lucky, a wave would crash into the building, sweeping her away. Away from prying eyes and inquiring stares. Away from old men who asked too many questions. Away from that ever-present emptiness.

But luck wasn't on her side.

A familiar tightness rose in her chest, and she gasped for even the shallowest breath.

Oh, not again! Not with an audience and no place to lie down.

She tried to fill her lungs as a band squeezed around them. The ground shifted, her whole world tilting as she stumbled toward the chair she had just vacated. Squeezing her eyes shut against the black spots that danced in the edges of her line of sight, she leaned forward, fighting for a breath. Pain shot down the middle of her chest, but no amount of rubbing soothed the throbbing.

She was going to pass out in front of everyone.

A hand grabbed her forearm, and she jerked away from the searing touch. "You getting sick?"

The old man's now familiar voice made his hand on her shoulder barely tolerable, but she couldn't fight the blaze in her chest enough to get the air needed to reply. Finally, she wiggled her head, her hair swiping across her shoulders.

"You sure?" His hands guided her all the way into the chair, his breath warm on her face as he sat beside her. "You look a little green. And we're not even on the water yet."

Shaking her head again, she gasped, this time rewarded with a loosening in her lungs. They weren't full, but the relief lessened the spinning in her head and the pain at her sternum. She arched her back and again managed a wheeze.

"Now boarding the nine thirty ferry to Wood Islands. All ticketed passengers should be in the boarding area." They both turned toward the girl in the fleece vest holding the microphone.

"Can you make it to the boat?"

Marie blinked into the wrinkled face, pinning her gaze on a particularly deep crevice between the corner of his eye and his jawline. "Going to miss . . ."

"Well then, let's get on there before they leave us behind." He held out a ticket, the white slip contrasting his tanned, weathered fingers. "Take this."

"Can't." The ticket didn't budge. Had he not heard? Or had the words not passed her lips?

Finally he squatted before her with an unusual agility for a man his age. "Why not?"

She couldn't possibly repay him. She had no money. At least none that she could access without drawing undue attention. But she wasn't so low that she had to accept charity.

Another pang seared her heart.

Well, maybe she was.

He shot a glance toward the entrance to the ferry boarding area. "If you don't use this ticket, it'll just go to waste."

"I don't even know your name."

The lines around his mouth grew deeper, his eyes catching a shimmer from the ceiling lights. "Jack Sloane from . . . well, I suppose I'm from North Rustico, PEI, now."

"Marie." Twisting her hands into the hem of her sweater, she continued, the words barely making it to her own ears. "I can't pay for it."

"Didn't ask you to, Marie." He winked at her, adding in a conspiratorial whisper, "I'll make you a trade. The ticket for your help in picking out paint colors."

The attack had left her too weak to argue, but the trade was certainly in her favor. "All right." She dismissed his outstretched hand, and they stood together, his knees creaking like the old screen door at her father's beach house.

When she slipped her fingers around the ticket, it fluttered like a flag caught in an ocean breeze, and she clutched it to her chest, finally catching a full breath.

But could he really expect so little in return?

◆◆◆◆◆

"What color would you call that?" Jack gestured to the point where the open sea met the roiling gray clouds.

Marie squinted in the direction of his finger, hugging that silly pink bag to her chest but finally breathing normally. He'd been afraid she wouldn't make it onto the ferry, the way she'd been gasping for air, but she'd refused his arm as they boarded. And the salty sea air turned her pale cheeks pink like his wife's favorite flower.

After several long seconds, she shrugged one shoulder. "I don't know."

"Sure is pretty." She nodded slowly, thoughtfully, as she leaned back against the railing, tucking her chin again into her chest, nearly hidden behind the bag that was just about half her size. The pack wasn't so big, really. She was just a wisp of a creature. "You think I could paint the house that color?"

Without turning toward the sky again, she whispered, "I think it'd be perfect."

"Even with a red door."

"Especially with a red door." She offered him a tiny lift of the corner of her mouth, an obligatory smile. But she didn't mean it. He had a hunch she'd be a stunner if she really smiled, which she hadn't all morning. Not even when he pointed out the Caribou Lighthouse as they headed into open water. Rose had always smiled at the little lighthouse, delighted by the red roof.

"Maybe we should buy a lighthouse and become light keepers," his Rose would muse, leaning into his embrace.

"And give up on the bed-and-breakfast?" He only said it to watch her forehead wrinkle in distaste. "I'd be happy to take up light keeping, if you really want."

Rose had laughed and smacked his arm. "No so fast, Mr. Sloane. You aren't getting off the hook that easy."

Even after forty-one years, he'd loved it when she called him Mr. Sloane. Without fail it was accompanied by a twinkle in her eyes that reminded him of the day they'd met. The day he'd fallen in love with her.

But there wasn't a twinkle in Marie's eyes. They eclipsed her face, blue and haunted, as she gazed at the deck. Free of humor and good spirits, they made his heart ache.

What between here and heaven had caused such a pretty little thing to be so sad?

"So what brings you to the island?"

She turned those anxious eyes on him and without a hint of irony said, "You."

She may not have meant it to be funny, but he couldn't keep the laughter inside, letting the mirth roll from deep in his belly. Marie's eyes remained fixed on him, but she didn't say anything more. "You're quick, aren't you?" One bony shoulder poked up, and she wrapped a finger around the gold chain at her neck, twirling it. "I meant, why are you headed to PEI?"

She turned away from him, putting her shrugging shoulder between them before whispering, "In the books I read as a child, it sounded like a magical place." Her head turned farther away from Jack, as though she were looking back at the gray horizon, but she'd closed her eyes, taking deep breaths through her nose and releasing them slowly through tight lips.

"Where are you staying?"

His gut flipped when she didn't answer him, and he knew. She didn't have sixteen dollars to buy a ferry ticket. She didn't have two pennies to rub together. She didn't have a soul to ask for help or anyplace to go.

As if sitting on his other side, Rose whispered in his ear,

"It's a fine how-do-you-do when you can't help someone in need, Jack. Give the poor girl a place to stay."

Of course, Rose didn't bother with any particulars. She never had. Always a big-picture thinker, she wasn't concerned with the details. But Marie wasn't going to accept anything else for free. She'd fought him on the ferry ticket. What would she say about a room at his inn?

"They sure don't make these benches for seventy-two-year-old backsides." He shifted, relieving pressure from a sore spot and, in the meantime, leaning closer to her.

Marie nodded, but her shoulder dipped enough that he could see her whole face.

Apparently, if he wanted more of a response from her, he was going to have to ask direct questions. "How'd you get to know so much about colors and paint and stuff?"

Several seconds ticked by, the only sounds the hum of the ferry's motor and the squawking of a lone gull. "I took—" Her voice broke, and she had to clear her throat before she could continue. "I took a few art classes in college after a friend showed me a few things."

"You must have been pretty talented. Ever consider a career in it?"

"That wasn't really an option."

"Why not?" That barrier jumped into place again, and he tossed a less invasive question her way. "Do you know anything about decorating?"

"A bit."

He scrubbed his chin, rasping his fingernails over his whiskers, and let his eyes grow bigger as though just thinking of something. "Say, you wouldn't be available to help me with a project, would you?"

The girl could teach a college course in shrugging. One for every occasion, but this one most likely meant she wasn't going to commit to anything without more information. She might be broke, but she wasn't desperate.

Jack nodded slowly, rubbing his hands together, for the first time realizing that the kid didn't have more than a light jacket to ward off the damp chill of the late winter air. Maybe that's why she hugged that bag so tight.

"Don't know how long you're planning to stay in the area, but I need some help. I'm renovatin' a home in North Rustico, turning it into an inn along the harbor."

"Sounds beautiful."

"Oh, it is. The core renovations are almost done, but it's missing something."

Marie shot him a look and leaned in just enough to ask her question without having to speak.

"It's missing a woman's touch." He waved toward the sky. "That certain something from someone who knows what color the clouds are. It's missing the details that will make it a home."

Her forehead wrinkled. "I don't understand."

Over her shoulder, the green pine trees on the shoreline quickly approached. Soon they'd be on the island. Soon he'd miss his chance to help her. And to get her help.

"My inn opens in a couple months, and I need help getting it ready for guests. I have beds but no sheets. I have a little furniture but no decorations. I have rooms with no soul. And I could use a woman with an eye for color and details."

Marie's eyebrows lifted as she bit her lower lip. "Really?"

His hands jumped into the air, warding off too much hope.

"I can't pay much, but you can stay in the basement apartment until we open the first of May."

A flicker of hope disappeared almost before he noticed it was there. "What's the catch?"

"No catch. I need help turning this house into a home." And as he said the words, he knew they were true. He did need help.

Rose would have called this meeting positively providential, and she'd have been right. The big guy upstairs clearly knew that Jack needed a hand before Jack even knew it.

Marie's eyelids drooped, and she turned away from him again. He had to do something to get her on board before the ferry landed and he was left with the ugliest bed-and-breakfast on the island.

"I could pay you four hundred dollars a month, and I'll cover all your living expenses."

The terse shake of her head made his stomach churn.

"Fine! Six hundred for the month, the best room in the house, and a bonus when the inn is done."

"I can't take your money."

"But you'll be earning it."

"Ladies and gentleman, please prepare for arrival at Wood Islands, Prince Edward Island." The disembodied voice sent both Jack and Marie turning toward the overhead speakers. The humming motor suddenly went silent as they floated to the dock, but Jack's heart revved. It was now or never.

"I've owned three auto shops, and I've always paid a fair wage. I won't start shorting employees now."

"Employee?" Chin still tucked, she looked up, her eyes glistening. It could be the wind making them water, but he had a feeling it was something else.

"Until the inn is ready."

"What's its name?"

"The inn?" She nodded, and he scratched at his hairline. "Well now, I haven't quite decided on that yet, but I'm thinking about the North Rustico Red Door."

2

The door in question was white. Not ecru or cream or even ivory. Quite the opposite of the red door Marie had pictured. And it stood wide open.

"Is someone here?"

Jack looked a bit surprised. "Of course. I told you about Seth."

Her eyebrows jumped just as her stomach fell to her foot, raised to cross the threshold of the two-story house. The front porch, with its brand-new boards mingled sporadically with weathered and colorfully painted beams from the house's previous life, blocked some of the wind, but the cold still seeped to her bones.

"I don't think so." She twisted her fingers into her hair, trying to tame it in the residual breeze, as she replayed their conversation in his truck on the drive from Wood Islands. It had been mostly one-sided, Jack telling her about North Rustico and the bed-and-breakfast and how much he loved this island. For her part, Marie had done little more than take in the beauty he mentioned. Tall pine trees and swerving two-lane roads. Small towns made up of three farms, and rolling meadows to the horizon, peppered with the remnants of the last snow. And a cloudless blue sky over it all.

"I didn't?" He scratched his chin and tapped his lip, his eyes focused on a point beyond her shoulder somewhere in the house.

The purposeful and powerful footsteps behind Marie betrayed that Seth wasn't a boy or a shuffling old man. His shoes thumped on creaking hardwood floors, each step bringing him closer. As she turned around, her eyes leveled with a blue, cotton T-shirt stretched across a broad chest, paralleled by tan arms.

And her heart joined her stomach.

This could not be happening. How could Jack conveniently forget to tell her the only thing that would have changed her mind about helping him at the inn?

Taking a stuttering step back, she lifted her gaze past the dark brown stubble on his neck, over the tight-mouthed grimace splayed across his lips, beyond his slightly crooked nose, and into a whirlpool of something akin to horror.

He held her stare for a silent second before looking over her head. With raised eyebrows he nodded in her direction. "Are you kidding me?" His voice, so loaded with venom, seemed almost too heavy to make it the two feet to Jack.

Clearly she and Seth had at least one thing in common. They didn't want the other one here. But she had no claim to the inn, absolutely no reason to be there beyond Jack's invitation. Spinning to face the older man, she shivered as Seth's breath fanned the top of her hair. "Thank you very much for the ferry ticket and the ride, but I should go."

"Nonsense!" Jack waved off her words, his eyes locked

on Seth. "Marie, this is my little brother's boy. He's handy with tools and has been helping me with the restoration." Crow's-feet from years of laughter deepened at the corners of his eyes as he shifted to look into Marie's. He reached out to rest his hand on her shoulder, and she stiffened, steeling herself for even that contact.

"Seth." Jack didn't bother to break eye contact with her as he addressed the younger man. He squeezed her shoulder twice, like she imagined a kind uncle might. "Marie has a woman's eye."

With equal parts gravel and sarcasm in his voice, Seth said, "Oh really. You don't say."

The corners of Jack's mouth turned down with the first true frown Marie had seen him wear, and he pushed his chin into the air. "We can use her help getting this old place in shape for the opening."

"Really," Marie cut in. "I'll go." She moved to step around Jack, her breath already catching in her throat, hands beginning to shake. If she didn't move quickly she'd completely embarrass herself. She blinked against the strength of his grip, her shoulders shaking.

"Not while you're under my roof." Jack's voice brooked no argument, despite the fact that she had yet to make it beyond the porch. The pressure of his hand on her shoulder increased.

But it didn't stop her from trying, even as a wheeze caught in her throat. "I'll be fine." She gasped for another breath, her heart pounding at a pace it couldn't possibly sustain. "Don't worry about it." She sighed as her knees buckled, forcing her to lean against the edge of the doorway.

Jack shook his head again, his shoulders suddenly more

stone wall than Silly Putty, his hand slipping to cup her elbow, providing support she wished she could decline. "I need your help. I need someone to find the right towels to match the bathroom faucets. I need someone to add candles or flowers or those little soaps in the shape of seashells. Do you think an old man like me knows the difference between a duvet and Dalvay-by-the-Sea?"

"Dal vay?"

A harrumph from behind her reminded her why she needed to leave. Now.

Jack might think he needed her, but she had needs too. He could easily find someone else to help decorate the gorgeous old house. Saving her sanity around the likes of a man like Seth Sloane wouldn't be nearly as simple.

"Has she even been to the island before?"

Jack's glare returned in full force. "You're talking like you're island through and through, like you aren't here on a temporary visa."

Seth grumbled something else about a dal vay before saying, "It's your inn. You can borrow as much trouble as you like," and marching away.

"I don't want to get between you," Marie said. The stiff back of the retreating man disappeared through the door at the end of the hallway. "Really, I don't mind going."

The sparkle returned to Jack's eyes, and he laughed as though she'd told an amusing joke. "No more talk like that. I want you to stay. And if I'm not mistaken, you don't have anywhere else to be." Waving for her to enter through the open screen door, he laughed again. "Besides, it'll be nice to have a polite conversation over dinner. Seth has been about as fun as a month-old jug of milk." Jack's eyes shifted back and forth, making sure they weren't being spied on, as he leaned in with a wink. "Between you and me, he wouldn't be here if he had anywhere else to go."

"He doesn't? Have anywhere to go, I mean."

Maybe they had more in common than she'd thought. But that didn't mean he had to be so rude.

Jack ushered her toward the same door through which Seth had exited, his voice hushed but still echoing between the cherrywood floors and ten-foot ceiling of the empty hall. "He's not an orphan, mind you. Just going through a rough patch, and this seemed like the safest place for him to be."

"What? Are the police after him for unlawful use of sarcasm?"

The words popped out before Marie even realized they were on her tongue, and she clamped her hands over her mouth. She couldn't remember the last time she'd made a snide remark or an ironic comment.

It felt good.

Actually, she felt . . . free.

Not all the way free, but freer. Safe, at least, to say such a thing.

Jack patted her back, his laughter rolling over her like a blanket, and she barely shied away from his touch. "Something like that." He pushed open a door off the foyer, motioning for her to step through. "Let me show you around."

Seth had disappeared, leaving the room empty except for streams of light flooding every corner of the poorly painted dining room. One wall boasted what she hoped was supposed to be a hunter green. Of course, it wasn't actually anywhere close to that pretty of a color, and she squinted away from it, hoping that it would change colors on its own. It didn't, leaving her to wonder if the paint color was named Simply Seasick.

Windows covered nearly every inch of the adjacent wall, so bright in the afternoon sun that she couldn't even tell if the color on that wall matched the hideous green.

A large oval table dominated the room, the only indication that this was meant to be a dining room. Several wooden chairs surrounded the empty tabletop, two pushed in and the other three sitting haphazardly along the walls.

The far wall boasted the ugliest piece of furniture she'd seen in years, a tall credenza, its wooden frame nipped and scarred by years of use. One of its legs had been replaced by a wooden dowel. The pathetic piece drew Marie to it, and she ran her fingertips along the dark grain, past the chipped details across the backboard, and over the broken knobs on the drawers.

"A friend of mine had one of these." She wasn't really speaking to Jack, instead remembering the sweetness of Georgiana's blueberry tarts. "She put treats on it every afternoon and told me to eat as many as I wanted."

"You didn't do a very good job of it."

Jack's words pulled her back from the ripe tang of those berries. "Excuse me?"

"If you'd really indulged, you wouldn't be quite so skinny now."

Marie's gaze dropped toward her toes. Sure, she'd lost a few pounds over the last couple months. Who wouldn't after all she'd been through? But she wasn't absurdly thin. She certainly didn't have a problem with eating enough. Her appetite had just . . . dropped off.

She bestowed Jack with a half grin and resumed her tour of

the room. "I suppose I could have eaten a few more." With a toss of her head meant to dismiss Jack's comment, she spotted a brushed silver chandelier covered by years of dust. "Where did you get this?" Her voice remained low, as though in reverence of the six curling arms, each holding a candle-like lightbulb.

"Came with the house." Jack crossed his arms, nodding over his shoulder. "You want to see the kitchen?"

Marie, still staring toward the ceiling, shook her head absently. "You could design a whole room around this piece. Matching silver candlesticks. White napkins with swirling silver embroidery that complement silver table runners." Her smile was genuine, if not quite full, as she glanced to the wall of windows. "Red curtains over there that match the door. And pictures of Prince Edward Island framed on the walls. And"—she waved at the credenza—"if you replace that, you could set out glass plates of treats for your guests."

"Replace it?"

"I'm sure it was once a really beautiful piece of furniture, but it's seen better days. A dining room should be beautiful and homey. Not filled with pieces that make you want to eat faster so you can leave."

Jack's eyes crinkled at the corners, his arms still crossed. "You've done this before."

"Not really." She scooped up her backpack and hugged it, taking her first deep breath since entering the house. "But I like to put colors and pieces together."

"You don't say."

◆ ◆ ◆ ◆ ◆

Seth wasn't interested in hearing about the scrap of a girl Jack had decided to bring back from his trip to Nova Scotia,

26

but that didn't stop him from leaning into the crack at the door and listening to their conversation. Like a stray kitten, she'd shivered even inside the house, looking equal parts lost and terrified.

He didn't have time to deal with this.

Jack probably thought he was doing the girl a favor insisting she stay. In all honesty, he did a disservice to everyone involved. The girl needed a permanent home. Well, she was probably older than a girl. At first glance, he'd thought she wasn't much out of high school. With a closer look he knew she'd seen some life. But she needed somewhere to live where Jack wouldn't have to watch out for her. Having her around just distracted them from getting the inn ready to open.

And kept Seth's mind on things he'd much rather forget.

After all, he'd come to the island with a plan. Forget about his business and the bank that had been so quick to repossess the tools of his trade. And try not to think about the pretty face responsible for the whole thing.

But count on Jack to throw a wrench into his blueprint.

Suddenly the kitchen door swung in, slamming into his forehead and sending him stumbling into the rolling island that did little to slow his staggered steps.

Rubbing his head, Seth squinted at the pair walking into the room. Maybe he imagined it, but he would have sworn under oath that she shot him a you-deserved-that look. Almost immediately her face returned to its original expression, void of any distinguishable emotion. With the exception of her eyes, which reminded him of a mouse he'd once trapped as a kid.

"You're still here." Jack's grin came far too easily. "I thought you'd be halfway to Charlottetown by now."

Seth grunted, looking around for a hammer. Or a screw-driver. Any tool would do. The old inn still needed plenty of work, and he was more than happy to think about installing the new sink in the second-floor bathroom. Anything beat thinking about . . . well, what he'd been thinking about for eight months.

Righting the island, he frowned at Jack and tried to make his escape.

"I have to run to Charlottetown tomorrow to meet with the loan officer at the bank." Jack's words stopped Seth in his tracks. "I'll get an early start of it, and I'll run a few other errands while I'm about."

"You're going to leave her here by herself all day tomorrow?" Marie blinked big eyes, the same rich blue as Rustico's harbor, and wrinkled her nose, clearly as happy at the prospect as Seth.

Jack laughed. "You'll be here, boy, won't you?"

"That's not what I meant."

"I know." Jack clapped his hand on Seth's shoulder, and the wrinkles around his eyes deepened. "She won't bite. You could even help her get the lay of the land."

Refusing to even look at the little imp, Seth growled, "I have work to do. Besides, we're behind schedule."

"We're almost on schedule. And once Marie is up to speed, we'll work that much faster."

"I don't want to get in anyone's way," Marie said. "I'll be fine on my own tomorrow."

Both of the men looked at her as though she had no say in this argument, but it was Jack who responded first. "Of course you would be. But Seth is happy to help you get settled in."

Seth opened his mouth to contradict his uncle, but Jack's

hand whipped up, palm facing Seth, and a look in his eye said, *Hold that thought.*

"Fine." Seth sighed. "I'll be around tomorrow."

But Marie didn't seem at all pleased as she shrank into the far corner, holding on to her bag like a lifeline. It took everything inside of Seth not to march over to her and demand to know her game. One minute she and Jack had been talking in the dining room, the next she was practically climbing into the kitchen cabinets to hide from the world. Was it all a ploy to get Jack to feel sorry for her and let his guard down? If she was playing him for a fool, Jack would just sit back and let it happen.

"I suppose you're worn pretty thin there, Marie." Jack held out his hand, offering to lead her back through the kitchen. "Maybe we should get you set up in your apartment." Shooting a pointed glare at Seth, he said, "Get her bag, son." Jack nodded at the bright pink backpack, the only colorful thing about her.

"No," she whispered. "I've got it."

Seth squinted at her but nodded to the hallway at his left. "The door to the apartment is down there. We don't have sheets or anything for the bed. I wasn't expecting any guests until May."

Jack smiled like Seth had made a joke, ignoring the younger man's glower. "I can pick up some sheets and towels when I'm in Charlottetown in the morning. In fact, I can get all the linens we need."

Marie started another silent nod, her gaze locked on her feet, but suddenly looked up. "Have you thought about how the sheets will go with the bedspreads? And what kind of colors you want for each room?"

THE RED DOOR INN

Jack shook his head, confusion clearly painted on his features.

"Before you buy for all of the rooms, maybe consider some alternatives to white."

Seth narrowed his eyes. "Why would we do that?"

"I was just thinking about a bed-and-breakfast that I stayed at one time. The sheets were green paisley. And they made the room . . ." She bit her lip for a second. "I guess they made it feel homey. Simple touches like that make an inn memorable."

Jack's face cracked, a smile breaking through. "I like that. How do we know what sheets to get?"

"Well, they should match the comforter. And the island is known for its quilting. Maybe we could start there."

"Good." Jack beamed, his grin spreading all the way across his grizzled cheeks. "Make that your first project." He paused for a minute and scratched his chin. "Where exactly would you find quilts for sale?"

Marie's lips puckered to the left, and she glanced toward the ceiling. "Is there a fabric store close by? Or an antique store? I could even look for other statement decorations while I'm there."

Seth put his hands on his hips. So this was her angle. Spend all of Jack's money on useless junk at jacked-up prices. She hadn't even been there fifteen minutes and she was after his savings, the only funding for Rose's dream.

"There's an antique place down past the bakery. Seth will show you where it is."

Seth hadn't been joking when he said he had things to do. Besides the upstairs sink, the walls in the second-floor rooms needed to be sanded for painting, and he'd promised Father Chuck that he'd check out the roof at the church.

He opened his mouth to tell them that he had prior engagements, but Marie beat him to the punch.

"I'm sure that Seth is busy. Would you mind just pointing me in the right direction? I'm sure I can find it."

The hair on Seth's arms stood on end. Sure. Send her off on her own to buy only God knew what. That would turn out well. But maybe Jack wouldn't fall for her innocent routine. Maybe he'd show her the no-nonsense attitude that he'd been giving Seth for months.

"How much money do you need?"

Maybe not.

Jack's hand dove into his back pocket, and he had his wallet out faster than Seth could say *gold digger*. "Here's seventy-five. Will that be enough?"

Seth jumped between Jack and Marie, shaking his head at his uncle. "Are you serious?"

Jack nodded, dipping his hand back into the stash of green twenties. "You're right." He held another handful of bills out to Marie. "Antique stores can be expensive."

One measly suggestion from the blue-eyed girl, and Jack had dropped over two hundred dollars without even seeing what she was going to buy. He had lost all of his senses.

If Jack wasn't careful, he'd end up broke and conveniently free of the headaches of owning a bed-and-breakfast. Someone had to watch Marie to make sure she didn't swindle him out of his retirement. And someone had to watch out for Jack if he wasn't going to watch out for himself.

3

The front door clicked behind her as Marie stepped onto the inn's wraparound porch. The brisk March wind blew her hair into her face, and it took two hands for her to capture the wayward strands behind her neck. Her cheeks stung even more with each step farther into the open.

But oh, the open. How had she not noticed it the day before? She'd completely missed the rich blue of the bay across the street from the inn. The ground dropped off on the far side of the road, straight to the shoreline. Straight to the line of pine trees, two months late for Christmas but still decked out in their finery. The gentle waves from the wake of a fishing boat beckoned her like the beach at the Hamptons never had.

If only she could find a place to sit and watch it. Just her and the sea. And the goose bumps breaking out across her arms.

She picked up her pace, hurrying in the direction that Jack had pointed the night before. If she wanted something more than the flimsy blanket he'd given her to ward off the chill of her underground room, she had to find the antique shop.

And it had to carry the bedding she needed. If it didn't, her first attempt at helping Jack would fail. And likely his patience along with it. He wouldn't put up with her wasting his time or spending his money frivolously. She didn't know him well, but she knew business owners. It took guts and a strong will to run a business. He wouldn't hesitate to do what was best for his bed-and-breakfast, even if that meant sending her packing.

Maybe she should just keep walking and not go back.

The thought froze in her mind as her gaze met two of the biggest brown eyes she'd ever seen. She stumbled back a step, her stare glued to the unblinking eyes. Until the cow mooed.

Black and white spots swayed as it lumbered toward her, chewing like it had never met a piece of cud it didn't like.

Did cows charge like rhinos? Would it attack?

Panic bubbled in her chest, gripping her lungs and sending her heart into overdrive. Again. This always happened at the worst possible moment. The horizon tilted, nearly sending her to her knees, and her vision narrowed. She couldn't possibly run if the beast charged her.

Bending at the waist, she sucked in a stilted breath just as tears formed in the corners of her eyes and slipped down her cheeks. What was she thinking leaving Boston? There were no cows in Boston. No four-legged creatures set on attacking her for no reason. Why hadn't she just done what her father wanted her to do?

Because he'd cared for nothing and no one but himself.

Even thinking of his words made her stomach roll like

she was going to retch. Or maybe that was the memory of an attack she hadn't been able to ward off.

Either way, she needed to be free. But she didn't need to have a heart attack along a road in Nowhere-ville, Prince Edward Island. She needed the freedom of the open space, not a hulking black and white monster charging her.

Leaning her hands on her knees, she tried again to grasp the edge of a breath like the string on a balloon before the wind carried it away. There it was. A wisp of air seeped in, and the spinning in her head slowed down.

The next breath filled her lungs almost halfway, enough to give her the strength to look back up to meet her attacker— who had apparently decided she wasn't interested in Marie anymore. The heifer tossed her head, training those big brown eyes on the far side of the green pasture, and ambled off toward a water trough beside a bright red barn set at least fifty yards off the road. The weathered wooden panels served as a portion of the fence, connecting to thin wire that followed fence posts all the way around the pasture where Big Brown Eyes and six others lazed away their morning.

Of course there was a fence. No farmer would risk his cows wandering into the road. Even if not a single car had passed in the five minutes since Marie came face-to-face with the cow.

Of course.

Feeling every bit the fool she was, she pushed aside the remnants of the panic attack, managing a shaking breath with every step toward the antique shop. The buildings grew closer together, businesses and tourist shops lining the road. At an odd three-way stop, traffic picked up, and North Rustico started looking more like a town and less like a village on the harbor. Passing a hole-in-the-wall restaurant, she turned where Jack had told her to.

But twenty minutes later, the same pasture and same brown-eyed cow loomed before her.

Looking over her shoulder, she squinted hard enough to make out the outline of Jack's house. She hadn't passed it again. She was sure. Almost.

So how had she gotten back to these same cows, which had graciously given her a wide berth this time? Maybe she should go back to the house and ask for directions again. But she'd heard Jack drive away while she was still curled in her blanket, which meant Seth was the only one there.

She'd rather have breakfast with these cows than ask Seth for help.

As Marie started her second attempt to find the store, the wind picked up, tilting the tops of the pine trees and sending a shiver from her head to her toes. She snuggled as deep as she could into her lightweight jacket, but temperatures hadn't been quite this cold when she'd left Boston. Now she longed for her faux fur-lined parka. Or at least a scarf and gloves. Shoving her hands into the deepest corners of her pockets, she leaned into the wind, which blew a blanket of gray across the sun.

By the time she reached the three-way stop again, the tip of her nose could have held an icicle. She needed to find a place out of the wind to warm up, but this early in the morning the restaurants were still closed. Besides, she only had the money that Jack had given her for the quilts. She couldn't spend it on anything else—even breakfast—without giving him a reason to kick her out.

Then her eye caught a blue sign on a white house on the

opposite corner. A bakery. She hurried around a car, stalked up to the wooden deck, and reached for the door handle. Before it even cracked open, the smell of heaven surrounded her. Inside, the aromas of cinnamon and sugar mixed with apples and peaches and ginger, each complementing and accentuating the one before.

The bell on the door jingled as Marie's skin tingled with the warmth of the cozy room, every nook lined with shelves laden with breads and rolls and packages of mouth-watering brownies.

"Be right there!"

Marie jumped at the voice coming from around a corner behind the cash register. First a cow—a fenced-in one at that—and now a disembodied voice sent her out of her own skin.

"Get it together," she chided herself as the body to the voice appeared.

She was the type of girl who would have been shunned by Marie's childhood friends in Boston. She wouldn't have been invited to the cotillion in high school or had a date for prom. The boys at her elite private school hadn't dated girls who looked like they enjoyed a meal. Even at Wharton the student body had snubbed the girls who didn't and couldn't wear designer clothes.

They also missed out on smiles like this one.

The young woman's grin—punctuated by dimples on either side—filled the entire bakery, as sweet as the spicy scent lingering in the air. Hands tucked into the pockets of her white apron, she leaned against the counter next to the cash register. "Hi there. What can I get you?"

The smile that Marie offered was an involuntary response

to the other woman's kindness, and it felt strange, like she'd forgotten how to use those muscles. The grin dropped away quickly, replaced by a feeling of chagrin. At the same time she said, "I was just looking for directions," her stomach growled violently, betraying the fact that she hadn't eaten anything before leaving the house that morning. It just hadn't felt right, eating without asking Jack first.

An alarm chimed in the background, and the woman waved her hand before disappearing into the back room again. "I'll be right back. Just a second." Suddenly a loud groan accompanied the ringing, followed by the sound of several metal cookie sheets falling onto wire racks.

A few moments later she slunk around the corner, smile gone, carrying a plate piled with dark brown rolls. "I'm trying a new recipe, and I think I overcooked these cinnamon rolls." Her blue eyes moved between the stack of treats and a garbage can. Then they lifted to meet Marie's gaze. "Would you mind trying one? They're overdone, but we could pick off the overcooked parts and you could tell me what you think of the flavor."

Marie glanced over her shoulder and around the empty room, sure that the woman must be speaking to someone else. But there was no one else there. Tucking her finger around the chain at her neck, she twisted it several times, wanting to accept the offer as much as she knew she had to decline.

The other woman didn't bother to wait for a response, wrapping one of the steaming sweets in a napkin and holding it out. Marie hesitated for a beat before taking it and holding it close to her chin with both hands.

"Are you visiting or new to the area? I haven't seen you around before."

Marie nodded before picking a bite off the roll and popping it in her mouth. Flavors exploded across her tongue—cinnamon and nutmeg mingled with the sugar of the cakey bread, like a coffee cake in roll form. Her smile returned, and she pointed at the roll, too consumed with experiencing it to make any sound except a sigh of pleasure.

"Really? You think it's okay?" The chef extraordinaire took her own and nibbled on a corner, her lips pursing and dimples disappearing as she analyzed it. "It's all right."

Marie shook her head. "It's so much better than all right. It's amazing and delectable. Light and spicy. It's like an L. M. Montgomery story in edible form."

This made the other girl laugh. "No one has ever compared my baking to any author, let alone Maud Montgomery. This deserves a cup of hot cocoa on the house." She pulled a paper mug from beside a silver machine and pressed a lever, filling it to the brim before holding it out. When Marie took her cup of deliciously hot chocolate, the other woman filled her own. "To Maud, then." They held out their drinks in a toast, then sipped carefully.

The heat coated Marie's stomach, warming her toes and fingers and every bit in between. With tingles and pricks, feeling returned to her nose, and she blew into her cocoa just to watch the steam rise. After several minutes of eating in silence, Marie glanced up, warm, renewed, and ready to find the illusive antique shop.

"I was told there's an antique shop close by. Can you tell me how to get to it?"

"Sure. It's just down the street. About five minutes."

"How many miles—I mean, kilometers—is it?"

The woman's laugh was as rich as her cinnamon roll. "I'm

from the island. We only know it by time. But it's very close. In fact, if you walk it, I can give you a shortcut."

Marie nodded quickly, paying closer attention to the directions than she had when Jack told her how to get there.

"Thank you so much. You've been so kind . . . and I don't even know your name."

"Caden Holt."

"Marie Carrington."

"How long are you in town?"

Marie shrugged, not sure how to even begin answering that question. "I haven't figured that out yet."

Caden leaned over the counter and whispered, "Watch out or the island will lure you in. You'll never want to leave."

The facial muscles that hadn't had a workout in months bunched again, Marie's smile growing wide. With views like the Rustico Harbor and people like Jack and Caden offering kindness to strangers, Marie didn't have any trouble picturing PEI capturing someone's heart. In fact, she was as much at risk of falling for the island as any girl who'd grown up reading about the redheaded orphan. And she'd love to leave her heart there, if only she could stay. But she'd be leaving as soon as she made good on her promise to help Jack.

And part of that promise meant finding bedding for the queen-size mattresses at the inn.

Tossing her empty napkin into a trash can and wrapping her fist around the roll of bills in the pocket of her jeans, she slipped toward the door. "Thank you again."

"I'm just glad you liked the cinnamon roll."

"That was entirely my pleasure. I'll be your guinea pig anytime."

"Don't offer it unless you mean it." Caden chewed on the

corner of her bottom lip, her eyes rolling toward the ceiling. "I have an orange scone and berry brownie recipe I've been dying to try out."

"Then I will definitely be back."

With a wave Marie stepped into the chilling wind, the ringing of the bell muted as the door closed behind her. Replaying Caden's directions in her mind, she turned right, passing a gas station and a small grocery store, then ducked between a bank and what appeared to be a family-run restaurant. Right past the Lions Club building was the little blue house, just as Caden had described it. With the white trim around four-pane windows on either side of the red door, it looked like the building was sticking its tongue out at her, but the sign next to the door said COME ON IN!

No bells as Marie snuck into the surprisingly large room, and despite the towers of furniture and knickknacks stacked nearly to the ceiling, a small woman with gray curls shuffled toward her.

"I thought I heard someone come in." She stuck out a wrinkled hand with skin so thin that her veins stood out bold and blue. Marie offered her own hand, but instead of shaking it, the older woman clutched it in both of hers. "Aretha Franklin. No relation to the singer."

Aretha had to be joking. The petite ghost of a woman would never be confused with the robust soul singer of the 1960s, except by name. And the humor broke the ice, leaving them more friends than strangers. "Marie Carrington."

Aretha tugged on Marie's hand, which she still clasped firmly in her own, leading the way through the narrow maze toward the cash register. Marie barely had time to take in the enormous collection of worn and weathered treasures, each a story in itself. What stories had the ancient Underwood typewriter from the turn of the century put on paper? What ships had the brass compass navigated to safety?

There was no time to wonder at any of it as Aretha pushed Marie toward a wooden stool at the long counter, then settled onto a matching one beside her. "Hope you don't mind sitting a spell. My ankles swell when I stand too long."

Marie wasn't sure how to respond, but it didn't matter. Aretha didn't give her a chance to do more than shake her head.

"So your accent sounds like you're from away. From the Boston States?"

"Yes." Pricks swept down Marie's back as though someone was watching her, and she fought the urge to sweep her gaze around the room. Her father couldn't possibly have tracked her down already. "How did you know I'm from Boston?"

Aretha's laughter tinkled like an afternoon rain on a covered porch. "Oh, honey, us old-timers call all of the United States the Boston States. My daddy called it that, and his daddy too. Not so many of the young ones do anymore, but those of us born and bred in the Maritimes picked it up. Something to do with fishing boats and sailors and trading between the island and Boston."

"I see." She didn't, but she didn't think she would, no matter how much Aretha slowed her rapid fire.

"Where are you staying?"

Marie pointed over her shoulder, in the direction she hoped was the harbor. "I'm helping . . ." She trailed off, unsure of how to refer to Jack. "A friend. We're working on his bed-and-breakfast."

"The two-story Victorian on the bay?" A quick nod was all the encouragement Aretha needed to dive back in. "Oh, what a beautiful house. It sat empty for well over a year, you know. Such a sad sight with peeling paint and a few broken steps up to the porch. And right along the water. I take my evening walks there. And it was so sad to see it dark every night, no hustle and bustle. Who are the new owners? Is it that handsome young man? The one with the black hair, broad shoulders, and snug T-shirts? I've seen him around a bit at the grocery and one time in line at the bank. I said hello, but he only nodded. Seems a sad sort. Is he married? Or are you two . . ."

Throwing her hand up to stop even the suggestion, Marie said, "Jack—who's retired and in his seventies—owns the house, and he's the one turning it into a bed-and-breakfast. I'm just helping him out."

"And is Jack married?" The gleam in Aretha's eye wasn't altogether innocent.

Marie jumped to change the subject. "I don't think so. But the reason I came is to look for quilts. I need to find bedspreads for the guest rooms."

Aretha's smile turned thoughtful, the wrinkles between her eyebrows deepening. "This is an antique store, sweetheart. You can find those reversible feather-filled sets at one of the bedding stores. There are several in Charlottetown."

"I know. But I was hoping you might carry something tied to the island. Something made by a local quilter. Something that stands out, sets the bed—and the inn—apart. And I'm looking for some pieces that I could theme an entire room around too."

Aretha leaned her elbow on the counter next to a row of

flyers about upcoming antique auctions, her gaze roaming from Marie's eyes down to her tennis shoes and back up again. "A woman who knows what she wants." Nodding slowly, she continued, "I'm running a little low on bedding, but let's take a look."

4

Aretha flipped to the fourth hand-crafted quilt hanging from the rack in the back room. She watched the little scrap of a woman run a hand over the blue and green pattern, her finger following the hand-stitched heart pattern as it swung and looped.

"It's beautiful." Marie looked up with a hesitant gaze. "How much is it?"

"Six fifty."

Immediately the delicate hand dropped to her side as Marie shook her head. "I don't have enough."

Aretha hated to break the girl's heart, but she sold the quilts on consignment for one of PEI's best quilters and could take no less than the listed price. "Maybe there will be something in your price range at one of the antique auctions later in the season."

With a quick nod, Marie said, "Thank you for showing these to me."

"My pleasure, dear." Aretha put the quilts back to rights, and as she did, her hand brushed a sheet of ivory linen.

"What's that?"

She flipped back the bedspreads to show off her only antique sheet set. "I picked this up at an estate sale. It broke everyone's heart when old Mrs. Donnell passed on and her son decided to sell off all the treasures in her house to pay off his gambling debts. They said she'd embroidered this set of sheets herself right before marrying into the Donnell fortune. I just couldn't let it pass."

Somehow Aretha knew that the girl understood how special these simple sheets were as her eyes grew large and round, and she ran slender fingers over the red needlepoint in the corner of the ivory linens.

Her lips mouthed the monogrammed letters in turn. R. D. I. The middle letter dipped and swooped, its tail circling and embracing the other two.

Still running her fingers around the scalloped edges of the fabric, Marie whispered, "This is amazing."

"I sell to a lot of tourists, and also to inns in the Canadian Maritimes looking to redecorate. But for some reason I can't seem to part with these."

Marie's gaze broke away, and she squinted until her beautiful blue eyes almost disappeared. "I'm afraid to ask. How much is the set?"

"Three hundred and sixty-five for the top sheet and two pillowcases."

Her shoulders fell, her face going even more sallow in the dim lights of the shop's back room.

It was clear to anyone with a soul that this young woman needed something in her life to go right. And maybe she needed a friend too.

"I thought you were looking for quilts. Are you looking

for sheets as well?" She reached to pat Marie's shoulder, but stopped just short as the girl twitched it out of reach.

She sure was a nervous sort.

"Not really. Jack gave me 225 dollars, but I was hoping to take back some change. Seth already—" She pressed two fingers to her lips, her eyes again wide. But this time she wasn't lost in the beauty of the embroidery or the silkiness of the fabric. Color pinked high in her cheekbones as she checked herself.

Leaning in with a wink, Aretha chuckled. "Seth, eh? So, he must be the handsome young man I've seen from time to time. And Jack is his . . ."

"Uncle."

Aretha stretched to the side, leaning her elbow on a low-slung table. "And does Uncle Jack have a last name?" His name tasted like fresh clams cooked on the beach.

Jack suited the man she'd seen only in passing. Strong and simple. Just the way she liked them. There were only so many available men of a certain age on the island. She'd have to be blind not to take note of his full head of silver hair and weather-loved features.

"Sloane. Jack Sloane." Marie peeked over her shoulder at the door, clearly looking for an exit. Apparently she didn't find the only door easily available, so she hunkered down on her stool and swallowed quickly. "But that's really all I know about him."

"All right then. What about this Seth?" As she folded the linen sheets with the red stitching, she winked at the young woman, who didn't look up from where her fingers gripped the edge of the table. "What should I know about him?"

"I don't know. I don't know anything about him."

"Well now, I don't believe that for a minute. You must know something about him. After all, you are sharing a roof, aren't you?" She tapped her lip and then smoothed a hand over her curls as Marie looked at her own hands like she'd forgotten what to do with them.

When the girl finally looked up, her eyes shimmered like the sun glistening on the morning's gentle waves.

"My word, child. I'm only teasing you." She grabbed Marie's hand, refusing to be shrugged off again. The taut skin over elegant fingers quivered inside her grasp. "I didn't mean any harm."

"Of course." She swiped her free hand down the leg of her jeans before tucking it behind her back, her gaze intent on a point just beyond the rack of quilts but not quite to the wall lined with shelves of antiques waiting to be priced and sold.

More skittish than a newborn foal and prettier than the sunrise over the bay, this girl was what Aretha's mother would call a posy, beautiful and fragile. She needed kid gloves and a safe haven. Someone needed to tell that Jack and Seth how to treat a lady like this.

And if that meant she'd have to drop in for tea, then that's just what she'd do.

It couldn't hurt to meet the most eligible bachelor to arrive on the North Shore in five years.

And if she could help the poor girl at the same time, well then, all the better.

Setting the rack back to rights, she nodded toward the front of the store. "Perhaps we should look around for a—what did you call it?—a theme piece."

Marie followed her up and down the aisles until they discovered a framed map of PEI from the early twentieth century.

The thick black line of railroad tracks ran almost the entire width of the island, winding between streams and inlets, marshes and bluffs. The pinks, yellows, and greens of the map had faded over time, leaving it softened, romantic.

"Could this find a place in your inn?"

With a tender touch, Marie traced the intricately designed, brushed silver frame. When she finally spoke, her voice was hushed in wonder. "Oh, I think it would be stunning in the dining room under the chandelier."

"Perfect. Then it's yours. A gift." Aretha carried it to the front counter, where she could wrap it up.

By the time Marie reached the other side of the divider, her face was pained. "I can't accept it."

"You said it would fit your dining room, right?"

"Yes, but it's too much for a gift."

"Nonsense." She taped two pieces of brown paper around the frame and slid it into a bag. "Consider this a welcome present from one islander to another—with a condition or two."

Marie's mouth dropped open, eyebrows disappearing beneath a curtain of dark bangs. This time the girl wouldn't miss her wink and accompanying smile.

"Now you can take all your money back and prove Seth wrong. Am I right?"

"I—yes. I'm sure. But what conditions?"

"How about you ask Jack about those quilts and bring him back to see them."

"Oh, I'm sure he'd love them. I'll ask him to stop by as soon as—"

The squeak of the front door cut her off. Aretha called out a morning greeting to the tourists who walked in, their gait stilted, unsure. With a wave the tall man dismissed her assistance. "We're just browsing." Which translated roughly to, "We spent all our money on our bed-and-breakfast."

No use looking for a potato in a cornfield. She couldn't make their money appear no matter how pristine her inventory.

Holding out the bag with Marie's map, she leaned in. "Now, tell me more about Jack."

◆◆◆◆◆

Marie picked up speed, her feet matching the rapid intake and exhale of her breath as she clutched the paper-wrapped gift to her chest.

At least it wasn't another panic attack. While her lungs worked quickly, they weren't hindered by the band that always accompanied the unbearable episodes.

Glancing over her shoulder, she half expected Aretha to run after her, saying she'd made a mistake. The store owner couldn't possibly give away her inventory. Even if their agreement had included a promise to recommend Aretha's store for all of the inn's antique needs. And as many details about Jack as she could come up with.

It had been too easy.

Aretha had been too accommodating, too eager to give the piece away.

How thick were the attached strings?

Marie stopped just steps from the bakery, and not just because the scent of Caden's treats demanded to be savored. It would be best to turn around and return the map. Then she'd owe no one anything.

The sweet aroma of baked cinnamon and apples swooped

past her, carried on a gust of wind that rattled barren tree branches, and she shut out everything but the accompanying goose bumps. That fragrance couldn't be extracted from this moment any more than the ocean could be removed from the island shores.

Anytime she smelled fresh-baked apple pie or applesauce, she'd return to this spot, to this instant.

The moment when she turned back, thinking the worst of a woman old enough to be her grandmother, thinking the worst of the world.

But her only other option was to press forward, to take the gift to Jack and face down Seth's sour smirk when she returned without the one thing she'd set out to find. But she hadn't spent a cent. She was coming back with more than just change. She was coming back with all of it. Waving the bills under Seth's nose might even knock him off his high horse for a minute.

That was enough to carry her another step and one more after that. And pretty soon she couldn't even catch a hint of the bakery's aroma as she pushed open the front door of the inn, slipping from the porch to the foyer to the hideously green dining room.

As she pressed her hand on the door to the kitchen, a deep voice rang straight through the wooden panels.

"She can't stay here." Seth's words were anything but unclear, his voice catching on the last word. He was probably pointing adamantly straight through the floor and into the basement apartment.

"I'm not sure I like this color." In the style she'd come to expect from Jack even in less than twenty-four hours, he sidestepped Seth's comment. "Not sure it's right. Especially for the kitchen. Here. Look at the color sample. Don't really match, do they?"

"Jack, be serious for a minute. What do you know about her? How do you know she's not running a scheme or just trying to get at your money?"

The older man's laugh bellowed to the far corners of the house. "What money? I've sunk nearly every penny I have into this place."

"That's what I'm talking about. What if she's trying to make you feel sorry for her?"

"I already do."

Her stomach knotted at a brand-new sensation. No one had ever pitied her before. Envied and imitated? Certainly. But no one felt sorry for the heir to a multimillion-dollar real estate conglomerate.

Except she wasn't the heir anymore. She'd given up her rights to all that her name claimed by getting on one bus.

And that decision had stemmed from eavesdropping on another conversation.

Seth sighed, probably putting his hands on his hips. "Try to hear what I'm saying, Jack." His words rang louder and clearer. Had he turned to face the door? "She's trouble."

"How do you know?"

"I just do. Who shows up out of thin air like that just when you're about to be a success?"

"Rose wanted this inn more anything, and I promised her I'd open it. Success isn't a guarantee." Jack's voice cracked. He sure loved Rose.

"And would Rose want you to lose it all to a pretty hustler with glistening blue eyes and a pert little nose? She's already been gone long enough to walk to Rusticoville and back again. Three times. Maybe she's not coming back. Have you checked to see if any valuables are missing?"

Silence hung heavy on the other side of the door, and she held her breath, suddenly afraid of being discovered. If they found her listening in on their very private conversation, they'd throw her out.

Nothing good ever came from eavesdropping.

If she hadn't stood outside her father's study with her ear pressed to the door, peering through the crack, she never would have gotten on that bus. She wouldn't have left home at all. And where would she be? Somewhere else she wasn't wanted. Or at least somewhere she wasn't loved.

She'd be in Boston, doing exactly what her father wanted, helping him get his way. He certainly wanted her back there now. That was the only way he could use her situation to blackmail a man she'd never met.

Pain throbbed at her temples, and she closed her eyes against the building pressure.

Which was better? Used in Boston? Or unwanted on Prince Edward Island, the home of L. M. Montgomery, the place where her childhood dreams had always begun?

At least here she was free to leave, to find another place to hide until that ache in her heart began to ease.

She began to take a tiny step away, but stopped with her foot still six inches off the floor.

"Rose would have wanted me to take that girl in. She has nowhere else to go. I can see it in her eyes. And I won't turn her out just because you're worried that she'll abscond with two stories of a badly painted, half-renovated bed-and-breakfast."

"That's not what I meant and you know it." Though his

words were no softer, Seth's tone hummed with a compassion she hadn't heard in him before. "I'm just worried about you. I want to make sure that Rose's dream lives on for years and years."

Apparently she owed Rose for the roof over her head the night before, but it didn't mean she had to stick around to accept any more hospitality.

As she finally stepped back, her foot found the worst groan in the floorboard. Like her weight caused the house to weep, it went on for hours, loud and painful.

She closed her eyes, wishing that the old boards would open up and swallow her into her basement, where she could pick up her backpack and run until her legs wouldn't carry her any farther.

She wasn't quite so lucky.

When she opened her eyes, Seth stood before her, eyeing her with more disdain than the day before. She wouldn't have thought it possible then, but there was no doubt now. The glint in his eyes meant she was in for it.

His nostrils flared, lips disappearing in his anger.

"Marie, so glad you're back." Jack efficiently cut off Seth's ire with a quick motion for her to hurry into the kitchen. "I need your advice on this color." He held up two color swatches, one in a family of orange and the other in the seaweed green clan.

This was her chance to run. She could put distance between them until she couldn't see the blue of the bay or smell Caden's pastries. It was time to go. Time to run.

But her feet refused to move.

Seth's gaze swept over her as goose bumps exploded down her arms. She grabbed the lapel of her sweater, tugging it closed beneath her chin and covering every inch of skin. The rush of fear that zipped down her spine had nothing to do with being in this house, but there was no denying that the hazel gaze trained on her sent her pulse sailing and her mind racing to a dark night and a midnight morning.

"Well? Which one?" Jack waved the cards again. "I need ya, kid."

Run.

She just had to put one foot in front of the other and run.

Before they sent her packing. Before it broke her heart to have to leave.

Instead, she followed the lines on Jack's face like streets on a map and ignored the steam nearly coming out of Seth's ears. She hugged the door frame, calculating each movement to ensure she wouldn't brush even a hair against Seth, and slipped past his broad chest. When she reached the older man, she accepted the outstretched cards, her hair swishing with each shake of her head. "Neither."

"Neither?"

"They're all terrible kitchen colors."

Jack's face fell, his eyes jumping back and forth between the cards in her hands like he was watching a never-ending tennis match. Finally, he pointed at the middle color on the green swatch. "What's wrong with this one? It'll match the dining room."

"You say that like it's a good thing."

Seth, who still stood at the open door, coughed, but his eyes crinkled at the corners. Was that a smile? She hadn't even known he knew how.

"It's not?"

Again her hair swayed. "No."

"Need to paint the dining room again?" His eyebrows curved to match the frown tugging at the corners of his mouth.

"Only if you want your guests to enjoy eating in there." She glanced toward the ugly room. "Did you paint it that color yourself?"

He nodded and swept an age-spotted hand around the room. "What are we going to do? We have to open in just under two months." He leaned his forearms on the kitchen island, hanging his head to his chest and plunging his fingers into his hair. "If we miss the tourist season this summer, I won't be able to pay the mortgage on this place for the rest of the year."

Seth swept past her, his arm brushing her shoulder. She sucked in a quick breath, recoiling from even the briefest touch, but he didn't seem to notice as he charged toward his uncle.

Placing a hand on the older man's shoulder, he sighed. "It's going to be all right. We have enough time."

Jack's words, muffled against the counter, knocked her against the wall. "I'm not so sure."

What would he do if the inn didn't open in time? She could go. But what would Jack do with a house he couldn't pay for and no rooms to rent?

"We'll get it done." Seth pressed both of his hands to his hips and closed his eyes, pinching his lips together. "We'll figure it out."

How could this man be the same one who had suggested she was after Jack's money? How could he be so set on tossing her out one minute and so kind to his uncle the next?

Jack straightened, pressing his hair down where his fingers had yanked on it. "Going to take all three of us."

"I think you and I can—" Seth's words stopped at a sharp glance from his uncle.

"I said it'll take all three of us to make this house into the inn that Rose dreamed of." He stepped around Seth, reaching out to Marie, though not quite touching her. "And you'll stick around, right? You'll stay here until we're ready to open. You'll make sure we don't paint the wrong colors or end up with mattresses on the floor."

The urge to run washed over her again, but she swallowed it down twice, still hugging the brown paper package like it was a life vest on the *Titanic*.

This was her chance to bolt. There were really only two choices. Freedom and uncertainty or commitment and stability—for the time being. The stability only lasted as long as Jack offered it, and there was no telling when he would change his mind.

The wrinkles at the corners of his eyes sagged as he peered at her, silently nodding her into agreement. He wanted her to stay. He wanted her.

It had been so long that she'd nearly forgotten what it felt like to be needed. And, at least on Jack's part, wanted.

She couldn't leave now. After all, she still owed Jack for the ferry ticket.

She'd go before Seth forced her to. But for a little bit she'd stay. Until they didn't need her anymore.

"I have a pretty good idea where to start." She held the map out.

"Oh really?" Seth's words dripped with sarcasm.

"What's that?" Jack's eyebrows rose.

Their words tumbled together, and she chose to respond to only one. The crinkling of the paper would have masked her breathing—if she hadn't been holding her breath as she revealed her treasure.

Jack's forehead wrinkled as she handed it to him, and he traced the pattern of the frame. "For the dining room. It matches the light fixture."

"I thought so too."

Even Seth's eyes brightened at the old map, his jaw going slack as he leaned in to look at the legend. Suddenly his eyebrows snapped together, the familiar cynicism returning. "You blew two hundred bucks on this thing?"

5

No." Marie swung her arms around her middle in an instinctively protective motion. "It wasn't like that."

Seth's eyes narrowed, and he jerked a hand toward the white sticker on the glass that clearly stated the price. "Then, what? You stole it?"

Jack snorted at the suggestion, but Marie wasn't so sure that Seth had been joking. He leaned a hip against the far counter, crossing his arms and scowling at his uncle, whose finger still traced the detail of the frame.

"Where did you get this? It's perfect. My Rose would have loved this. She loved this island so much." Jack's eyes glistened, and he blinked against the pools beginning to form there.

"I got it at the antique store you told me about. Aretha Franklin, the owner, pointed it out to me, and I knew it would fit in this house." Her hand hovered over Jack's forearm long enough for her to take a deep breath before she risked touching him. Her skin burned at the first voluntary contact she'd had in weeks, and she yanked her hand to her chest, cradling it there.

Seth, oblivious to the enormous step she'd just taken, pointed his chin toward the map. "So is that all you got? I thought you were going to look for some bedspreads."

Twisting a finger into the collar of her sweater, she stared at the planks of the floor. "They were a little more than I expected."

Jack looked up from where he inspected a tract of land. "How much?"

"Between six and eight hundred." She managed a swift breath. "Each."

"I told you the antique store was a waste." Seth's words bit so hard they nearly broke her skin. Even though he addressed his uncle, the reprimand was clearly for her. "We don't have time or money to throw away on frivolous knickknacks."

She reached into her pocket, pulled out all the money Jack had given her, and held the bills out to him. Seth's jaw went slack.

"Close your mouth, boy, or you'll start catching flies." Jack shot him a hard look. "And keep it closed unless you've got something constructive to add to this conversation."

"Aretha gave the map to me. It's kind of a welcome-to-the-neighborhood gift, but I promised that if we need any other antiques for decorating the inn, we'll look at her store first. And there were so many interesting things there. We can easily find one or two key pieces for each room in the house. Our paint colors and linens will accentuate them. For example, this silver frame would pop against a dusky blue, so we should look for that when it's time to repaint the dining room."

Jack lifted his brows just enough to tell her he knew she was teasing him about the green walls, but he said only, "Well done."

Something sparked in her chest, but she couldn't quite name it. She'd found just the right piece to start, and Jack approved. Perhaps it was just pride in a job well done, but somehow this felt different than graduating with honors from Wharton with her MBA or winning a high school swim meet.

What she'd done mattered to someone. It was more than bragging rights to his buddies or closing another deal.

The inn mattered to Jack. And to Seth.

Maybe she was a part of that. Because it mattered to her too.

"And I saw these sheets—beautiful antique linens."

"For this B and B?" Seth cocked his head like she'd almost certainly lost her mind.

She waved her hand to stall his train of thought. "They were hanging with the quilts, and there was a gorgeous embroidered monogram. R. D. I. And I thought . . ." She shrugged, not sure where she was going or at all how to get there. "I thought the name of the inn should be simple. Straightforward."

"The Red Door Inn." Jack's eyes turned misty.

Goose bumps erupted down her arms as her gaze locked with his. He heard the same ring of rightness in the three simple letters.

"Very well done, young lady."

"And the bedspreads? What are we going to do about those?" Seth's questions ripped her from the cozy world of mattering. "As far as I can tell, we still only have the sheets Jack picked up and a handful of blankets in the entire house."

"Well, the quilts are still there. And so beautiful." She squeezed her hands together. "And I told Aretha that we'd be back to look at them again."

Seth recoiled like he'd been struck. "You did what? We

can't afford eight hundred dollars a room on bedding. You had no right to promise something like that."

Her heart stopped, and her words in the antique store settled like a brick in her stomach, bile rising in the back of her throat. It had all seemed so right at the time. That morning Jack had been on board with the idea of adding an island-made quilt to every bedroom.

But that had been before he'd seen a price tag.

He'd been careful about giving her 225 dollars. How ridiculous to hope he'd be willing to part with three times that much for just one quilt.

Tears pricked at the back of her eyes, and she tried to blink them away, but they rushed in again and again. Her cheeks burned, and she covered them with fingers cold as icicles.

Now she'd have to either break her promise to Aretha or spend money that Jack didn't have.

Jack cleared his throat, tilting his chin toward the open package on the island and tapping his cheek. "No harm in looking. I'll have to think about those quilts a bit then."

"Oh, Jack. I didn't—" Her lip shook so hard she had to bite deep into it to keep the tears from flowing, to keep her fears from showing.

His rich baritone laugh echoed through the room. "Don't worry, my dear." He patted her hand. "We've a name for the Red Door Inn and a connection at the antique store. Worth the trip, don't you think?"

She shook her head, still pinching her lip between her teeth for fear that the rush of tears would spill if she let go. Silence fell over them, the weight of four eyes trained on her sending sharp pains down the middle of her chest.

Her breath vanished in an instant, and she wheezed twice

before dark spots flashed in her periphery and her skin lit from a fire within.

She pointed to the hallway, dashing away before they could object.

Down the stairs. She had to make it down the stairs to her room. She'd be safe there, protected from Jack's curious stares and Seth's . . . Seth-ness. Those disapproving glowers and crossed arms, like a sentry standing at the inn's entrance, keeping the unwanteds at bay.

She pushed the door closed behind her, crashed onto the pillow-soft mattress in the center of the bedroom, and pressed her arms open as wide as possible. Air had vanished, replaced only by the binding around her lungs. She tried again and again to find any trace of oxygen left in the room until her line of vision narrowed, then vanished altogether.

◆◆◆◆◆

"What was that all about?"

Seth paced the narrow confines of the kitchen, the hair on his arms on high alert. Though Jack's tone wasn't sharp, the seriousness underlying the words was clear. Or maybe it was his own regret at the way he'd spoken to the girl. "I might have been a little hard on her."

Jack stepped in his path, standing firm despite giving up at least three inches and thirty pounds of muscle. But his eyes flashed like he had the entire United States Navy backing him up. He waited for the artillery to sound, for Jack to lay into him like he deserved.

He'd been downright mean to Marie. And why? Because he didn't want to be near a pretty woman? Because it might remind him of what he'd lost when Reece ran out on him?

Those excuses were weak.

The truth stung more than Jack's next words.

"You think you were a little hard on her?"

"I'm sorry."

"What's gotten into you, boy? I know you're hurting, so I've let you be sour. But this"—he waved to the door where Marie had disappeared—"this isn't like you. You're a better man than that. She's a guest in this house, and you've treated her worse than an enemy. How are you going to make it right?"

He could just avoid her for the rest of his time on the island. They were under one roof, but it was a pretty big one. With a little planning he might be able to dodge her for a few months.

Like a coward.

"I haven't told you enough since your dad died, but you know that I love you like my own son. If Rose and I had been able to have a kid, I'd have wanted him to be like you."

The old man had never strung so many consequential words together in one conversation.

Jack cleared his throat, staring hard into Seth's eyes.

Seth's stomach flipped, and he picked at the paint stain under his thumbnail, fighting the urge to escape to the bathroom on the second floor in need of a mirror. Those nice words were just a setup. He was about to get hammered. He'd seen that look in Jack's eyes before. He'd been a boy then and deserved everything Jack had said.

But he wasn't a kid anymore.

Which made this infinitely worse.

Jack jabbed his crooked finger again at the spot where Marie had disappeared. "I know you've been hurt. Understand that Reece hurt you."

Seth flinched at the mention of her name. She'd stolen everything. Including—apparently—his mind.

"I've given you leeway to be cranky and unpleasant, but we're all that girl has."

"How can you be so sure?"

"She'd have bolted if she had any other option." Jack took a steady breath, then let it out like an angry steed.

Seth prayed the worst was over.

"Rose had big plans for this house. She'd have taken in every single stray on the island if she could, so don't you dare dishonor her memory by running off our first one."

"Yes, sir."

A wrinkled hand clapped him hard on the back. "Fix it so it's sweeter than a lobster tail covered in butter 'round here. And take her back to the antique store to get started picking out decoration pieces like she was talking about."

Seth stepped back, crossing his arms again. "I've got lots of things to do around here. That sink upstairs isn't going to fix itself, and I still need to install that closet rod, put up the shelves, and hang that door."

Jack turned to the counter next to the double-sided sink, collecting a handful of paint samples and ignoring the excuse. Which is exactly what it was. "And buy at least one of those quilts while you're there."

God help him, he had to apologize, or Jack would send him back to an apartment filled with nothing more than lousy memories and condolence cards. And most of those were probably from wedding guests who had missed the chance for a party more than the opportunity to see him marry the woman he'd loved.

"I have a few errands to run this afternoon, so don't expect me back early." Jack stopped at the laundry room door, tucking the money Marie had given back to him into his pocket. "Make it right."

Seth glared at the clock on the microwave as though he could turn back the time. A year might just do it. That was enough time to get back his life and livelihood. If he'd never met Reece, never gone to that party, never popped the question, he wouldn't be where he was.

He wouldn't be stuck in small-town Prince Edward Island, trying to figure out what to say to a woman he wasn't ready to trust. Jack might think she was a lost puppy in need of a home. Seth wasn't convinced. She was more than the down-on-her-luck kid that Jack saw.

And he'd have to stick close to her side to figure her out before she could do any real damage. But he'd have to earn her trust in order to do that.

His stomach growled, and he pulled open the refrigerator door, staring hard at the empty shelves. Two bachelors true to the stereotype. They didn't shop for more than the bare essentials. And they certainly didn't cook. So they didn't eat well.

He grabbed a carton of yogurt out of the door, pulled a plastic utensil from the spoon drawer, and beat the yogurt into submission before shoveling it into his mouth. It disappeared sooner than he was ready to make his trek down the stairs, but the longer he waited, the more time Marie had to fester in her anger. If Reece had taught him anything, it was that a woman could make a mosquito of a grudge into a mammoth if left to her own devices.

Hoping something had magically appeared in the three seconds it took to finish off his snack, he peered back into the fridge. Still empty except for one more yogurt.

Maybe Marie was hungry too.

It never hurt to take a peace offering.

He thumped down the stairwell and stopped at the four-paneled white door at the bottom. The last time he'd knocked on a woman's door, her apartment had been as empty as his bank account.

But Marie wasn't Reece. And he had to get close to her for Jack's sake. No matter what it cost him, he'd make sure it didn't cost Jack everything.

He rapped his knuckle on the door twice and waited.

Nothing.

Hope curled his toes. Maybe she'd decided to leave.

He knocked with his whole fist just to make sure.

"Who is it?"

His hopes fell at her clear voice, and he leaned a shoulder into the door frame. "Seth."

"Please, go away." She clipped her words despite the soft volume.

"I thought you might be hungry. I brought you something to eat."

When she opened the door, her dark hair was pleasantly disheveled, a gentle wave sticking out above her ear. But the bags under her eyes weren't as sweet.

Probably for the best.

Thinking of her as a pretty woman was bound to throw him off his mission.

Hugging the door between them, she chewed on her lip as she eyed the carton in his hand. He held it out to her, and she whipped it open like she hadn't eaten in a month, filling her mouth with giant spoonfuls of the pink yogurt. For a wisp of a thing she could sure put it away.

Her spoon scraped the sides and bottom, and after one final lick, she handed back the container and spoon. "Thank you."

The door was nearly shut before he pressed a flat hand against it. "Hey, wait."

Her eyes glowed in the afternoon sunlight from the windows at the top of the stairs. Long lashes framed their innocence as she asked a question without speaking.

"Listen, I'm sorry about what I said earlier. Jack is really interested in the quilts, and his is the opinion that counts here."

She blinked twice as her brows furrowed. Uncertainty splashed across her face. "All right."

He'd apologized and the best she could give him was "All right"?

She moved to close the door again, but this time he gave it a solid push, and she scurried into the depths of the room, putting the corner of the bed between them. Eyes wide and wary, she drew tight fists to her stomach like she was planning to slug him.

He might deserve it, but he'd bet money she didn't have the gumption.

One of her fists cocked under her chin as he took another step in.

Maybe he was wrong.

He shuffled back to the door, holding up his empty hand in submission. One after the other, her hands dropped to her sides, still curled tightly.

"Jack wants us to get started picking out antiques and stuff like you said."

She glanced around the room like she was looking for

someone else to join them. When she came up empty, she said, "I'll just stay here."

"Come on. Jack is running errands, and if he comes back and we haven't been to the antique store . . ."

"What? What will he do?"

Seth tapped the empty carton in his hand with one finger. "I'm not really sure. But it might involve either risking our necks cleaning second-story gutters, or worse, grocery shopping."

A little pop of breath jumped out of her like she couldn't hold it in. It wasn't quite a laugh, but it was a pleasant sound, one he hoped he'd get to hear again. She ran her fingers through her hair, dislodging that misbehaving strand over her ear, then fidgeted with the zipper on her sweater. She looked away, then back at him, then quickly away again.

She was every bit as unsure what to do with him as he was with her. Why hadn't he noticed before?

"Tell you what, I don't want to find out what Jack would do if we don't get started looking for those antiques. So I'll make you a deal. Come with me for a quick shopping trip, and I'll buy you dinner."

"Do I have to sit with you?"

"That's the generally accepted custom. But hey, if you want to sit by yourself, I won't stop you."

She rubbed her hands together, breathing quickly.

"So? What do you say?"

6

"Are you going to get in?" By the time Seth opened the door of his truck, Marie had made it to the rear bumper. "Were you planning on walking to the antique store again?"

She nodded and shook her head at the same time, sending her hair whipping across her face. As she leaned forward, she took a matching step back, just confirming his suspicion. She did not want to go with him. She'd probably only agreed to make the shopping trip to get a free dinner.

When was the last time she'd eaten a real meal?

She couldn't afford to lose any weight. Her elbows already poked at the sleeves of her jacket, her collarbone sticking out below her neckline.

Aunt Rose would have tried to fatten her up. Which was exactly what Jack would try to do too. Which meant that was what Seth would do as well.

"Just get in." He sighed, pointing to the passenger side of the cab.

What was it with this girl? She couldn't stand up to a stiff wind and shook like a lost puppy in a thunderstorm. But she had no problem telling Jack that he'd picked out ugly paint colors.

Seth hadn't even been able to do that.

He couldn't afford to discourage his uncle, who needed every bit of support Seth could muster. Especially after Rose's death more than a year before. So he'd been party to the dining room fiasco, slopping moss-green paint across the wide walls, cringing with every brushstroke.

Before his trip to Halifax, before he'd met Marie, Jack had been nearly ready to give up on Rose's dream. Ready to throw in the hammer, close up the inn, and retire in a quiet Phoenix suburb.

Ready to leave Seth with only that empty apartment as home.

He couldn't let that happen. He wasn't ready to go back to—

"California. Is that where you're from?" Marie's question barely made it across the bench seat of his pickup. Her fists grabbed the old fabric, twisting into the cushion as she tried to pull herself up.

He almost offered to help after watching her struggle for several long moments. Finally she jumped far enough to wrench herself the rest of the way into her seat.

When she settled in and slammed the door, he rolled out of the driveway, pulling onto the road lined with classic and refurbished homes to the right. A fishing boat in the bay to his left wove between rows of mussel-sock markers, the late afternoon sun glistening on the ripples in the vessel's wake.

As they reached the stop sign at the end of the road, he finally responded to her question. "How'd you know about California?"

"Your license plate."

Right. And she'd probably noticed the outline of the decals that he'd pulled off of the doors too. He wasn't the best contractor in Southern California anymore. He was just handy with a hammer in North Rustico, middle of nowhere. But at least he could watch Jack's back from here.

Her wary eyes tracked his movements as he shifted gears, rolling through the three-way intersection. "What part of California?"

"San Diego."

"Oh."

"Yeah. You ever been?"

She shook her head, her mouth opening like she wanted to say something more, but then she snapped it closed.

As he navigated past the bakery and the bank, she pointed. "I think the store is right there."

"The bank doesn't appreciate non-customers parking in their lot."

"Oh." Again, she looked like she had more to say, but instead she clung to the door handle with one hand and her shoulder belt with the other.

"You have something against that door?"

Her eyes shot in the direction of her death grip. Without looking back at him, she uncurled one finger at a time. "Not really."

His laugh burst out before he even realized how funny her comment was. "Not really? So . . . maybe just a little bit?"

Her eyes flashed with either anger or embarrassment. Or, more likely, a combination of both, and he chuckled again as she folded her hands into her lap, back straight as a nail.

Tempted to tease her again, he bit his tongue as she jumped

out of the truck before he'd even put on the brake in front of the antique store. The front door was already closing behind her by the time he reached the cobblestoned front walk.

"Welcome to Aretha's Antiques," a disembodied voice called over the jingle of sleigh bells as he walked in. "I'll be right there."

The maze of artifacts towered above him, blocking his view. Marie had disappeared.

Probably picking out useless things.

At least he had control over the money this time. And he refused to let her waste it.

An overhead light caught the edge of a large brass lantern straight ahead, and he blinked against the flash just in time to step on something that shrieked like it had just lost three of its nine lives.

"Was that Chapter? Silly thing acts like you gave her a sallywinder."

Whatever that was, he didn't want one.

The gray-striped cat darted between a matching pair of seven-foot china hutches before he could catch it, but as he wandered farther from the front door, the tabby began purring as if she'd never met the underside of his work boot.

He rounded a turn in the maze and bumped into Marie, jostling the cat tucked in her arms. Chapter hissed, baring her teeth at him and immediately snuggling back into the warmth of Marie's embrace.

"I think you've made an enemy." The corner of Marie's mouth lifted, and a wicked spark flashed in her eyes.

So she *could* smile.

Her good humor lingered as she ran her fingers between the pointy gray ears, following a black line all the way to the middle of the cat's back. The hum coming out of the little beast was pure bliss, and Marie's drooping eyes weren't far from that either.

Risking a finger, he moved his hand to follow Marie's motion, only to be swatted away by a fully clawed paw. He inspected twin red scratches on the back of his hand as Marie let out a full-on laugh.

"She really doesn't like you." Marie hooked a finger under the furry chin and looked into the monster's black eyes. "Smart girl."

Before he could form an adequate retort, a thin woman with silver and gray hair appeared at the far end of the aisle, her hands clasped beneath her chin in delight. "Well, well. Marie, you're back so soon. And who have you brought with you?"

Marie flashed her bright white smile toward the older woman, who patted the cat's back without losing a hand in the process.

Maybe the creature didn't like men.

That was it. It couldn't have anything to do with being on the losing end of an encounter with his size twelve boot.

Whatever his fight with the cat, it sure knew how to show off a new side of Marie, whose smile persisted as her gaze shifted from the fur ball in her arms to an antique typewriter on the shelf in front of her, and back to him.

"This is Seth Sloane."

"Aretha Franklin. No relation to the singer." She reached around Marie and grabbed his hand, shaking it hard. Her eyebrows bounced, and he got the feeling that if she were twenty years younger, her whole body would have been bouncing. "You're new to the area—well, nearly everyone is new next to an old-timer like me. But I've seen you at First Church, haven't I?"

"Yes, ma'am." He'd probably seen her at the church too. After all, there were only about a hundred people in attendance on any given Sunday, and he and Jack had been faithfully attending since before the New Year. But unlike her, he stuck out like a thistle in a rose garden. The average age of church members in the area was well over sixty, and most of them looked just like Aretha.

Thankfully he wasn't on the island to make new friends his own age. He was there for Jack, and it was good for Jack to connect with his peers. There were plenty of them at First Church of Rustico.

Besides, the fewer young people he met, the less likely he was to meet single young women hoping for more than he could offer.

Aretha's gaze swept over him, and an unheeded chuckle rose from deep in his stomach. He turned his head to cover it with a cough, but his shoulders still shook.

He had a feeling that if she were thirty years younger, he'd have had to worry about her more than the other women in town.

Marie shot him a glance filled with questions, but Aretha asked hers first.

"So what brings you back so soon? Is everything all right with the map?"

"It's perfect," he said. "Jack loved it."

Aretha's face shone with delight. Marie's just filled with more questions. He could only offer a lift of his shoulder and half a smile in response. No need to let Aretha in on his rotten behavior.

"Marie had an idea for decorating every guest room in the inn with a unique piece, so we're back to see what you've got." For reasons he couldn't begin to identify, he dug into his pocket and pulled out Jack's small-business credit card, waving it slightly. "Jack sent me with the money, so let's get started."

"Oh, I have some fabulous ideas!" Aretha clapped her hands, sending Chapter, who was apparently tired of being ignored, jumping to the ground and disappearing beneath a desk.

A phone rang from the back of the room. "I'll be right back. Start looking, you two," Aretha called, already vanishing at the end of the row.

"Thank you." Marie glanced at him, then quickly back at the round keys of the typewriter.

"For what?" He already knew, but he wanted to hear her say it, wanted to hear her say he'd rescued her.

She couldn't meet his gaze as she whispered, "You could have told her how stupid I'd been, promising to buy things when I didn't have any right to."

"You're welcome."

Their first civil exchange. No slams. No teasing. No scowling. They'd managed to speak politely to each other for three whole minutes.

Jack would be pleased with the progress. It wasn't exactly butter-covered lobster tail, but it was better than three hours ago.

And if Marie didn't hate him, it made keeping an eye on her all that much easier.

Who knew? If she smiled at him every now and then like she was grinning at the typewriter, sticking by her side might not be as miserable as he'd thought.

◆◆◆◆◆

Marie wanted that Underwood typewriter. The black one shining in the light coming through the window across the store. The one with the round keys and worn letters from years—probably decades—of use.

She ran a finger along its cool edge. What had been typed on this machine? Had someone written a book or a story on it, hoping to replicate the literary magic of L. M. Montgomery's island tales?

"So where do you want to start?"

Seth's question jerked her from the image in her mind of Maud Montgomery's protégé at work on a masterpiece, her story taking shape one keystroke at a time.

"What do you think about making one of the rooms into a book lover's retreat?"

His brows knit together. "Doesn't that kind of limit the type of guests we could invite?"

"Oh, it's not just for people who love books. It's for anyone who needs a retreat, but we'll use pieces like this typewriter and maybe an old secretary desk and lots of old leather-bound books." Her voice rose with each word until she rested her folded hands under her chin. "Can't you just picture it?"

His grimace told her that he most definitely could not picture it.

But she could make him see it. "Stories are part of the island's heritage. We could theme every room around part of the history. Like the ocean and lobster fishing and . . . and . . ." Clearly she needed to do a bit more research on PEI.

"And potatoes."

"Potatoes?"

"Sure. There's a potato museum toward the West Point Lighthouse. I think Irish immigrants brought them over a hundred years ago." His face remained completely passive as he pointed in the general direction of the museum. "I think a potato room is a great idea."

"Well, that's not exactly . . ." She bit her lip and stared at her hands. He couldn't be serious. What color brown would the walls be? Would the mattress be lumpy and the comforter made out of potato sacks? And they'd have to put pitchforks in the corner next to the bed.

Laughter erupted from somewhere deep inside him, rattling the glass panes of the hutch that he leaned into for support. The guffaws kept coming. "Did you think I was serious?"

She crossed her arms over her chest and shook her head. When it was clear he didn't believe her, she walked away in the direction Aretha had gone. The older woman was bound to like her idea and could certainly give her more background on the island.

Seth's laughter followed her from aisle to aisle, rubbing every one of her nerves raw. How was she supposed to know about the grand history of potatoes? All she knew about the island she'd learned from reading about a redheaded orphan.

That didn't give him the right to tease her. The most he knew about the ocean was probably surfing the Pacific. At least she'd been born and raised on the Atlantic seaboard.

Well, he could tease her all he liked. Her idea was a good one. She'd always had an eye for trimming a house. At least that was what her mother's best friend and interior designer Georgiana McWilliams had always said. When Georgiana had decorated their beach house at the Cape, she'd asked Marie to help.

Seth might be too thickheaded to know it, but he and Jack needed her.

At least Jack knew it.

As she approached the counter where Aretha stood, Seth's chuckles finally died out.

Aretha hung up her phone, a broad smile wrinkling her features. "Did you find some things you like?"

"I was thinking about using writing-related pieces for one of the rooms."

"Honey, I have the most beautiful Underwood typewriter."

Marie nodded enthusiastically. "I saw it. And I was thinking about some vintage books and maybe an old wooden secretary to go with it. Any ideas?"

"Plenty, my dear." She led the way to a wooden bookcase along the far wall. The edges of the shelves had been worn smooth from years of borrowing and returning books. Many of the books still sat there, just waiting to be loaned out once again.

With a tentative touch, Marie brushed her fingers along the red leather spines of Shakespeare and Dickens and Austen. The brown ones on the far end were only a few reads away from losing their threadbare casings, and she dropped her hand before she could add to their wear and tear.

Would she have liked reading the classics in high school any more if they'd been this beautiful?

Probably not.

"Do you have any first-edition Montgomery?"

"Maud?" Aretha spoke as though she were old friends with the author who had made the island famous. "Oh dear.

I can't keep Anne on the shelves. I've had three first editions and fourteen second or third." She shook her white hair. "But the tourists eat that stuff up. They can pack it into their rollers and carry it back to wherever they come from. It's easier to move than the whole case."

"I suppose that makes sense." Even if it wasn't what she'd hoped to hear. The beautiful antique bookcase would look stunning in the inn with or without a first edition of the classic island tale.

She flipped the price tag so she could count the zeros there, and her breath caught in her throat.

Nothing could look *that* good.

Aretha patted her shoulder. "I'll keep my eyes open for a first edition for you."

"I'd appreciate that. Thank you." Marie pulled an early-twentieth-century *Pride and Prejudice* off the shelf and turned it over. No price tag. "Are these for sale?"

"By the set."

"How much?" Seth's voice made the women jump.

Aretha looked up into his face, her smile knowing. "For you? We might be able to make a deal. Let me just check my records to make sure I'm not giving them away."

She wandered toward the back room where they'd looked at the bedding just that morning, leaving Marie to stare at her feet while Seth stared at her.

"Books and a typewriter, huh?"

He sounded so much like Jack, trimming his words until he had to speak only the essential ones.

"And a writing desk too, I hope." She glanced down the wall, brass and iron pieces lining every inch until there were none to spare.

Which of these pieces would fit in the Red Door? Which would make it feel like home for the guests who would spend their vacations in its rooms? Which would seal memories in their minds, keeping them coming back season after season?

There were iron animals and fireplace pokers. But they were cold and heavy, like the weight of Seth's ever-watchful gaze.

She needed something beautiful and strong. Something that showed Seth that she knew what she was doing. Something like the large brass light right in front of her.

Stepping around a wooden pedestal topped by a porcelain washing pitcher, she hurried to inspect the lantern with its faded gilded edges. "What is this?"

Marie had meant to ask Aretha, but Seth stepped to her side, even as she pulled away. "It's from a lighthouse. See, the light would stay still, and the outside panel would spin like this." He made a circle in the air with his finger.

"Are there lighthouses on the island?"

Aretha joined them, her laughter booming through the store. "I should say so. There are more than fifty active lighthouses."

A smile tugged at the corner of her mouth, but Seth piped up before she could voice her idea. "Let me guess. A lighthouse room." He didn't have to go on. His tone said it all. He thought it was a ridiculous idea.

"What a splendid idea." Aretha clearly didn't agree with his assessment. "I have a few other pieces."

She grabbed Marie's hand, pulling her deeper into the maze, and pointed out a captain's wooden box—which contained a seafaring compass—and a ship in a bottle. They danced around the room so fast that Marie's head spun and her chest tightened.

Fighting the panic attack that had, of course, shown up at the worst possible moment, she jerked her hand out of Aretha's grasp to cover her mouth as she sought the air that had turned thin.

Aretha's eyes filled with concern. "Are you all right, honey?"

She nodded, then shook her head. The floor jolted, and she stumbled against the movement. It couldn't all be in her mind. "Restroom?" she asked between her fingers.

"Right inside the back room. Go on. You're whiter than a sheet."

Marie ran to the room, flipped on the light, and sank to the floor. The cool porcelain of the pedestal sink felt good on her forehead as she breathed in through her nose and out through her mouth. She closed her eyes and the world went black, the ringing in her ears blocking out even the sound of Aretha's worried voice.

In about five minutes they would check on her and find her passed out on the bathroom floor.

Perfect.

Seth would pick her up, holding on to her until she awoke. Until she promptly had another attack from being that close to him.

Just perfect.

That scenario didn't work in her imagination, and she certainly couldn't let it play out in real life. Pushing her feet beneath her, she grabbed the sink to pull herself up. The oval mirror on the wall said exactly what Aretha had. Panic had robbed her of all color.

Splashing water on her face helped a little, and she sipped from a cupped hand until she could swallow normally.

Then came the knock on the door.

"Are you all right?" Not Aretha.

Taking a shaky breath, she turned the knob and faced Seth. "Much better."

His eyebrows furrowed, his lips tight. He didn't believe her.

"Ready to go?"

He stared at the top of her head as she staggered past him, hoping she could ignore the rope around her chest until they got back to the Red Door.

"Aretha's just finishing ringing up your antiques."

"My what?"

He didn't bother to answer, and she saw why when she reached the counter. Aretha smiled as she wrapped the ship in a bottle in brown paper and tucked it into a cardboard box.

"Mr. Sloane here has already taken your typewriter out to his truck. And I have the compass, lighthouse lamp, and ship right here for you." She motioned to a second box. "We took the liberty of selecting a few classics to get your book room started. And he said you were to have that blue and green quilt. That was your favorite, wasn't it?"

Marie's chest loosened as her gaze traveled between Aretha and Seth. It finally settled on Seth's grumpy grin. "If Jack says you get antiques, then who am I to put a stop to it." He picked up the box of books. "Besides, you have pretty good taste."

"Now you just come back here when you're ready for more." Aretha patted her hand. "Oh, and I almost forgot. I have another little gift for you."

"For me?"

"For all of you." Aretha's smile broadened as Seth's forehead wrinkled in confusion. She pulled a thin paper bag from under the counter and laid it on top as though it contained the crown jewels. "After you left this morning, I remembered that I had a photo album of The Crick—that's what most of the locals call this area—from almost seventy-five years ago. And what house do you think was featured in one of the pictures?"

Marie's heart stopped for a long second as she held her breath. It couldn't possibly be the Red Door.

But it was. There was no mistaking the gabled roof and wide porch. Even in black and white, it was Jack's inn. Except it wasn't entirely in black and white. Someone with a steady hand had painted the front door. Red.

Her stomach lurched as Seth leaned over her shoulder to get a better view, his mouth open and eyes narrowed. "So it was red back then?"

"It sure seems that way." Aretha looked more than satisfied with herself, tucking the picture back into its protector before holding it out to Marie. "I thought you might like this."

With still trembling hands, she accepted the gift. "Jack. I'm sure Jack will appreciate this. Thank you."

"Well then," Aretha said. "We'll see you back here soon."

Yes. They'd have to come back. Soon. After all, she hadn't gotten any real furniture. Of course, it would be easier to finish painting before the rest of the furniture went in, but she'd promised Jack. She had to show him that she could do the job, get the inn everything it needed. She'd earn the roof over her head until she had to go. For now that meant rooms full of armoires and nightstands. Not just decorative pieces.

"We're going to need furniture too."

Glancing into the back room, Aretha tapped her pursed lips twice. "You mentioned a writing desk, eh? I do have a beautiful one."

Marie's stomach flipped with anticipation.

Aretha showed her to the piece, but it didn't strike her interest. What did catch her eye was the cherry buffet sitting right beside the desk. Strong and detailed, it would be stunning in the dining room, the perfect place for afternoon treats for the guests.

"What about this?" She ran gentle fingers over it, enamored with the swirled hardware handles and curved legs.

Aretha frowned. "I'm afraid that one is set to go on auction next week."

7

Seth took the bump at the end of the driveway slower than usual, his eyes on the figure in the passenger seat. Marie still hugged her knees under her chin, tucked into the corner as far away from him as possible. She hadn't moved more than the barely-there rise and fall of her shoulders in the seven-minute drive from Aretha's.

"You feeling any better?" He tried to keep his voice low, but it filled the cab, where there had only been silence for the entire drive.

She turned her head, resting her ear against her knees and squinting at him. The faint pink of her lips struck a stark contrast to the ashen tint of the rest of her face. She mumbled something incoherent before hiding her face again and tucking her shoulders up to her ears.

She'd pulled this a few times in the two days he'd known her, turning pasty white and eerily silent. She was either annoyed with him or seriously ill.

If she was sick, it wouldn't do to have her dying on his watch. Jack wouldn't overlook that, and given the recent animosity between Seth and Marie, Jack might even suspect Seth was responsible. Perhaps it was time to smooth things over, just in case she passed that near-death look and went all the way.

Without saying anything, he hopped out of the truck and walked around to her side, reaching her just as she pushed the door open with a shaking hand.

"Can you make it inside?"

She nodded, but as her foot slipped on the side panel, he grabbed her arm to keep her from falling.

Jerking her elbow out of his grasp, she whispered, "I'm fine." Leaning against the closed door, she took an unsteady breath. Apparently noticing his doubt, she added, "I'll be all right in a minute."

He wasn't so sure, but arguing with her wasn't going to get them on the road toward a truce. Swallowing the retort on the tip of his tongue, he shoved his hands into his pockets and glanced at the bed of the truck. They'd brought in a good haul for their first trip to Aretha's, but it wasn't nearly enough to decorate two full stories, a basement, and five guest rooms. And Aretha's mention of the credenza up for auction next week had definitely caught Marie's attention. Maybe he could tempt her out of her shell with a promise to get it for her.

"I'll take you to the auction on Monday."

She perked up, pink finally appearing in her cheeks.

"If you want to go."

She wrapped her fingers into her shirttail, her gaze firmly settled on the ground between their feet. "Yes." When the word popped out, she looked as shocked as he was. Her eyes grew wide, and she pressed her palms against her cheeks, burying her fingers into her hair. Completely missing his amusement.

He let his shoulders shake but kept his laughter silent.

No need to counteract their step forward.

"Good." With that, he took off for the bed of the truck and slid the monumental typewriter toward the tailgate. As he hefted it off the lip of the tailgate, he turned back to where Marie had been, only to find her gone.

"Don't worry about me," he muttered, lumbering toward the porch. "I've got this."

It took a flick of his foot and a bump of his hip to get the screen door open. But at least she'd left it unlocked for him.

Voices rose from the parlor as he stumbled over the threshold.

"Don't do that." Marie's voice carried a note of panic, and his pulse jumped into overdrive.

Was she in trouble? Was someone else in the house?

Storming down the narrow hallway, he crashed into the door frame, chipping the molding at his elbow and sending fireworks up his arm. His grip on the typewriter waning, he bent until he could drop it onto the tarp-covered hardwood floor and cradle his aching arm.

Before he'd even lifted his gaze, he demanded, "What is going on?"

Two blank stares met his when he finally straightened enough to survey the room. Marie chewed on her lips, wide-eyed and unblinking. Jack's eyebrows nearly reached his hairline, his mouth hanging open.

"What's gotten into you, boy?" Jack stepped forward, tipping his chin down and drawing his eyebrows closer together.

Seth blinked several times and pointed over his shoulder, half turning toward the hall. "I heard Marie . . . she sounded . . ."

Jack's grin spread across his face as he scratched at a few days' worth of white whiskers. There was no saving face now. Seth had overreacted. They all knew it. And Jack wasn't going to let it go without a few snide comments.

The old man wiggled his finger between Seth and Marie. "You two finally getting along?"

He wouldn't go that far. He didn't trust the little wisp or like that she'd invaded his recovery time. But it didn't mean he wished trouble on her.

He just wished she'd found somewhere else to stay.

Dodging the question at hand, he motioned around the room. "So what had you all worked up in here?"

Marie didn't say anything—to either of the inquiries—instead she pointed at a bucket of paint. Given the twist of her mouth and the clench of her other fist, the color in question seemed to cause her physical pain.

For good reason.

He jerked his gaze away from it, blinking against the neon yellow glaring from the bucket.

"It didn't turn out quite like the swatch." Jack shrugged. "But it's okay, isn't it?"

"No. It's most definitely not okay." The tone of Marie's voice reminded Seth of his first surfing coach, who had kept strict control of her students with the same snap. "This is the parlor. A place for mingling and relaxing. That color"—she jabbed a finger at the offending bucket—"is for obnoxious billboards and ugly gym clothes. That is not serene and inviting."

Jack rasped his beard stubble again. "Where'd you learn

that?" He voiced the question Seth had been wondering also. She spoke with authority on colors and paint and knew something about antiques. Enough to pick the heaviest typewriter in Aretha's store. The most interesting one too.

She lifted a shoulder, staring at her hands clasped in front of her. "A friend."

When it was clear that she wasn't going to elaborate, Seth laid a hand on Jack's shoulder. "I guess it doesn't matter so much right now. Just trust me when I tell you that her taste is better than yours."

He'd never intended to be on Marie's side about anything, but the girl wasn't afraid to speak her mind. And this time, at least, it had saved them having to repaint the entire room. As long as she was here, he might as well let her be useful.

"So what should we do?" Jack said. "We've got to get paint up in here soon."

"Let's go into Charlottetown tomorrow and pick up some other paint."

"We've got church tomorrow."

Marie frowned at Jack's announcement, but he didn't seem to notice.

"Perhaps on Monday?" Jack suggested.

Seth hiked his thumb over his shoulder in the general direction of his truck. "I said I would take her to the antique auction in Cavendish on Monday."

"All right then. Tuesday we'll go to Charlottetown for new paint." Jack looked back and forth between them as though expecting an argument. "Can't wait any longer than that or we'll run out of time to get the walls painted, dry, and the furniture in."

Marie nodded. "That's good. At least by then we'll have

our central antique pieces and a good idea of complementary colors. But we should talk about tables and dining room linens and curtains and . . . There's so much more to cover." Her hands fluttered in front of her as her voice rose.

Jack rested a hand on her shoulder. "It's all right. Let's talk about it tomorrow night. Make some lists and divide and conquer." His gaze swung around to Seth, his eyes crinkling at the corners. "You'll join us, Seth?"

He held up his hands, backing slowly out of the room. If he didn't get out of there fast, he'd end up roped into spending more time with Marie than he'd already agreed to. He could keep an eye on her and still keep his distance. "I have plenty on my to-do list already. So count me out of that particular brainstorming session."

Marie's bright blue eyes flitted in his direction, her black lashes long and sweeping. She didn't say anything, but it sure seemed like she was asking him to be there. But he was no good at fabric and color. His expertise was structure and drywall. Let him make it a house. Jack was in charge of making it a home.

And if Jack trusted Marie to help him, so be it. It didn't mean Seth would let his guard down. No matter how pretty her eyes.

◆ ◆ ◆ ◆ ◆

Marie pulled her covers under her chin, shivering in the cool morning. Jack had picked her up a set of generic sheets and a scratchy blanket in Charlottetown, but they weren't enough to ward off the Atlantic chill creeping through the basement walls.

Then again, she hadn't been warm in a bed for more than

two months. The memory of being forced onto another bed brought chills from deep within every night. It didn't seem to matter how many layers she wore or how many quilts she pulled up to her chin. The chill always won.

She'd even tried to sleep on the floor once. She'd hoped the hardwood in her bedroom back home would take the teeth from the vile memories enough to give her some rest.

It hadn't.

Now she tried to focus on the worn paperback open in her hands. Tried to lose herself in the story and forget the reasons for the chill.

It didn't work.

Three solid thumps on her door had her shooting out of bed, wrapping the blanket about her shoulders, setting aside her book, and shuffling across the room.

She'd left her white silk robe in Boston. Not that it would have done much to combat the morning air. It had been for show. Like most of her life.

When she opened the apartment door, Jack stood at the bottom of the steps, grinning hard. "We'll leave for church in about thirty minutes. Do you want something for breakfast before we go?"

"Oh, um . . ." She swallowed the hesitation in her voice. "I thought I'd just sleep in this morning. It's been a long couple of days."

His smile widened. "Sure has been. Long, that is. No time like the present to find some refreshment in the Lord's house."

She shook her head. Maybe he hadn't understood. "I'd rather just stay here this morning."

"I'd rather you go with us." His voice turned rock solid, a bit of the strength visible in his shoulders suddenly audible.

What was his deal? Why was he so intent on getting her out of the house and into a church building? Maybe it was more about not wanting to leave her alone in his precious house. "Maybe I'll just go for a walk this morning."

His head began shaking even before she'd finished speaking. "I like you, Marie. You're smart and have a good eye. You can stay here as long as you like. But as long as you're here, you'll go to church with us on Sunday mornings." He couldn't possibly have read the question in her eyes as he gazed into the distance, seeing something that wasn't even there, but he answered her anyway. "My Rose loved the good Lord. And she loved people. She prayed for this house and the people who would stay here for years. Long before we'd ever heard of North Rustico. She'd want to know that the people working on this house love God too."

But what if Marie didn't love him anymore? What if she couldn't?

What if she couldn't even begin to comprehend a loving God—who was supposed to be her Father—who let terrible things happen?

Jack reached out and cupped her ear, smoothing down her bed head in a motion that her mom had used over and over.

Maybe he could read her mind or see the tension in her shoulders. "Even if you're having a hard time loving him, he's not having a hard time loving you. Come to church with us."

His voice creaked with age, like the floorboards of the old house. And even though he didn't seem the enforcer type, he'd drawn the line in the sand. If she wanted a roof over her head, she'd go to church with them.

Her stomach clenched, and she waited for the telltale tightening in her chest. If ever a moment called for a panic attack, this was it. She'd feared the inability to catch a breath, the inevitable dizziness since the attacks had begun just after New Year's Day. But this moment it would save her from sitting in a building surrounded by people praying to a God she could no longer trust.

But it didn't come. Her breaths were as easy and smooth as they'd ever been. Her head didn't swim, and her hands were rock steady.

Wrapping her traitorous arms around her middle, she closed her eyes for a long moment. Jack stood before her, silent except for a small cough.

They remained like that for what felt like hours, and she shifted from one foot to the other.

She couldn't turn her back on the only man who'd ever helped her. He'd asked so little of her in exchange for a safe place to sleep every night. And it was safe. If the way Seth had charged into the parlor at the first hint of trouble was any indication, this home was secure.

Jack's offer had only one string. And it was only for a couple months. By May the inn would open and she'd have enough in her pocket to move on. Enough in her pocket to find a new place for a fresh start.

When she opened her eyes, Jack grinned at her. "I won't make you sit next to Seth. I promise."

She couldn't help but match his smile.

The light slowly dimmed in his eyes, and he squeezed her hand. "I don't know what's haunting you, girl, but you have a home here. As long as you need one."

If only that were true.

8

The cross atop a white steeple pierced the cloudless blue sky, its call reaching far and wide and filling the unpaved lane with churchgoers. Marie leaned toward Jack and said, "I had no idea so many people lived around here."

The wrinkles around his eyes deepened. "First Church has members from across the parish."

They stopped in the green grass beneath the empty branches of an old tree, joining a line of smartly dressed middle-aged women leading to a man with salt-and-pepper hair. His black clothes and white collar gave away his role at the church, but his smile wasn't like that of any priest she'd seen at the cathedral in Boston.

After several moments, the women dispersed.

"Father Chuck." Jack grabbed the other man's hand, pumping it several times in quick succession.

"Jack Sloane." The younger man clapped Jack's shoulder. "Good to see you this morning, as always."

When Father Chuck's eyes shifted to her, Marie sucked

in a quick breath. His eyes were the color of amber. Just like her dad's. He held out his hand, and she gave it a cursory glance, unable to shake it. That required touching this man who reminded her far too much of the past she'd much rather forget.

"Chuck O'Flannigan, parish rector."

"Marie Carrington." Her voice sounded hollow even to her own ears, but she didn't attempt to try again in a warmer greeting.

It took several seconds for him to realize she wasn't going to shake his outstretched hand, but his smile didn't dim as he dropped it back to his side. "What brings you to the Gentle Island, Marie?" Before she could come up with a useful answer, he turned to Jack. "Another family member helping you out? Another one of your brother's kids?"

Seth nearly coughed up a lung behind her, and she covered her mouth with trembling fingers.

"Not quite." Seth snaked an arm around her, brushing the side of her arm, to shake Chuck's hand. If he noticed her jump, he didn't let on. "Just a friend."

"A friend?" Chuck's tone turned teasing, only missing a wink and an elbow nudge to border on church social gossip.

Marie had wanted to ask the same question but for an entirely different reason. Friendship seemed like a bit of a stretch. Sure, they hadn't killed each other after two nights in the same house. But that wasn't exactly friendship. They'd gone antiquing together, but that was entirely at Jack's prodding.

If she had to guess, Seth wanted to be around her about as much as she wanted to be around him.

"Just friends." Seth's tone brooked no argument or further teasing, firm and without doubt.

All right then. Just friends it was.

She could be friendly toward him. Well, at least nonantagonistic.

As long as he kept his space. And didn't insist on being alone with her for longer than a heartbeat. And never touched her again.

He pressed a hand to her lower back, the imprint of his fingers on her coat sending fire through her stomach. He yanked his hand away like the contact burned him too, and she stepped closer to Jack, away from Seth's touch.

She glanced at him out of the corner of her eye as Chuck and Jack chattered about the inn and renovations.

Seth stared at the wide palms and long fingers of his hands as though they'd betrayed him. Had they? Maybe brushing against her was a reflex, something he'd grown used to with someone else.

Well, it didn't mean she couldn't nip that in the bud right away.

Putting another foot between her and Seth, Marie slid closer to Jack. She nearly jumped out of her skin when a hand landed on her shoulder.

"Marie!"

She spun at the singsong sound of her name, catching the raised eyebrows and curious glances of Jack and Seth before coming face-to-face with the woman from the bakery the day before.

"It's Caden. Caden Holt."

"Yes, of course." Marie let herself be pulled into a quick hug, fighting the urge to push away. This was good. She should practice letting people touch her again.

As long as it wasn't Seth.

"I didn't expect to see you here." Caden's bright eyes flashed toward Seth, then to Father Chuck, who earned a quick nod and a wider smile as he excused himself to prepare for the service. "You didn't come back to the shop yesterday, so I assume you found Aretha's."

"Yes. Thank you for the directions. I did." She waved a hand over her shoulder toward Seth. "We found some great pieces."

"I'm so glad."

An awkward silence settled over them before Marie's childhood training kicked in. "I'm so sorry. Where are my manners? Caden, this is Jack Sloane. He owns the Red Door Inn."

Caden and Jack shook hands vigorously as she smiled. "Is that what you've named it? The Red Door?"

"Would seem so." Jack chuckled.

Caden's cheeks, rosy from the morning breeze, drooped. "But the door isn't red, is it?"

Jack all-out hooted at that. "Not yet, my dear. Not yet." As he wiped his eyes, he continued, "This is my nephew Seth. He and I have a lot of work to do on the old house before we open."

Caden waved at Seth, flashing her teeth at him. "When will you open?"

"In May."

The smile faded, leaving Caden with scrunched-up eyebrows. "May? That's two months away."

Jack nodded with a wide grin while Marie pressed her hand over the stone rumbling in her stomach. Why did Caden seem worried that they wouldn't be able to get the doors open in May? Of course they could get the inn ready. Right?

"Well, I'm sure it'll be lovely." Caden nodded toward

a row of redheaded little boys and girls standing at the stairs leading up to the front door. "Would you like to sit with us?"

"Are they yours?" Marie clapped a hand over her mouth. If her mother was still alive, she'd have been mortified. A lady didn't say things like that. She didn't act surprised at the thought of having half a dozen kids.

The other woman's laugh filled the churchyard. "Oh, no. They're my nieces and nephews. That's my brother and his wife over there."

Flames brushed from Marie's collarbone up to her ears. "Of course."

"So, would you like to sit with us?"

Marie stared at Seth, who had twisted toward his uncle, his shoulders pulling tight against his button-up shirt. Those shoulders probably took up more than their fair share of a church pew.

"That would be very nice."

But as they settled into the wooden pew, worn smooth over the years, those imposing shoulders were right in front of her. Jack turned and gave her a smile, but she could only glare at the back of Seth's head as it blocked her view of Father Chuck.

Why was he always in her way? And he was far too close for anyone's comfort.

A little finger poked her leg, and she glanced at the child sitting next to her. With red braids and freckles dancing across her nose, she was as close to a living version of Montgomery's fictional orphan as Marie had ever seen.

"I'm holding the hymnal, so you've got to turn the pages."

"What?"

The girl shook the book in her hands, yellowed pages flapping as the melody from the piano began to fill the square room. "It's two pages. You have to turn the page when it's time." Her little eyes squinted hard as if she wasn't sure Marie was up to the job.

"All right." She leaned toward the girl and lowered her voice, but it still filled the silence in the split-second pause before nearly one hundred people began singing.

Every eye within a two-row radius spun toward her.

Every eye except the ones right in front of her.

The pianist pounded out a lively tune, his foot stomping with the crescendo. He sounded like he belonged at a piano bar rather than a Sunday morning church service.

There had been a pianist at the New Year's Eve party two months before. Of course, he'd been playing classics in the hotel ballroom. He hadn't even deigned to play a Billy Joel or Elton John song. Too bawdy for the tuxedo-clad guest list. Too common for the exceedingly expensive tastes of Boston's elite.

She'd heard that music deep in her toes. Her laughter had mingled with it as she let *him* kiss her, let him dance her out of the room. Let him lead her to the elevator. He'd promised to show her the view of the fireworks from his balcony.

From the penthouse the city shone like a sparkler on the Fourth of July. They could even make out the roiling, teeming crowd in the square. Another year about to begin. Another year—

"Now. Turn the page." The whisper in her ear and poke in her side sent her nearly to the ceiling, and she pawed at the page, ripping it at the top near the center.

Caden's niece scowled at her, but she could only shrug

and mouth her apology before it was time to flip the page back for the start of the second verse.

There'd be no tuning out during this song. Or the sermon either, given the pointed fingers and even more pointed glares of her pew neighbor.

That was all right. She'd rather not dwell on New Year's Eve. She was much better off forgetting Boston. For the moment she could rest in Rustico. And when she needed to leave, she'd go. If the memories got too close or the nightmares too strong, she'd go.

If she stayed put too long, her father would track her down and convince her that he needed her help to close the land deal. That he needed her presence in his office in order to make his threat viable.

She couldn't let that happen. She'd find the right time to move on, before it was too late.

But in this moment she'd turn the page. Very carefully.

◆◆◆◆◆

After the service ended, Aretha bid Father Chuck a good day before sailing down the stairs. She brushed past Betty Robertson with little more than a pat on the back, her gaze never wavering from Marie, her tall young man, and the silver fox next to them.

She was still several meters away when they turned toward the parking lot. Throwing decorum aside, she waved and hollered, "Marie, honey."

The girl's chestnut waves flopped over her shoulder as she turned, clearly surprised at first. Then she bestowed a rich smile, as though she'd long missed having a friend with whom she could share it.

Aretha hustled across the lawn, her breaths coming in quick gasps.

A woman her age was inclined to avoid exercise at every opportunity. But a single man in Rustico, well, he was worth a bit of a jog.

"Aretha." Marie greeted her with an outstretched hand that she quickly pulled back then held forward again. As though to cover her indecisive movements, she hurried to add, "I wasn't sure I'd see you here today."

"And why not? Did you think me such a heathen that I wouldn't even attend a church in my own backyard?"

Marie's eyes opened wide, her mouth pumping like the handle on an empty well and her cheeks turning red. "I just meant, maybe we wouldn't bump into each other."

The poor girl thought she was serious. Aretha tossed her head back and let her laughter bubble over. For several seconds, she could only pat Marie's arm as she let the mirth overtake her.

Finally she wiped the pool of tears from her eyes and leaned into the mute girl. "I'm only teasing you, child. We must teach you to loosen up."

Fear flickered in Marie's eyes, and Aretha's humor vanished. Whatever had caused this girl so much grief still haunted her. It had probably chased her all the way to the island. All the way to North Rustico. In good time, she'd have to address that. But she was young. There would be time to uncover the pain, lay it bare, and reveal the truth. And then she'd learn to find joy again.

Aretha knew a thing or two about finding joy. And about the pain that made it so hard to claim.

But that had been so long ago. Now she had the store of

her dreams, a new little friend, and a very handsome man standing right in front of her.

Wrapping a loose arm around Marie's shoulders, she nodded toward the two men shooting her strange glances out of the corners of their eyes. "Seth, it's good to see you again."

"You too, ma'am."

His handshake was stiff. Overly formal. Like she hadn't swiped his credit card for more than a thousand dollars the day before. Like she hadn't asked him to knock on the restroom door to check on Marie. Like she hadn't seen the tenderness in his touch as he helped Marie to his truck.

His smile was as stiff as his shake, his gaze bouncing from her to Marie and back.

Where was that gentleness and concern today?

But the man on his other side didn't have to force anything. His teeth shone in the noontime sun as he leaned forward, the crinkles in his cheeks deepening where he once probably had dimples. Now they were covered with lines of age and life.

"I'm Jack Sloane." He bowed ever so slightly, a mere slant at his waist.

Boys didn't do that anymore. Neither did most men, for that matter.

But clearly courtesy wasn't a lost art. Jack knew how to introduce himself to a lady. Even one pink in the cheeks from a jog across the lush grass.

"It's a pleasure to meet you, Jack. Aretha Franklin of Aretha's Antiques. No relation to the singer."

Jack's white brows lifted, his lip curling. "You're the woman responsible for the state of my credit card bill."

"Guilty." She wiggled her eyebrows. At least she hoped

that was what she was doing. "But you'll thank me for it when you see the finished rooms."

His laugh was deep, like the baritone who had just sung the closing hymn. "Marie has quite the eye for antiques."

The girl still tucked under her arm squirmed at the praise but didn't pull completely away. Aretha tightened her squeeze just enough to keep Marie in place, her gaze never leaving Jack's face. "I couldn't agree more."

A pleasant flush crept up Marie's neck, and she stared hard at her simple black flats as though without careful supervision they might run off by themselves.

Leaning into the young woman, Arctha continued. "She picked the very best typewriter in the store without a single suggestion from me."

Seth shifted his weight to his other long leg. "The best? It wasn't the most expensive. Not by a long shot."

"Why should the cost make it the best?" She shot Marie a look that the younger woman immediately nodded to. Some things about shopping, men just didn't understand. "Marie chose the only antique typewriter in my store that actually works."

"What?" Marie's head whipped up, her blue eyes alight. "I didn't know that. But how could it possibly be in working condition? It's got to be at least ninety years old. And the nicks and scratches on the keys—it's seen plenty of use over the years."

"The man who owned it before you, the man who sold it to me, was a bit of a tinkerer. He spent hours with that thing, fixing the letters, replacing the ribbons, greasing the levers. He showed it to me when I bought it. The old girl works like a charm." Aretha turned to Seth. "I hope you'll write me a letter on it." She winked at him without losing sight of Jack's full-on grin. The man had joy in his eyes and a full-throated chuckle that made her spine tingle like a woman half her age.

Jack thumped his nephew on the back. "Just don't trifle with Miss Franklin's affections, son." His laughter mingled with her own.

Maybe those tingles were more like a woman a quarter of her age.

"How are the rest of the renovations coming on the inn? Nearly ready to open?"

"Not quite." Jack scratched at the back of his neck, dipping his head low.

It sounded like there was more to be done than time to do it.

Seth rubbed his stomach, his long fingers making slow circles over his flat belly. A man working on a home needed to eat. And from the size of both him and Jack, they needed to eat regularly. It couldn't hurt to offer them a meal.

"I made up a pot of potato stew. Care to join me for a bite and a little furniture talk? Perhaps I could even give you a peek at the other pieces selling at the auction this week."

Marie's posture straightened. She had the girl's attention.

"My stew's not much, but it's a sight more than a pork and jerk."

"Pork and jerk?" Seth and Marie asked at the same time.

Aretha laughed. "I suppose it's not a common phrase anymore, but my mother often used it to refer to a meal so small it didn't suffice. In the old days of the island, if a family had only one piece of ham for dinner, each person got a chance to chew on it. But if they hung on to the meat too long, well . . ." She held up a hand and mimicked yanking on the end of the string.

Seth and Marie both looked shocked, but Jack's chuckle bubbled over in unexpected delight. "I've never heard such a thing." His mirth choked him, and he pressed a hand to his side before taking two long breaths.

The young ones stared at each other, then at Jack as Seth grabbed his uncle's elbow, steadying the swaying man.

"Well? Shall I plan on noon guests, then?"

"We'd be delighted," Jack said.

Seth scowled, not nearly as enthusiastic as Jack, but whatever was poking the seat of his trousers would work itself out in due time. For now, she had a lunch date with her new little friend. And the first man to make her insides dance in more than forty years.

9

Seth twisted the wrench with a sure grip, the last piece of pipe below the kitchen sink finally in place. As he curled to fit his wide shoulders through the cabinet doors, he slid onto the neutral tile floor. Picking up the orange bucket that had lived under the leaking drain, he walked through the laundry room, toward the back door, and tossed the brown water into the yard.

The open door sent a chill up his arms, the wind making the damp ring around his shirt collar nearly frigid. Still, the cool fabric felt good against his clammy skin.

They wouldn't need the bucket again anytime too soon, so he threw it into the empty walk-in pantry, eyeing the walls and hoping to find something more than the freshly painted shelves. But it was as empty as his growling stomach.

He'd enjoyed the leftover potato stew Aretha had sent home with them on Sunday. Rich potatoes, chunks of ham, and cheesy goodness. It was the best meal he'd had since arriving on the island. But they'd finished it off for dinner the night before.

And the three-day rain that had postponed the antique auction had also kept him from making a real grocery trip. It was high time they had some food in the house.

But maybe not tonight. Tonight he wanted something sweet. Something cool and creamy.

He strode to his toolbox, which sat on the floor in front of the sink. His trusted monkey wrench fit back into its place just where it belonged.

The weight of his tools in his hands felt good. His fingers fit around the box's handle like they always had. Nothing had changed about his comfort or skill or knowledge.

Reece hadn't been able to take that away from him when she walked out of his life.

And the money she'd stolen, the bank account she'd emptied . . . well, that money could be made again. There was risk in every business endeavor. He'd known that when he started his own construction company in San Diego seven years before.

He just hadn't figured a threat would come from his own fiancée.

"Pretty color." Jack's voice carried through the swinging door, and Seth turned in that direction. He hadn't seen the paint they'd picked out for the dining room or the three bedrooms on the second floor.

"It's a perfect complement to the silver chandelier." Marie's voice rose with animation as he pushed open the door between the rooms. "And when we get the buffet and tables at the auction next week, the cherrywood will just sing against this wall."

"Singing wood? Sounds like you've got a bad batch."

The paint roller in Marie's hand tumbled, paint marks

skidding down the wall, until it thumped onto the tarp beneath her step stool. With little more than a surprised glance in his direction, she jumped to the ground to retrieve it.

She didn't reply to his mild joke, so he leaned against the doorjamb, admiring the slate-blue color that made the crown molding pop. "It's a beautiful color."

Without missing a beat, she said, "It'll be even better after the second coat. When you can't see the green behind it."

Jack grunted. "It's not that bad." It was his same old argument. And it still wasn't working.

"It really was." Marie resumed the smooth movements of her roller, forming perfect Ws with each stroke.

"Where'd you learn to do that?"

"What?" She sounded innocent.

But she had an eye for design and skills that were more than basic. Her movements were practiced and her design arguments solid. He'd worked with enough interior designers to pick up a few tricks of their trade. Hanging mirrors in a small room made it appear larger. An entire room could be designed around a single focal point. And the fastest way to overhaul a room was with a fresh coat of paint.

What a difference a new color could make. Even now, the long room was beginning to look like it could actually serve as the dining hall. At least the color of the walls no longer made his stomach roll.

"Where'd you learn how to stand up to stubborn old men with no sense of aesthetics?"

"Hey, now." Despite the tone of his words that implied offense, Jack's grin gave him away.

Marie shrugged, never taking her gaze off her section of the wall as she stepped from her stool and moved it closer to the corner. "Here and there, I guess." She swiped the back of her wrist across her forehead, the roller in her hand precariously close to the knot of brown waves tied on top of her head.

When it was clear she wasn't going to continue, he prodded her. "Like where?"

"Like, I might be more interested in telling you if you picked up a brush and finished off that corner."

Jack's snort ricocheted off the high ceiling, until Seth joined in with a chuckle of his own.

Picking up a soft-bristled brush, he dipped the very tip of it into Marie's pan. He caught her eye and nodded to his hand, reminding her of her promise to expand on the heres and theres of her history. After a week under the same roof, he didn't know any more about her than he had when Jack had first brought her home.

"This will go so much faster if we don't have to go back and do the corners."

He nodded as he daubed into the corner, filling every crevice with the new color, covering the offending one. As he lifted his arm over his head and brought it back down to his side, he cleared his throat. Silence remained.

Had she forgotten her end of the deal? It was high time she filled in some holes of her own.

He coughed again.

"Got something in your throat, boy?"

"I'm just fine." He caught Marie glancing in his direction, the corners of her mouth quirked in the slightest grin. So her smile at Aretha's wasn't a fluke. She couldn't be bothered to show any emotion most of the time, and this unexpected moment between them made his heart thump a little heavier than usual.

He couldn't help the grin he offered in return. Before she could look away, he prompted her. "So, Marie, tell us where you learned all about fancy antiques and color swatches and such."

A cloud slipped across her face before she ducked back into the paint pan. "A friend."

Could she be more vague? "What sort of friend?"

"A very kind one." Her voice nearly disappeared on the last word, and he leaned toward her to make sure he wouldn't miss anything she might add. But she was done.

"Where's this friend now?"

Jack coughed, clearly a bid to draw attention from Marie and save her from having to answer Seth's personal question, but she didn't seem to get the message. He frowned in his uncle's direction. No need to keep her from opening up.

"I'm not sure. We lost touch when my—when I left for college."

Whatever she had been about to say, she shut down, afraid to say the truth.

But why? What had she come so close to sharing?

And more importantly, what secrets was she intent on keeping?

It had been his experience that women with secrets did whatever it took to keep hidden things in the dark. At the moment she was spending more of Jack's money than her labor was worth. And that was an investment he couldn't risk without knowing more about her.

Maybe he could ease her into talking more. Once the conversation flowed, she might let down her guard just a bit and actually tell them something more than Boston. "Where'd you go to college?"

She shook her head without looking up from her paint pan.

"Boston University? Harvard?"

"No."

"MIT?"

Her snort was more sarcasm than humor, but it was still the closest to a laugh he'd heard from her.

"Science not your thing?"

He expected a shake of her head to be her only response until she said, "Not even close."

"Seth here was an—"

Seth cut Jack off with a loud cough, quickly moving the conversation into safer waters. He might want to know her background, but it didn't mean he was going to tell her all about his own degree in engineering or his penchant for number games. "So what is your thing?"

Her roller flashed in the air. "Today it's painting. Next week it's antique hunting. And one of these days it's going to be quilting." She looked up at the ceiling and pressed her lips together. "That's not quite right. I'm going quilt shopping."

"Will there be some at the antique show?"

"Aretha said she thought so. I'll definitely check."

Jack poured more paint into his tray, shooting a wistful glance in her direction. "Wish I could go too."

The rescheduled day of the auction hadn't worked any better for Jack, who had another one of his endless meetings. But Marie had been as excited as ever.

While her back was turned and her gaze focused on the path of blue left by her roller, Seth stole another quick glance. Escaped strands of dark hair hung over her narrow shoulders, which tapered to a slim waist, no matter how hard she tried to hide it under baggy sweatshirts. She couldn't be much more than five feet tall, but as she stretched across the wall, she managed to reach all the way to the line that he'd painted from the corner.

Another swipe of her forearm to get the hair out of her face left a blue stripe along her temple, and he chuckled.

"What?"

"Blue's a good color on you."

Her pert little nose wrinkled and her pink lips pursed. "What does that mean?"

He pointed to the spot above his own ear with his brush.

Reaching around with her left hand, she patted her hair. When she pulled her fingers back, she shot him a scowl like he'd been the one to throw paint on her.

"Hey, why are you looking at me like that? That's not my fault."

She opened her mouth, then snapped it closed. Ice-blue eyes still flashing, she shook her head and returned to the work at hand.

The suddenly silent work.

Except for Jack's off-tune whistling, the room was quiet. Not even the walls groaned as they slathered on another coat of paint.

Jack hit a particularly sour note halfway through "Yankee Doodle Dandy," and Seth glanced at his uncle's hunched shoulders that rose and fell in quick succession. Marie seemed happy enough to talk with Jack. So why wouldn't she open up to someone closer to her own age?

Maybe it's because you've been about as welcoming as a hungry shark.

He silenced the voice in his head with a quick shake.

Even if it might be true.

Maybe it would help if he was a little warmer. He could

do that. In fact, if he just got her alone for a bit, maybe she'd talk with him about what had brought her to the island. And he'd find out why she didn't want to tell them where she'd come from. Or what her intentions were with Jack's property.

"I was thinking about getting some ice cream after we're done here."

Out of the corner of his eye he caught a quick jerk of her head. Definite interest.

"There's an ice cream shop at the end of the boardwalk, near the beach, by the fishing village."

"The boardwalk?" Marie squinted at him as though trying to envision the wooden path to the creamy treat.

"Yes." He pointed toward the bay. "The one that's practically right outside the front door."

She shook her head slowly and looked at the ceiling.

Had she really missed the two-kilometer footpath around the bay's inlet? The tree-lined boardwalk where couples strolled at dusk. The one filled with equal parts tourists and locals. The one along the bay that sometimes matched the color of Marie's eyes.

"I don't think I've seen it."

Jack laughed as he scooped the last dregs from his can of paint. "Been inside quite a bit with the rain and all, huh?"

"Well . . ." She frowned.

Three days of rain and sleet had kept them mostly inside. Except for Marie and Jack's trip to Charlottetown to pick up paint. As far as Seth could tell, Marie had been responsible for the paint while Jack went to the hardware store to pick up the u-bend pipe that Seth had just installed.

There had been plenty to keep them busy. Seth had finished the grout work in one of the downstairs bathrooms while Marie painted the upstairs bedrooms. Those walls were nearly dry enough for them to move the furniture in.

Which meant working with her again.

She'd managed to mostly avoid him during their confinement, and he hadn't argued the point. It was easier keeping his distance.

Just not if he needed to know her secrets.

Maybe the shining sun that morning had signaled more than just a change in their freedom. It could mean a chance for them to start new projects and finish conversations like the one she'd been avoiding for the past forty-five minutes.

At this moment, it certainly meant the ability to walk the boardwalk. Of course, it wasn't quite spring in the Maritimes, so he'd probably regret his craving by the time he arrived at the hole-in-the-wall ice cream shop. But a few goose bumps had never kept him from a frozen treat in the past.

"I'm pretty tired. I think I'll go to bed early." Marie sounded like she immediately regretted her decision. Good. Maybe she'd be easily swayed.

"Are you sure?" He gave her his best, least sharklike grin. "It's not a far walk, and they have the best ice cream on the island—besides cows, of course."

"Cows?"

"Come with me. I'll tell you all about it."

Hope flickered in her eyes, then vanished as quickly as it had appeared. "I'm really tired. I'm going to clean up my roller and then go to bed."

He motioned to the nine-paned window. "But the sun is barely setting."

She shrugged and hopped from her ladder. "It's been a really busy day." Scooping up her materials, she hurried toward the kitchen and thumped against the laundry room door before it slammed behind her.

"Wow." He breathed the word before remembering that he wasn't alone.

Jack chuckled. "Never seen a girl run from ice cream that fast. Maybe that's why she's so small."

Seth couldn't help but laugh, despite the twist in his stomach that implied true regret. Of course he wished she'd go with him. He wanted answers.

Not a romantic stroll along the boardwalk.

His gut rolled again. Patting a hand over it, he said, "I guess I'm hungry. I'm going to take a walk. Do you want anything?"

Jack shook his white hair, resting a hand on Seth's shoulder. "They won't all run away."

The old man had clearly lost his sense. He was talking like Seth wanted alone time with Marie for reasons far removed from revealing her true intentions.

Jack of all people should have known that he wasn't interested in another romantic relationship. At least not anytime soon.

His face must have telegraphed his confusion as Jack just patted his back and lifted a sloped shoulder. "We'll see about that, I suppose."

There was nothing to see about. He had no deeper need to know about Marie's background except to protect Jack's investment. His rumbling stomach was just hunger. The sandwich and potato chips he'd had for lunch clearly hadn't lasted very long.

His concern—his only concern—was to make sure Marie didn't walk away with Jack's money. And that was plenty of reason to spend time with her. He just had to keep reminding himself of that.

"I'll take care of that." Jack nodded at the brush in Seth's hand. "Go get your cone."

"You're sure you don't want anything?"

Jack shook his head as Seth handed off his paintbrush and strolled toward the front entry. After pulling his jacket over his sweatshirt and zipping it up to his chin, he grabbed a cap from the top shelf of the coat closet and pulled it low over his ears.

The wind whipped at his jeans as he left the porch's protection, and he squirmed deeper into the jacket, thankful for its wind-resistant lining.

He waited for a car to meander down the otherwise empty street before dashing across and trotting down the steps to the walkway. Leaning into the wind, he trudged toward the big yellow barn beyond the point where the path veered back across the road to the white sand beach.

He barely gave the sputtering fishing boat in the bay a second glance as it made a pass through the buoys marking the mussel-farm stockings, collecting the day's haul.

He had eyes only for the ice cream shanty.

And he couldn't seem to drop the thoughts of the girl who had so easily turned down his invitation. Whatever her past, whatever her plans, he'd figure them out. She may have turned him down this time, but he wasn't going to give up easily. There would be other nights of ice cream. And they had more rooms to paint. Of course, the upcoming auction meant time together too.

One way or another, he'd get her alone. And he'd get her to answer some real questions.

10

The morning sun hadn't made its first appearance over the wide berth of the bay when Marie closed the front door behind her. The latch fell into place with a soft snick, and she tiptoed down the steps in case her movement inside had stirred Jack or Seth.

She closed her eyes and sniffed the air. The breeze carried a familiar scent, but not quite like the Atlantic shore she'd grown up with. Even the sound of the waves was different, the force of the sea a gentle rocking against the coastline. She could hear the waves from wherever they lapped at the beach, singing a sweet song of peace.

The one thing she hadn't been able to find in Boston after that night.

The waves called to her, and she let her feet guide her across the street and then down the set of stairs she'd seen Seth use on his ice cream run.

Oh, how she'd wanted to go with him, to treat herself to her favorite dessert, the one her Boston friends had considered too pedestrian. Her school friends were crème brûlée and tiramisu. And her father's business partners were more edible gold than waffle cone.

After three long days, caged by the rain and surrounded by paint fumes, all she'd wanted was a scoop of strawberry on top of a classic sugar cone.

But she'd turned down the offer.

She stomped her running shoes harder than necessary on the boards worn smooth by thousands of feet, lit by the brilliant moon and fading lamplights.

Why had she refused Seth's invitation?

He wasn't a threat to her. A bit grumpy maybe. What had Jack called him? Sour milk? Yes, that was about right. He could certainly be sour, and she didn't appreciate his nosy questions about her past. But those were easy enough to dodge. Besides, they would have been in public the entire time.

She'd sworn never again to put herself in a situation like New Year's Eve. But this wasn't the Old Liberty Hotel.

Her feet moved quicker, punishing the ground for her regrets.

And they hadn't been sipping champagne for hours.

Sweat beaded across her upper lip, and she wiped her sleeve across it.

And she hadn't gone to Seth's room to see the view.

Her heart thudded, building speed to equal the rhythm of her feet, matching the echoes of her shoes.

And she hadn't let him kiss her.

The wind chapped her lips, and she bit them together, pressing harder, pulling from somewhere deeper as the evergreen trees and a white gazebo flew past.

And Seth hadn't pushed her onto his bed. And then again after she stood, trying to slip to the door.

She had ears only for the waves, only for the never-ending ebbs and flows.

And he hadn't ripped the strap off her golden dress, sending a shower of beads across the hotel room's carpet.

She squinted at a cluster of brightly painted buildings beginning to take shape ahead and leaned toward them. Her arms pumping faster and stronger. Her breaths coming sharper and harder.

He hadn't whispered slurred commands to her to be quiet as he pawed at what was left of her dress.

Even when the wooden boardwalk turned into the paved road, she never stopped running. Answering the call of the waves. Craving that song she'd heard even a mile away and the peace it promised.

Seth hadn't held her shoulders down, his forearm pressed against her throat.

Her shoe caught a patch of loose sand spread over the pavement, but she didn't slow down as she crested the gentle hill before a white shoreline.

He hadn't pushed his hand over her mouth and slapped her face when she bit him. Or ignored her sobs as she begged him to stop.

Seth hadn't done any of those things. He wasn't Derek.

She fell to her knees at the cusp of the wet sand. Through pinched eyelids, tears somehow managed to leak down her cheeks, mingling with the spray of the waves. Her heart still thumped painfully, and a familiar tightness in her chest promised another panic attack.

She sucked in several quick breaths, waiting for the air to turn off and the pain she knew so well to begin. She'd wait it out, kneeling before the lapping waves.

Pressing crossed hands to the base of her throat, she prayed the ache wouldn't come. That it wouldn't leave her more depleted than the memory had already.

Still she waited. It was useless. Prayer hadn't stopped Derek from stealing her hope and leaving her broken. God hadn't even been listening when her mom died. Maybe he just didn't hear her anymore.

If he did hear her, he didn't care enough about her pain to step in.

Once Father Niles, with his clipped British accent and handsome flourish of salt-and-pepper hair, had told her God was her heavenly Father. He'd compared God's love for people to the love fathers have for their own kids.

That made sense. Her dad didn't care much for her either. At least he didn't care enough to stand by her when she'd tried to tell him the truth. He'd told her they'd find a way to make it right. And she'd believed him. She'd thought they would go to the police station together, that he'd hold her hand while she made her statement. Each time she suggested it, he told her it wasn't the right time. They'd have to wait.

That was what she'd done. Despite her therapist's encouragement to report the crime, she'd waited.

Until she'd overheard his phone call with Derek's dad and the threat to use her pain as leverage for the land he wanted.

He'd picked a business deal over her, profit over his only child.

And she couldn't wait anymore. She wouldn't be a pawn in her father's sick game.

If that was how God cared for her, no amount of prayer could stave off the dizziness and narrowed vision or the knot in her stomach. No amount of begging would heal what had been broken. No amount of crying would restore her heart.

If God was like her father, he cared only about himself.

She focused on the orange glow peeking over the horizon as it slowly broke free of the fog. As the sun rose, donning all of its pink and purple glory, she didn't move. One little movement could trigger the attack, one hiccup could make the world black.

Then again, waiting helplessly for its imminent arrival wouldn't make the assault any less painful or end any faster. Delaying the inevitable wasn't her style. Better to just get it over with. So she took a slow breath through her mouth.

The misty air swirled inside her, filling her chest, pushing against the restrictive band.

Strange.

After exhaling through tight lips, she risked another breath that pushed even harder against the crushing pain in her chest.

With each gulp of air, the weight lifted until it vanished like the darkness as the sun displayed its power.

"Good morning." Marie nearly jumped into the water at the sound of another voice. "Isn't it beautiful today?"

She nodded mutely at the woman in a black wetsuit, who dipped her toe into the water before yanking it back quickly and wrapping her arms around her middle.

"It's a bit cold, eh. But there's nothing like the North Shore in the morning." Her gaze was curious but kind as she nodded toward the water. "Are you swimming today?"

Marie shook her head, and the woman smiled widely before wading into the water. "Well then, have a good one." Then she was gone, her flapping arms heading toward the end of the rock jetty the only trace of her.

Pushing to her feet, Marie stumbled in the loose sand and backed away from the waves with each easy breath. And they were so easy. Unencumbered by the usual tightness.

Her panic attack hadn't come. For the first time in more than two months, her body hadn't shut down at the very thought of Derek or hint of danger.

Maybe there *was* something special about this place. Just like the books had claimed.

She'd return to this spot, but she couldn't linger just now. She hadn't told Jack where she was going, and if she disappeared, he'd worry. And Seth would assume the worst of her—whatever he thought that was.

As she hurried back along the boardwalk, she took the time to soak in the island's beauty. The majestic green trees thrived even this early in spring. And the sun reflected on the water, leaving the inlet a rich sapphire that belonged in the best Tiffany necklace money could buy. The sputtering hum of a fishing boat on the far side of the water set a rhythm for her slow jog, the whistle of the morning birds a bright soundtrack.

Prince Edward Island. It was at once everything that she had imagined as a child and far beyond anything she'd dared to hope.

Could any place be so beautiful *and* have the power to lift the weight of her nightmares and a father's betrayal from her shoulders?

As she climbed the steps to view the Red Door Inn, she sighed. Only time would tell if the island's magic held more than pretty views and rolling ocean swells. If they were to have the inn ready to open in two months, there would be little time to think about it.

She swept through the front door into the foyer, only realizing the force of the wind when she was free of it. Her cheeks stung in the warmth of the home as she hung up her jacket, thankful she'd left Boston with at least some protection from the elements. She'd only brought three pairs of pants and four tops. That was all that would fit into her backpack. Running away with a Louis Vuitton roller bag just hadn't been inconspicuous or practical.

People always assumed that a woman with designer luggage would have more than three hundred dollars to her name. But that's all the ATM had allowed her to take out before hopping that bus to Bangor. She didn't need bus drivers asking why she was taking the bus toward Canada while raising their eyebrows about her bag. As far as the border agent who had checked her passport in Woodstock, New Brunswick, was concerned, she was just another tourist visiting his country, traveling in a bus full of the same. Anything more would have raised a few eyebrows.

And those sorts of things always had a way of getting back to her dad. He needed her in Boston, needed to dangle her in front of Derek Sr. He'd be looking for her, and flying under the radar meant giving up the amenities she'd long enjoyed.

Except she didn't really miss them. Not at the Red Door.

She walked into the kitchen, surprised that she hadn't heard the men's voices, as they looked up over their cups of coffee.

"Up early?" Jack's morning conversation was more clipped than usual.

She pointed over her shoulder. "Went for a run."

Seth lifted his eyebrows. "So you found the boardwalk?"

What gave her away? She smoothed her hands over her

wind-whipped hair and fought the urge to drop her gaze to the floor. That was what she would have done a week before. But today she'd already run more than two miles, seen the sun rise over the ocean, and conquered a panic attack.

It was going to be a good day. No matter what.

"We're just making a plan for today." From on top of his daily *New York Times*, Jack picked up a white sheet of paper, the simple kind she'd use in a printer. Or a typewriter.

Maybe she could track down a sheet of that and get to see the shiny black Underwood in action.

"What's on the list?"

Jack pointed one corner of the paper in Seth's direction. "He's going to install a closet rod in the bedroom upstairs and finish the grout work in that first-floor bathroom."

"I'm going to have to go pick up another tub of grout today." Seth disappeared behind his mug, white curls of steam spiraling past his temples.

"What about you, Marie?"

She glanced toward the dining room. "I guess I'll put another coat of paint in there. And then I thought I'd visit Aretha. After spending a day in the dining room, I realized that we don't have any dishes or flatware. Maybe I can pick some out. And I can stop by the grocery store on my way home and pick up a few things."

Seth's eyes brightened, his brows disappearing into the wrinkles on his forehead. He looked surprised. Did he think she didn't know how to fend for herself?

"Good. Good." Jack nodded, scratching notes onto his list. "Been too long since we had enough decent food in the house." He dug into his pocket and handed her several bills. "First week of work."

He shoved the money at her, and despite suddenly numb fingers, she accepted it. The bills lying against her palm weren't much, but they brought a smile to her face. She didn't have a desk or her name on a door. She hadn't swindled or coaxed this money from anyone. This was hers because she'd earned every penny.

Jack shoved another wad of cash at her. "And here's for the grub." Seth's gaze came down heavily on her, but she did her best to ignore it. He couldn't possibly be angry that she was going to stock their pantry. Then again, he might not appreciate it if she tried replacing his sour milk with something more fresh.

As if on cue, her stomach rumbled, upset at still being empty after a run. Marie chuckled, pressing her hand to her middle. "Maybe I'll go shopping before I paint."

Seth nodded, his eyes flat and the merest hint of a smile playing across his face. It was clear he didn't feel it, but apparently he was trying. She offered him the same grin in response. She could try too.

He wasn't Derek.

She blinked several times against the punch to her stomach and swallowed the bile that rose to the back of her throat.

It was best not to think about him. Best to forget Boston, except to stay a step ahead of it.

Folding the money carefully in half and then in half again, she backed toward the door. "I guess I'll get going."

"Do you want a ride?" Seth's words were quiet and about as soft as cement. He wanted to offer her a ride about as much as he wanted to smile at her.

In spite of that apparent truth, the simple offer caught her off guard, and she bumped into the door in her hasty escape.

Getting the groceries home would be a lot easier in his truck. It would also necessitate one-on-one time.

"No. Nope. I'm good." Grabbing her jacket, she hurried outside before he could offer again.

She could spend time with him another day. No need to rush into these things. There would be plenty of togetherness between the auction and finishing painting.

As she hustled down the road, away from her beach, she yanked the zipper up to her chin. She'd been used to Boston cold, but PEI temperatures were an entirely new low.

She rounded the bend in the road at a pace that matched her frenzied run earlier. And just as her stomach reminded her that she hadn't eaten, the white bakery appeared.

A quick stop to see Caden couldn't hurt.

Neither could a cinnamon roll.

The bell on the door jingled as Marie stepped inside.

"Be right there." The voice didn't belong to Caden or any other woman, the deep tones nearly rattling the shelves on the walls.

"Um . . ." Her gaze swept around the empty room three times. All with the same result. It was empty, and she was alone with another man—one she didn't know. "No rush."

Maybe she should just forget breakfast. She could get something to eat at the grocery store. She put her hand on the doorknob, ready to turn it, until the sweet smell of cinnamon and sugar unfurled from the back room, keeping her feet grounded.

Suddenly the knob in her hand twisted, and the door swung open as she tumbled in its wake, still clinging to the handle.

"Whoa!" Caden jumped out of the way and then immediately reached out to steady Marie. Caden's wide eyes didn't overshadow her smile as Marie found her footing. Before she could move, Caden enveloped her in a hug that felt like she'd stepped inside all over again.

"Good morning."

Marie shivered as Caden let her go with a pat on the back. "I'm so glad to see you. Aretha told my mom that Jack isn't feeding you. They're all so worried about you getting enough to put some meat on your bones. They keep talking about stopping by the inn to check on you. But really, I think they just want to see what you've done with the old place. It's been empty for more than a year, you know. Are you hungry? Come inside. Dad is making pecan potato rolls. It's one of our specialties. You'll love them."

Her mind swirled as fast as the words gushed from Caden's mouth. But she'd definitely heard something about a pecan potato roll, so she followed Caden.

"Pumpkin? Is that you?"

"Yes, Dad. Are you done with—"

A man with a shock of red hair stepped from the kitchen. Maybe his hair just looked brighter against the head-to-toe white baker's uniform. He was clearly related to the little girl with the pointy fingers who'd given Marie the evil eye for accidentally tearing the hymnal page. From the hair to the round blue eyes to the little clefts in their chins, they were obviously family.

He stuck his hand out, and she slipped hers into the giant mitt. "James Holt. You must be the girl everyone's talking about."

Marie's jaw fell slack and her neck burned, the heat creeping up it faster than she could pull back her hand and make sure her jacket covered the blush.

"Dad." Caden's tone chastised her father, but the smile she added onto the end was anything but critical. "Be nice. This is my friend Marie. From Boston."

How did Caden know she was from Boston?

Caden answered the unspoken question with a guilty grin. "Aretha really likes you. She and Mom are best friends, and she might have let it slip."

"Very good." James smiled at his daughter and winked at Marie. An unfamiliar warmth spiraled through her stomach, drawing her to the flour-covered man. "Now about the business at hand. I need your opinion on the new pecan berry potato roll recipe."

Marie's stomach growled again, and they all chuckled. "I guess my opinion might not count for much. I'm hungry enough to eat a hippo."

"Well, we're fresh out of hippo, so you'll have to settle for sweet rolls. Be right back."

Caden rolled her eyes and whispered, "Sorry about my dad. He's been telling the same bad jokes for years. He's so happy to have someone new to use them on. Feel free not to laugh. You know how dads are."

Actually, this kind of father-daughter interaction was new to her. Her dad hadn't been playful or ever cracked a joke in his life. At least not to her. Of course, that would have required them to spend time together.

"It's okay." In fact, it was better than okay. It was kind of nice to have a man want to tell her a joke.

When James reappeared with a plateful of golden rolls overflowing with purple berry juice and a brown sugar and pecan crumb topping, she forgot all about laughing. There was only the sweet goodness of the blueberry center surrounded by the melt-in-your-mouth roll.

"A-maz-ing." The word was garbled by the second roll she was already stuffing in her mouth.

Her stomach finally appeased after her third treat, Marie bought a dozen to take back to the house and then bid them farewell. The sweets carried her through her grocery shopping, and despite balancing seven plastic bags, she still felt good when she reached the Red Door. Whether it was the sugar or seeing Caden or the fact that she'd managed to think about New Year's Eve without a panic attack, she didn't care. It was shaping up to be the best day she'd had in months.

She bounded up the steps, swinging a bag at Jack as he drove by. He rolled down his window. "I'll be back in a bit."

The house was silent as she filled the cupboards with her purchases. She put a roasted chicken breast in the fridge and caught another whiff of the fresh onion she'd chosen. They'd make a good chicken salad. Maybe she'd ask Jack to help her pull something together for lunch.

She left the bag of sweet rolls next to the bread box, but turned back to it before she could get very far. It wouldn't hurt to have just one more.

As she tore the pieces apart, savoring each bite, she bumped her hip against an open drawer. But it didn't budge. She glared at the white bottom before realizing that the white wasn't actually part of the drawer. It was more of the computer paper that Jack had used to write his list.

This was her chance to try out the typewriter, to see if Aretha had been right.

"Seth?" she called, peeking out the window to the backyard.

"Seth, are you here?" She raised her voice as hope bubbled in her chest.

The old home groaned, wind whistling along the paneling, but Seth didn't respond. She looked into the pantry and poked her head into the laundry room just to be sure she was alone before reaching a sticky finger into the drawer, then stopped just short.

"Georgiana would have a fit if I didn't wash my hands before using an antique Underwood." The image of her mother's friend with crossed arms and stern eyes danced across her mind, and she laughed out loud. Georgiana had loved design and antiques, and she'd have a conniption if she knew Marie was typing on the old black machine.

But Marie had to know. What did it sound like? How hard would she have to press the keys?

Some questions required answers.

Swallowing the rest of her roll in one bite, she hurried to the sink and scrubbed at the sticky residue. While she was at it, it couldn't hurt to work at the paint-stained creases in her knuckles.

Her hands nearly shone as she snagged a piece of paper from the broken drawer and stole through the house to the back room where Seth had stacked their antiques. Dust motes danced in beams of morning light that illuminated the classic tomes. On the floor beside them sat her mission.

Tiptoeing toward it, she looked over her shoulder one last time to make sure she was alone. She kneeled before it, slipped the paper into place, and turned the roller to feed the paper. Butterflies filled her stomach.

This had been her fantasy since Georgiana first showed her one of the classic writing devices. They'd spent hours speculating about who had used the machine and what had been written on it. Was it government directives or love letters? Wildly fictitious stories or heartbreaking memoirs?

What had been written on this machine?

More importantly, what was yet to be typed on it?

She wrinkled her nose and scratched her chin as she stared at the blank page. She needed to write something short and true. Just a trial run. She searched every corner and crevice of her mind, hunting out something to type.

This machine deserved more than gibberish or random keystrokes. She wouldn't use it just for the sake of throwing letters against a page to see what stuck. That would be a terrible waste of whatever life was left in the black buttons. Even if she was just going to throw the sheet of paper away as soon as she tried it out.

An idea came, slowly at first. Then it cemented into place, and she could see the words on the backs of her eyelids.

The truth. The very real and simple truth as it had struck her that morning.

She held down the shift button, the pressure required to budge it much more than she'd imagined. Then she pressed the *I* key. Then the funny little space bar.

Halfway through the single sentence, her fingers were tired, and she longed for the easy keyboard of her laptop, which was probably collecting dust on her desk at her dad's house. Of course, her computer didn't punctuate each letter with a sharp crack that made the paper tremble.

When it was all said and done, she leaned back, ran her hands over her thighs, and smiled.

I wish I had gone to get ice cream.

Georgiana would have been so jealous. She'd have been proud too.

Marie reached for the knob to scroll the paper out of the machine, but stopped short at a ruckus coming from right above her. A crash was followed immediately by a deep groan and a dull thud.

She jumped to her feet and ran up the stairs in the direction of the noise. "What's wrong?" she called out, trying to decide which of the rooms the sound had come from. As she passed the open door to the bedroom she'd finished painting just a few days before, she spied Seth leaning against a wall, his chin hanging to his chest.

Skidding around the corner, she reached him with outstretched arms. She grabbed his elbow without a thought, spinning him in her direction. The screwdriver in his hands fell to the floor, the sharp note of the plastic handle against hardwood filling the room.

Seth squinted at her, the line of his mouth tight, and she felt the full force of his displeasure.

"What is it? What's going on?"

"Why don't you tell me?" He flicked his hand around the room, motioning to the walls.

As the midmorning sun illuminated the room through the window, she spun in a slow circle. Immediately the backs of her eyes burned and her stomach plummeted to her shoes.

Her mouth opened and closed, but she couldn't get anything past the lump in her throat.

It was all her fault. Her good day had been ruined. By her own hand.

11

The next evening Seth sat alone in the work shed, swiping sandpaper over a closet rod. A shower of dust fell to his feet, and he brushed it aside with his shoe. Checking the rod for any splinters that had managed to escape his thorough sanding, he spun it around and around. But all he could see in his mind's eye was Marie's lower lip quivering as her shoulders fell when she saw what had become of the bedroom walls.

After two long minutes of utter silence, she had apologized over and over again.

"I don't know what happened," she said, her eyes glistening like she was about to cry. She ran her hands over the walls, the patches of mismatched color glaring in the sun's spotlight.

Just what he needed, a sobbing girl who was either the greatest actress in the world or not the sharpest tool in the shed.

And she wasn't stupid. The paint, clearly two different shades of green, had been applied with no rhyme or reason.

A patch of the lighter green made a three-foot-wide path across a section of the wall beside the window. Adjacent to the door was a four-foot square of the darker color, but the rest of the wall was the paler green, save for seven or eight circles. And the corners were a magnificent mess, each one a deeper shade than the adjoining walls.

The whole room would have to be repainted.

She was trying to either delay the opening, set them back a day, or waste Jack's money.

Mission accomplished. She had managed to do all three.

It just didn't make any sense. Jack had been nothing but kind to her. He was even paying her for her help.

And wasting money didn't make sense. If her aim was to swindle him, intentionally throwing away money was counterproductive. Unless she didn't care about the money. Unless it was more about keeping the inn from opening. Was she on a mission from another property owner to make sure Jack couldn't open the inn's doors in time to make the business profitable?

Seth laughed at his own ridiculous imaginings as he carried the closet rod out of the shed and pushed the padlock into place. The wind had died down, leaving the early night air crisp. His breath floated in white wisps toward the sky as he trotted across the backyard.

Marie wasn't a spy for the Secret Order of the PEI Bed-and-Breakfast Owners. She could barely make it from one day to another without a breakdown.

Whatever her motives, she wasn't undercover.

Underhanded? Perhaps.

He pulled up a stool in the mudroom, shed his coat, and laid newspaper on the floor. As he lifted the lid off a can of white paint, Jack strolled into the cramped corner, leaning his shoulder against the wall.

"How's it going?" Jack wasn't very good at small talk. Never had been. And his discomfort traced every word he spoke.

"Fine. You?"

The older man grunted as he tore off a piece of one of the sweet rolls Marie had brought home the day before and shoved it in his mouth. "Picked up another can of paint today."

"Uh-huh." Seth dipped a paintbrush into his own can. "Bet that cost you a pretty penny."

Jack grunted again before the rest of the roll disappeared into his mouth.

"What do you think happened?" He pushed his brush up and down the rod, giving it a quick coat. "She say anything else to you?"

"No. As soon as we got back from the paint store, she disappeared into her room."

Seth's stomach twisted. It wasn't right to think of the basement apartment as Marie's room. If Jack started thinking like that, he'd have a hard time getting rid of her when the inn opened. Besides, that apartment had already been assigned to another member of their team.

Spinning the dowel again, he eyed his uncle. "What's she been doing in there all day?"

Jack held up his hands before licking his fingers, a slow smile growing from the sugar that had been left there. "Why would I know?"

"Well, you're the only one of us who's ever been married."

Jack laughed like Seth had told the funniest joke in the world. "You think that makes me an expert on women?"

"Sure makes you more knowledgeable than me."

Jack just shook his head and crossed his arms. "Boy, I don't have a clue. I only had a great marriage to your aunt Rose because she was the next best thing to a saint. And after forty years, you start to learn the other person's tells. Understanding women is half poker game—who's bluffing, who's holding a full house—and half prayer. There's just no other way around it." He jerked his head in the general direction of Marie's room. "We've known her for a week. I don't have a clue what she's thinking."

The man had a point. Despite his resolve to keep an eye on her, Seth hadn't spent all that much time with Marie. He'd counted on spending time with her at the auction, but if he was going to get more than two words out of her when they went to that, he had to lay a sturdy foundation.

Seth balanced the closet bar on one end and walked over to the utility sink next to the commercial-grade washing machine. He turned on the faucet and washed the paint out of the brush with a vigor that wasn't required. "Do you think she'd come up for some supper?"

"Depends who's making it."

The two men shared a chuckle. "Sure wouldn't mind some more of Aretha's stew."

"Right about that." Jack's grin grew as his eyes rolled toward the ceiling.

Seth thumped the old man on the back with a matching grin. "You liked meeting Aretha?" It wasn't really a question. He already knew the answer because for the first time in his whole life, Seth had seen Jack speak more than three words to a woman his own age other than Rose.

"Sure I did. Nice woman. Good cook."

"And . . ."

"And what?" Jack led the way into the kitchen and stuck his head into the fridge.

"Nothing. I'm just saying. It's nice to see you talking to someone other than me."

Jack jerked up to look over the refrigerator door. "What's that supposed to mean?" He pulled out a white bowl, opening the lid and sniffing the contents.

"Just what I said."

"You make this?" His uncle handed him the bowl, and Seth pulled off the lid. It was full of chunks of white meat, onion, and green celery coated with mayonnaise and flecked with black pepper. The chicken salad smelled fresh and tart, like it had a squirt of dill in it.

Seth shook his head. "Nope."

"Marie?"

He set the bowl down and pulled two paper plates from the cabinet next to the sink. "If it wasn't you or me, who else would it have been? She must have made it last night after we went to bed. You don't think she'd try to poison us, do you?"

Jack's bushy brows lifted about an inch. "You? Maybe. Me? Never. We're safe."

Seth chuckled as he lifted the lid of the bread box to find a fresh loaf of wheat bread. He spread two slices on each plate and heaped a pile of chicken salad onto them. Handing Jack a sandwich, he squished his bread together and shoved a third of it into his mouth.

It wasn't fancy, but it sure tasted good after a long day of work. Celery crunched between bites of tender chicken, and he sighed as he leaned against the counter, crossing one leg over the other.

He popped an escaped cube of white meat into his mouth and licked his fingers before Jack was even halfway done.

"This would be pretty tasty with some of Aretha's potato stew."

If Jack was going to leave the door open like that again, then the least Seth could do was walk through it. "Speaking of single women, you ever think about getting remarried?"

"No." Jack chomped down on another bite of his sandwich.

"Not ever?"

"No."

Seth nodded and crossed his arms. "You're still pretty young. It might be nice to have a wife to help you run this place."

The older man's slumped shoulders wrenched to attention, his pale blue eyes flashing with something Seth hadn't seen in a while. Seth clenched his teeth while Jack deliberately finished chewing his food and swallowed.

"This is Rose's Red Door Inn."

Jack, usually all things good humor, tossed his plate in the recycle bin and stalked out of the room without another word.

All right. Clearly there were still some things off-limits. And suggesting that Jack consider bringing another woman into the Red Door was at the top of the list.

He snagged an orange out of a bag next to the bread box and peeled it before wandering into the dining room. He flicked on the lights to admire the even coat of slate blue that gleamed its perfection below the crown molding. It looked good. And it would look even better with a matching white chair rail all the way around the room.

He made a mental note to ask Marie about it.

He strolled from room to room on the first floor, past Jack's closed door and into the antique room. At least that was what he'd been calling it since they'd begun storing Marie's collection there.

The walls still needed paint, but he flipped the switch to illuminate her purchases, his gaze immediately drawn to the typewriter in the corner. A sheet of white paper had been threaded around the roller and left in place.

Had Aretha been right? Did the old machine actually work?

He squatted in front of it, only then seeing the single typed line.

I wish I had gone to get ice cream.

His stomach lurched. Marie had written this.

He glanced over his shoulder, suddenly expecting her to be staring at him, either angry that he was reading her personal thoughts or upset that it had taken him more than a minute to find her message.

The question remained. Was he supposed to find this? Or was it her secret?

More importantly, was it true?

He ran a hand over his face, the calluses catching on at least three-day-old stubble. "What am I supposed to do with this?"

Nothing.

The answer rang so clearly, he thought the word had been spoken aloud. But he was still alone in the room. Alone with Marie's regret.

His gut squeezed, realization jolting to his fingertips.

Marie's regret was his regret too. He wished she'd gone

with him. And not just so he could grill her about her past and her plans and the real reason she'd come to North Rustico. He wished he'd been the first one to introduce her to the boardwalk. He wished he could have seen that light in her eyes—the one she'd had when she got back from her run the morning before—when she first saw the white gazebo, old-time lampposts, and sprawling beach.

He wished he'd been kinder to her. He didn't know her motives for sure. And if Jack was right and she had nowhere else to go, he'd kick himself from here to eternity.

He still didn't have an explanation for the second-floor room with the disaster of a paint job, but maybe that would come. If he lowered his own defenses. If he tried to be kind.

If she turned out to be a snake like Reece, well then, he'd still be right there to stand between her and Jack when she struck.

Pushing to his feet, he turned his back on Marie's letter. Better to preserve their tense truce than cross a line by letting her know he'd seen it.

He walked to the door, flipped the light off, and was halfway down the hall when an unseen hook jerked him back. He marched to the typewriter and stared at the chipped keys. After several deep breaths, he scrolled the paper up until he had a clear line.

He popped the last slice of his orange into his mouth and licked the juice dribbling down his fingers before contemplating his message. He couldn't count on a delete button or Wite-Out if he mistyped. There was no spell-check and no fixing typos on this sheet, so he weighed each word with care. Finally, he punched in the first letter.

A single keystroke sounded like a gunshot that bounced

off the leather books and nautical devices stacked beside him. He jumped, but pressed the next letter and the next until he had left his message for her.

> *I wish you had too. Next time?*
> S

Satisfied with his message, he hopped to his feet and hurried toward the door.

She probably wouldn't see it anyway. But the rock in the bottom of his stomach suggested otherwise. Either she'd appreciate it or she'd think he was an idiot.

She might not be wrong.

Strolling back through the house, he shut off the downstairs lights and picked up his closet rod. He checked it with tentative taps. Dry enough.

Halfway up the back stairwell, a cold breeze whistled down the hall, sending a shiver across his shoulders. Someone had probably left a window open. He turned the corner at the top of the stairs to find not only an open window but also a wide-open door and the sharp odor of fresh paint.

He poked his head into the disaster room, where the light of the single fixture in the center of the ceiling illuminated Marie, roller in hand. Her hair pulled back in a loose ponytail and head cocked to the side, she wiped her forehead in a familiar motion.

Adding paint to her roller, she leaned to the side, revealing a streak of green down the leg of her jeans.

She kept working for several more minutes without any indication that she'd noticed his arrival. Finally he cleared his throat. Her shoulders jumped, and the steady sweep of paint hitched then resumed.

"What do you want, Seth?"

He held out the pole in his hand before realizing that she couldn't see it. "I came to put the closet rod back in. What are you doing?"

"What's it look like?" Her words were clipped, each one a barrier against whatever reaction she expected from him.

He swallowed the impulse to respond in kind. After all, he deserved that response. If not worse. Taking a steadying breath and praying for kind words—or at least benign ones—he let the night wind carry her question away. "Looks like you could use a hand."

"You don't have to. It was my mistake. I should have mixed them . . . I should have seen that they didn't . . . It doesn't matter. I'll fix it."

"I don't mind helping." He hoped he sounded sincere. But old habits died hard, and he'd been sharp with her time and again in the previous week. Maybe she thought he had something else to work on. "I've got nothing else to do tonight. Well, nothing that won't wait until tomorrow."

"I said I'll take care of it." She didn't even bother turning to look at him, her shoulders tense even as she bent over to add paint to her tray.

Seth stabbed his hand through his hair. If she wanted to be so stubborn, fine. She could do it all on her own. He backed out of the room but stopped at the door, the words that she'd typed flashing across his mind's eye.

She didn't really want to be alone. At least not nearly as much as she let on. And she'd wanted to go with him to get ice cream. He could finagle an invite to join her one-person painting party. And deep in his stomach he knew he needed an invitation, her permission. Picking up a roller without her approval would just put her more on edge, so he tried for a bit of levity.

"Are you always this inviting?"

She didn't speak, but at least his question earned a glare over her shoulder.

"So what happened in here before?"

"You saw it yesterday." Her words were abrupt, as though she was afraid her voice might crack if she spoke for longer than a moment.

He nodded slowly. But she couldn't see it, so he cleared his throat again. "I did. But I'm still not clear why—or how—it ended up that way."

He'd seen some painting mistakes in his day. Glossy and matte finishes in the same room. Oil-based paint running down water-based. Bad textures. He'd seen lots of gaffes, but never one so glaring.

The next glance she shot his way was less defensive and much sadder. The pace of her roller slowed as she nibbled on her lip and swallowed several times. As the muscles in her throat worked, threads of dark hair clung to the porcelain skin at her neck. He clenched his fists, tearing his gaze away from the lean line of her neck and shoulders.

It would be so much easier if she was about forty years older. A sweet grandmother would be much better for him. Better yet, why couldn't she go back to wherever she'd come from? That would be safer for everyone involved.

Instead, in an undeniably youthful tone, she said, "I'm not exactly sure."

He had to pedal back in his brain to pick up the string of

their conversation, and when he found it, he latched on like it was the only line between him and insanity. He didn't want to analyze how close to the truth that might be.

"You're not sure how the room ended up looking like it had a bad case of chicken pox?"

She shook her head, then nodded. "I mean, I have an idea."

"Which is?"

She stared at him for a long moment, her gaze sweeping from his head to his toes and finally searching deep into his eyes, which sent shivers up and down his arms. Whatever she was looking for, he hoped she found it. Fast. Because the look in her eyes was making something deep in his chest begin to melt.

Finally, she tilted her head toward an extra roller sitting on the tarp next to her paint tray. "Might as well help if you're just going to stand around talking."

A slow grin spread across his face, which he hid inside his shoulder as he bent to pick up the handle. They reached to load up their rollers at the same time, and she gave him a glare that he read to mean she was having distinct second thoughts about asking him to join her. Holding out his hand, he said, "Ladies first."

Her movements were smooth and controlled as she applied an even layer over the walls, the wet paint that glistened in the light covering almost an entire wall. She'd been at work for at least an hour before he showed up, and now she continued on in silence until he prompted her.

"So are you going to tell me what you think happened?"

He surprised even himself with the sincere question. As the words popped out, he realized he really did want to know the truth. And he didn't expect her to lie about it.

"It's just a guess." Her voice barely carried to his spot on the adjacent wall, but instead of prodding her to speak up, he leaned in her direction. "I've only seen this happen one other time."

She just had to dangle that bit about her past out there. Like a marlin eyeing a fish at the end of a hook, he almost took the bait. He almost asked where she'd seen it before and if it had anything to do with where she'd learned interior design.

He almost got them off track.

Instead he forced his mouth to form a pertinent question. "You've seen what happen?"

"We bought a gallon and two quarts of paint for this room. We picked out the color from the swatch and asked the guy at the paint counter for what we needed. And I didn't think anything of it. It's pretty normal to need more than a gallon for a room. Anyway, we went through the big can pretty quickly, and I used the first quart to finish off that wall." She pointed to the corner adjacent to the door and took a loud breath. "And when that ran out, I used the last quart to touch up a couple drips. On that wall."

When she motioned toward the wall that still sported pockmarks, he understood. "The paints didn't match."

She shook her head, pursing her lips to one side and twisting her free hand into the waist of her sweatshirt. "I should have mixed the cans together first just in case they didn't quite match."

"You didn't notice it while you were painting?"

She sighed. "Paint never looks like it should until it dries. I just figured that the wet paint would dry to match the original gallon."

"And you're sure that you bought the same color?"

"Uh-huh. Summer Pasture."

"So how could they be so far off?"

She lifted a shoulder, completely abandoning her wall to meet his gaze. "It could be any number of things, I guess."

"You said you'd seen it before."

"Ye-es." She dragged the word out, and when he tried to ask about that experience, she dove into an explanation, controlling the direction of their conversation. "That time there was a glob of color stuck to the bottom of the can. Even when we stirred it, it didn't mix in."

"But that didn't happen this time?"

"The can was empty when I cleaned it out."

"So what could have caused it?"

She broke eye contact and turned back to her canvas. "A jam in the mixing machine?"

"You mean a jam in the squirter that shoots color into the base paint? I guess that's plausible."

Her roller stopped in midstroke. "Sure—if the gallon got the right amount and the quarts only got half of the hue they were supposed to because of a clog. Or the ratios could be off."

"I thought you didn't believe in math and science."

Her giggle punched him in the chest, and he wiped the front of his shirt over and over to brush the sensation away. Where had that come from? She hadn't laughed like that even for Jack. Seth didn't want to make her laugh. He wasn't responsible for keeping her happy.

But man, he wanted to tell another joke.

"I don't think there's much argument about the validity of math." The lilt of her words mirrored the rise and fall of her arm and the gentle sway of her head.

When had he stopped watching his own painting?

He whipped his gaze back to his own wall as she continued. "It's pretty objective. And ratios aren't exactly calculus."

"All right." Back to business. "So maybe the paint machine miscalculated how much of the color is required to make the right shade in a gallon."

"Or in a quart."

This was all making far too much sense. The splotchy wall could have happened to anyone. A simple mistake. Her story made sense, and he was inclined to believe her.

"The sun could have come through the window and faded some patches of the wall," she said.

"The sun faded the wall? But only in certain places."

"Why not?" Her guilty smile gave her away. She was making a joke.

First laughter and then teasing. He couldn't begin to guess what had brought this on, but he wasn't going to question or complain. Sometimes God just smiled down on him.

"Or maybe the paint counter attendant thought you were cute and wanted to see you again." The words were out before he realized they were beyond a bad idea.

She didn't say anything for a long while, so he had to focus on the blush rising up her neck and turning her cheeks into bright red apples. "Well, actually . . . the woman at the counter was closer to Jack's age."

"Maybe *she* wanted to see *him* again."

Her laugh returned, and with it came a swelling in his chest. "You might be right. She was awfully chatty with him."

"And what did he say?"

"About the same as usual."

"So . . . nothing?"

She nodded and quickly turned away, her jaw cracking on a yawn.

He glanced at his watch, the digital numbers swimming in front of his tired eyes. "You know it's late when you can't even read your own watch. Maybe we should call it a night."

"All right. Let me just clean out this pan." She made short work of the last bit of paint in the tray as Seth hammered the lid back onto the can. "Are we still on for the auction?"

He wasn't sure if he should be offended that she had to ask or happy that she still wanted to go with him.

"I'm looking forward to it."

Oddly enough, he really was.

12

"Y ou're sure you know what you're looking for?"

Marie blew a rebellious lock of hair off her forehead and glared across the cab of the truck. Seth had asked her the same question at least four times as they headed toward the auction grounds, and her answer hadn't changed. In fact, she'd known what she was looking for two weeks before, on the original date of the auction.

"What?" He sounded offended, like her glare was more painful than his incessant questioning. "I just want to make sure we're bidding on the right things—the things we need. It's easy to get caught up in the excitement and drama of an auction and end up bidding on things that will just waste money."

"And you know this because you've been to how many auctions in your life?"

He looked up at the ceiling. "Well, I haven't actually . . . But that doesn't mean that I don't understand human nature. When the paddles are waving, it's fun to get involved, to put yours in the game."

She ran her hand down the leg of the new jeans that Jack had insisted on buying for her. Apparently her paint-stained pants were an embarrassment to the Red Door Inn. "I think I'll be okay."

"Are those new?"

The sharp turn in the conversation made her fumble for an answer before she realized he was pointing to her gift from Jack. "Um . . . yes. Jack said he wouldn't let me represent the Red Door in public with stains all over my pants. He made us stop by the mall on our way out of Charlottetown last night."

Seth grunted, his eyebrows pulling tight.

She sat up a little taller in her seat and crossed her arms over her chest. "What's that supposed to mean?"

He shrugged, his attention back on the road as trees and yellow road signs flew by them. "Nothing."

Why was he always so touchy about spending money? Or was this about her calling him out on his lack of auction experience? She followed the urge deep in her stomach that said his sudden grumpiness was more about Jack spending money on her. "They were an advance against my next pay-check. He's not buying me things."

His profile remained fixed in the direction of the road, but he shot her an uncertain glance out of the corner of his eye. "Except—" He slammed his mouth closed, chewing on his lips until they disappeared.

"What? What do you think he bought me?"

"Nothing. I'm not Jack's accountant."

His nonchalant words didn't line up with the stiffness in his shoulders or the way he worked the muscle in his jaw all the way down his neck. When he swallowed, his Adam's apple bobbed, and he rotated his shoulders, stretching the jersey fabric of his long-sleeved T-shirt. The gray fabric looked as soft as the muscles beneath it were solid.

Like a slap across her face, realization struck.

She'd just looked at him as a man. Not a person or a body, but as a man. A handsome man.

What on earth was she doing looking at any man, let alone Seth, who had made it clear that he only put up with her presence because of his uncle?

They'd had pleasant enough interactions after their late-night painting session. Their tense treaty had smoothed into a pleasant camaraderie. She offered him a smile in response to his morning nods. And he thanked her when she brought back bags from Caden's bakery.

That was fine. Simple. Safe.

Looking at him like she might have a year before. Recognizing the softness of his deep brown hair and the depth of his hazel eyes. Focusing on the breadth of his shoulders and the muscles in his arms . . .

That was anything but safe.

Especially since his jerk side had a bad habit of popping up unexpectedly.

And she'd come to PEI to be safe.

Besides, she wasn't ready for it. Wasn't ready to think about holding hands and kissing and . . . This wasn't an innocuous topic, especially where Seth was concerned. There were too many memories bubbling right below the surface.

Her stomach churned, and she leaned her forehead against the window, waiting for a panic attack to begin, waiting for her head to begin spinning and her vision to narrow until it was gone. In the truck she couldn't get to her beach, to the security of her private view of the sunrise, to the clapping waves greeting her each morning.

The best she could do was let the window's coolness wash over her and wish that she could jump into the chilly waters of the gulf. Every now and then she'd catch a glimpse of the blue expanse as they wound their way toward Cavendish. Between pines standing sentry on the far side of a farmer's field, blue flashes captured her attention and soothed the unnameable monster that stole her very breath with each attack.

But the panic attack didn't come.

The monster stayed at bay, and the memories of that New Year's Eve night stayed with it.

Good. Because stuck in close quarters with Seth was the worst possible place to dwell on the old memories and her disturbing new realizations, so she heaved a sigh and thanked God—even if he wasn't listening—that her chest wasn't tied in a knot.

The auction was safer territory on all counts, so she pushed her mind from its track and forced the words out of her mouth. "Here's what I'm thinking about for the auction." She held up her fingers as she ticked off her top priorities. "We have to get that cherrywood buffet."

"How much do you plan on spending on it?"

She hadn't actually given that much thought. But three thousand dollars seemed reasonable. Jack had given them a budget five times that for the day, so she could splurge on a focal piece. "Around three."

"Hundred?"

"Thousand."

"Three grand?" His voice rose half an octave. "What are we going to do with a three-thousand-dollar table?"

"What do you mean? It's an antique buffet. We're going to build a room around it. We're going to find complementary pieces and put them into the room so they look pretty and your guests have a place to eat breakfast."

"I mean, what's its purpose?" The volume of his voice increased with his conviction. "Day to day, what are we going to use it for?"

"Are you joking?"

He shook his head, taking his eyes off the road long enough to stare hard at her. "For that much cash, it should be a time machine."

"We're going to put food on it. That's generally what a buffet is used for, right?"

He nodded slowly, his lips twitching like he couldn't decide if he was going to laugh or cry. He decided on a snicker of disbelief. "You're going to get Jack's New York chef to put his food on a buffet?"

"What chef?"

The curve of his lips flattened, the faint dimple in his cheek disappearing. "Jack hasn't told you about Jules Rousseau?"

Jack hadn't said a thing about hiring a professional chef. She pressed her hand against a growing ache that radiated from her stomach. It wasn't a big deal. He'd probably just forgotten to mention it.

They'd been so busy. Painting and then repainting. Running errands. Picking out dishes. They'd focused on colors and design. Decorations and personal touches.

She was almost certain it had simply slipped his mind.

Unless he was keeping her on the fringes. Unless he purposefully kept her out of the loop because he didn't plan to keep her on board.

That wasn't implausible. In fact, it was pretty familiar.

Her father had kept his plans to himself until the truth came out. He'd told her to wait before saying anything. Told her that she should be sure before she ruined a young man's life. And all the while he'd made plans of his own, plans to use her pain to get the thing he wanted most.

Jack would do the same to make his inn a success.

"Jack did his research, looking for chefs trained at the best culinary schools in the area. He asked for recommendations, interviewed four candidates, and finally offered Jules the position of executive chef."

"Oh." She wanted to ask every question rattling around her mind but couldn't say the words without revealing her own fears. Instead she said, "When does he start?"

"He's on payroll April 25."

"And where's he going to stay?"

Seth ran a palm down his cheek. "We're still working that out. But maybe the basement apartment."

"Right. Of course. That makes sense." She nodded enthusiastically, smoothing out the imaginary wrinkles in her pants again and again. Pushing down the lump rising in her throat. It wasn't her room. They weren't giving away her apartment. They were just doing what they needed to in order to open the inn. After all, she wasn't a permanent fixture at the Red Door. She was a traveler. A stand-in for the feminine touch that Rose would have provided.

Pressing a hand over the ache in her heart, she welcomed the reminder. It did her good to remember that she was no more a part of Jack's family than she was her dad's favorite person.

Jack would ask her to leave. Oh, he'd be nice about it. He

didn't have a cruel bone in his body. But his priority was making Rose's dream a success. So he'd ask her to leave someday.

The only way to save herself the pain of that rejection was to leave before he could tell her to go.

Seth shot her several furtive glances, his eyes gentle as he turned his truck off the two-lane highway. "So, what else are you going to look for today?"

"Huh?"

"Other than the buffet? What are you going to bid on?"

She held up her fingers to tick off the other things on her list. "Authentic local quilts for every guest room, tables for the dining room to match the buffet—"

"Tables? As in plural? We already have one."

"Yes."

His eyebrows arched in an unspoken question.

"Have you ever even stayed at a bed-and-breakfast?"

He shook his head.

"Wait. You're telling me that you're refurbishing an old house to become a B and B, and you've never even stayed at one?"

He shrugged. "Sure."

She pressed her hands over her face, groaning into them. No wonder he was concerned by all the money she'd spent. He had no concept of how a B and B should feel. Like a home, only better. How the finishing touches made the experience. "I'm going to pretend I didn't hear that."

"Fair enough. But you haven't told me why we need more than one table."

"Picture this. You're on your honeymoon, and you just want to share secret glances with your new wife. You want to hold her hand and touch her knee under the table." She waved her hand in front of the windshield, hoping he could imagine the scene. "You want to feed her a fresh strawberry or offer her a bite of your cinnamon roll after she begs you for just a taste."

"Hey, if she wanted a cinnamon roll, she should have ordered her own."

Marie fought the urge to slug his arm. "She was too embarrassed. After all, you're newly married, and she doesn't want you to think she's going to stuff her face at every opportunity."

"All right. Say she wants my cinnamon roll . . . Did your friend make it?"

"My friend? Caden?"

"Yeah."

Where was he going with this? She whipped her finger around in a circle. "Stay with me here."

He nodded. "I am. Just trying to picture this scene. Did the cinnamon roll come from Caden's bakery?"

"Yes. Fine. She made it. What does it matter?"

A lopsided grin broke his focused expression, and his dimple made him look about fifteen years younger. "Oh, it matters. If it's from Caden, I'm not sharing."

She heaved a sigh, her shoulders deflating. "Seth! Focus here for a second. We're talking about tables, not sweets."

"Fine. But I'm just saying. I'm not going to share." He winked at her. Great. Now he was teasing her.

"All right. So you're with your new bride, and she wants a bite of your waffle." He opened his mouth, but she cut him off before he could pursue his thought. "There are no more cinnamon rolls in this story."

His mouth snapped closed, his lips pursed to the side. Finally he nodded. "Go on."

"There are little candles and vases of flowers from Jack's garden on the table. And all you really want to do is touch her face and wipe away the speck of jam stuck to the corner of her mouth. You got it?"

His head bobbed in slow succession, his features taut but eyes bright.

"Now imagine she's on the opposite side of a twenty-person table, and you're surrounded by strangers."

His mouth dropped open. "Got it."

"We need to have several table options. Maybe a six- or eight-seater for bigger parties or the people who want to talk with other guests. A couple four-tops and then at least one two-person table."

"And they all have to match the cherrywood buffet." He sat up straighter in his seat, clearly proud of himself for his flash of brilliance.

She tapped her fist into his shoulder. "Now you're getting it, Sloane."

Her hand dropped to her lap in a flash, fire running up her fingers. She had no business touching him. She hadn't voluntarily touched a man her own age since New Year's Eve.

Her only saving grace was Seth's utter oblivion as he pulled into the gravel parking lot of the auction grounds.

"Ready to go find some tables?"

"Absolutely."

As she slid from the truck, she squeezed a fist against the butterflies suddenly swarming in her middle. She hadn't been to an auction in more than ten years. Since her mom passed and Georgiana was not-so-cordially uninvited to the Carrington estate.

But an auction had to be like riding a bike. She hadn't

forgotten how to look for the values. She could still read people's faces, and Georgiana had taught her how to cut her losses when the bids rose too high.

She'd give Jack her best today, no matter how much longer she worked for him.

Seth led the way toward stalls of furniture spread across a green lawn. "Is this all for the auction?"

"I think some of it is just for sale." Her blood rushed through her veins as she peeked into the first stall to find hangers and stacks of bright quilts in every color palate she could imagine. "We're coming back to this one," she said.

"All right." He shoved his hands into his pockets, his gait relaxed as he strolled down the first aisle.

"Seth Sloane!" The voice was as recognizable as her famous singing counterpart. Aretha bounced from one of the stalls at the end of the row and clasped Seth's hand with a firm grip. "Did you come alone? Where are Jack and Marie?"

"Hi, Aretha." He pointed over his shoulder. "Marie's here. But Jack is running other errands. We're the Red Door contingent today."

Aretha leaned around Seth's shoulder, checking to make sure he had his facts straight. Marie waved the hand that still tingled from the brief contact with Seth in the truck and managed a stiff smile. "It's good to see you."

Aretha held out her hand, the palm facing down and fingers slightly curled. Marie reached out to grip the wrinkled hand, surprised by the strength of the squeeze as Aretha hauled her in for a hug.

"Sweet, sweet Marie. I'm so glad you made it."

"Well, I'm not going to let that buffet go to anyone else."

With a wink and a tug, Aretha whisked them into the

crowded confines of her booth. "I didn't think you would. And for about three thousand, I think you'll get it. But the auction doesn't begin for another hour."

Seth hiked a thumb over his shoulder. "We figured we'd look around a bit. Decide what tables would go with the buffet."

"Smart. Was that your idea, Marie?"

She could only look at her hands, not daring to meet Seth's gaze for fear she'd burst into laughter. Aretha had all but confined him to the halls of stupidity, and either he'd missed the comment or he didn't intend to defend himself. "We also need to sign up for a paddle number. Where's the registration table?"

"Oh, honey." The word rolled from Aretha's lips about as slow as the real deal straight from the comb. "We don't do paddles here. Your raised hand is your word."

Her father's friend, Gary Stinson of Sotheby's, would have fallen flat on his back. "You're kidding, right?"

Gray hair bobbed back and forth. "No need for it. We stick a hand in the air and make just enough noise to be sure we get noticed."

Marie still wasn't convinced that the older woman wasn't teasing her when another customer—a paying customer—strolled in to look at the merchandise. "We'll talk to you a bit later." Marie waved.

Aretha winked. "Good luck, kids."

"Kids?" Seth's voice carried only far enough to reach Marie as they neared the end of the aisle. "I haven't been called a kid since . . . well, since I was a kid."

He was looking for a reaction. A smile or a chuckle, but his whisper was too personal, too close. She angled her steps away from him, putting a few extra feet between them before giving him half a grin.

She needed a little space. Just some breathing room. "I'm going to go check out the pieces up for auction and make note of what might work for—" She stopped herself before ending with the word "us." After the reminder in the truck, she didn't need to get attached to anything else. "The inn."

"Are you okay?"

She swallowed, then nodded with an overenthusiastic smile in his direction. "Yes. Doing great."

"All right. I'm going to take a look at the booths in the other aisle. I'll let you know if I see anything."

"It's a plan." She spun and darted toward the tents where items were lined up behind a fence. A small crowd milled around rows of chairs to the side, waiting for the auction to begin.

She slipped in at the fence line next to a woman who was near Aretha's age but without any of the spunk and attitude. They exchanged polite smiles as Marie pulled a notepad and pen from her purse.

"That's a very nice armoire," the woman said, indicating a wooden closet in a medium shade. Its intricate scrollwork seemed at odds with its depth and width.

"It is."

"You in the market for a piece like that?" The woman's gray eyebrows rose, her stare hard and unblinking.

Marie leaned toward her and lowered her voice until it was barely a whisper. "I might be."

"It may go out of your price range."

Auctions were synonymous with head games. This woman just wanted to know who her competition was. But she'd played her hand too early. Now it was clear she wanted that armoire, and she was going to put up the money to get it. In effect, she was warning other buyers not to bid her up because she intended to win the antique regardless.

"Maybe." Marie shrugged, letting a hint of a smile lift her lips. "But probably not."

As she walked away, she laughed at herself. She wasn't interested in that kind of bulky furniture. Pieces like that clogged the open feeling of a room.

When she reached the corner of the fence, Marie spotted her buffet.

And she spotted someone else surveying the same piece.

The man wore a blue coat over a white shirt, gray peppering his temples and neatly trimmed goatee. He too jotted notes on a piece of paper in his hand, while his gaze roved and caressed the edges of the century-old item.

She squinted at him, hoping even from fifty feet away that he'd get the hint and move on to other pieces on the block.

He didn't.

The even grain of the wood and scrolled brass knobs of the drawers belonged at the Red Door Inn. She'd already envisioned them against the long blue wall of the dining room, where every afternoon Jules Rousseau would offer his éclairs and beignets. And guests would find a reason to return to the Red Door in the warmth of the afternoon for a cool cup of lemonade and a sweet.

Well, the Jules Rousseau part was new, but the plan hadn't changed.

Guests of the Red Door deserved an afternoon treat. And they deserved to pick it up on this piece of furniture.

She wasn't going to walk away from the prize without a fight.

"What are you looking at? See anything you like?"

She jumped at Seth's words, the pages of her notebook flapping in the breeze. "I'm—" Well, it probably wasn't wise to confess that she'd been giving the evil eye to another bidder. "I'm not sure." She surveyed the whole lot in three seconds and pointed at a square table with four chairs. "What about that? The detail on the back of the chairs complements the hardware on the buffet."

He nodded, squinting hard as he shifted to look back and forth between the items. "Sure. If you say so."

"I do."

He cocked his head so his ear almost reached his shoulder, his gaze settling over her like morning fog on the bay. "You're kind of feisty today, aren't you?"

His words spread warmth through her insides. "Am I?"

He chuckled. "Well, it looks like the chairs are starting to fill up. Maybe we should find seats."

She followed him toward the horseshoe-shaped setup, only glancing over her shoulder at her rival once.

The first several items on the auction block were of little consequence to them, the mind-game player's armoire and a set of end tables. Seth gave her a nudge when the nineteenth-century tables were announced, but she waved him off. He raised his eyebrows.

His lips were almost to her ear when he whispered, "Wouldn't they look good in the living room?"

She gulped at the lump rising in her chest and managed to respond, "The Red Door doesn't have a living room. It has a parlor."

The look he shot her suggested he thought she had lost any good sense, but she let it roll off her shoulders as she straightened in her chair, catching another glimpse of the man in the blue coat. He stared at his hands, apparently bored by the tables.

The winning bidder let out a whoop and the matching end tables were whisked away.

"Next up is a cherrywood sideboard or buffet made by craftsmen right here on the island."

Marie looked around the head of the person in front of her and caught her challenger staring at her. Instead of backing down, he nodded his head to her.

Her stomach flipped, and she squeezed fisted hands in her lap, her breath catching as she waited for the opening bid.

"You'll get this. It's okay to breathe."

She glanced in Seth's direction and then followed his arm from his shoulder down to where his hand rested over hers. She gently pulled her hand out, stretching her fingers and burying the unwelcome sensations that came with his touch. There wasn't time to think about that. Especially not now. She had three thousand dollars that said that piece was hers. And if she was lucky, she could get it for less.

"We'll start the bidding at twelve hundred." The auctioneer's voice filled the tent like a ringmaster. "Do I have a bid at one thousand two hundred?"

Marie stared down the blue coat, waiting to see who would take first blood. Who would be the first to get to three thousand.

"Twelve hundred." In the first row, a tiny woman with an enormous hat held up her hand, nearly sending Marie sprawling on the ground.

"Where did she come from?" The words barely slipped through her clenched jaw.

Seth didn't pick up that the tightness in her words might be a reason not to respond. "The Deep South, if her accent is any indication."

She glared at him as the ringmaster called for the next bid, and she slipped her hand into the air without even looking toward the podium. "Thirteen hundred."

"One thousand three hundred from the young lady in the fourth row."

Before the auctioneer could ask for another bid, a deep bass voice that could only belong to the man across from her called out, "Two thousand."

"Twenty-one hundred." From the woman in front.

"Twenty-two." Marie left the facilitator in the dust. If she waited for him, her key rival could jump the bid again. Better to keep control, keep the bids steadily climbing.

"Twenty-five hundred." This from an unknown, two seats down from Seth.

Her palms turned damp, and she rubbed her legs. The hat lady shot a venomous look over her shoulder, but the new addition to the party just crossed his arms and smiled like he couldn't care less.

But Marie could. She needed that buffet for three grand. She'd been counting on it, picturing it, planning on it, for more than two weeks. And if she went back to Jack empty-handed, she would give him a reason to send her on her way.

He might not recognize it as such right away. But it was only a matter of time before he realized that she wasn't delivering on the promises she'd made. She had to have this buffet.

Her breath hitched, the well-known band settling into place around her lungs. She froze. Maybe if she didn't move, the symptoms would go away. But the dizziness seeped in, and she wrung her shaking hands until they were clammy all over.

Dear God, if there was ever a time she needed to be clear-headed, this was it. *Please don't let this happen now.*

Seth put his hand on her arm again. "Hang in there. You've got this."

"Twenty-seven." The number died on her lips, so she fought for whatever air she could find, pinched her eyes closed, and tried again. "Twenty-seven hundred."

"Twenty-nine." Her blue-coated competitor sat calmly, a smug smile settling onto his face.

She raised a clenched fist and said, "Three thousand."

That was it, her last chance at the piece. She just needed everyone else to have the same limit she did. She couldn't afford to go any higher.

"Thirty-one."

13

Seth squeezed Marie's arm as the jerk across from them sent the bid over three grand. Like a deflated balloon, air escaped from her lungs in one rush. She met his gaze, sadness flickering in her eyes. She swallowed and took a loud breath that didn't quite seem to stick, as she immediately gulped at another.

The self-satisfied fool flaunted his win with a cocky grin, and a rush of indignation washed over Seth. Marie wanted that piece. And she deserved it after the late nights she'd put in repainting the disaster room, the long hours she'd spent kneeling in the dirt preparing the flower bed, and all the times she'd put up with his sharpness.

He elbowed her as the auctioneer called, "Going once."

"Do it."

Her eyes flashed. "We won't have enough money to get the other things we need."

He stared straight into her eyes, willing her to see that he understood how much she needed this win. "It'll be enough. Do it."

"Going twice!"

He pushed her arm into the air, and her blue eyes flashed once more—this time with a fight he hadn't seen before—before she upped the bid. "Thirty-two hundred."

Their competition flung his arms to his side and sat up, his face twisting with a glower that could have wilted a tulip. "Thirty-three."

"Thirty-three fifty."

Seth held his breath, tension building in his muscles, roiling and fighting for an escape. Marie wiggled in her white folding chair beside him, her whole body trembling like an idling car. Like she might fly apart if someone didn't hold her together. No one else seemed to notice, so he wrapped an arm across the back of her chair, around her shoulders.

She seemed to settle down to a dull hum as the auctioneer looked to the other bidder. And if having an arm around her helped Seth feel more grounded too? Well, that was just an added perk.

"That's three thousand four hundred to you, sir."

The man nodded. "Thirty-four hundred."

Seth glared at him, but before he could squeeze Marie's shoulder, she said, "Thirty-five."

His gut twisted like a washcloth being wrung out as the silver-haired man at the podium began his final count. "Going once."

Marie sucked in an audible breath, her eyes wide and unblinking.

"Going twice."

The jerk scowled.

"Sold to the young lady in the fourth row!"

Marie's hands flew to her mouth, but they couldn't cover

the smile that crinkled the corners of her eyes. He pulled her into his side for a split second before she wiggled free.

"Thank you." Her words were soft, and he saw in her eyes something he couldn't remember seeing there ever before, almost as though a fence had been taken down. As though she was beginning to feel comfortable with him.

He hadn't even known that was missing. But now that he saw it, it was clear. She'd kept a distinct distance between them. He'd just been too focused on keeping her at arm's length to notice.

Today was different. This was new. And it was good. They'd moved to a new stage, a new level.

It would certainly make living under the same roof easier. And Jack would be happy. But it didn't change the fact that she was hiding something.

"I can't believe we got it."

He would still celebrate with her for the moment. "Congratulations. You were great."

She looked down, and her cheeks turned a very pretty color of pink. She always looked so embarrassed when someone praised her, as if compliments were few and far too infrequent in her life. Was that what Jack had first seen in her? He'd bet that was the thing that had tugged at Jack's heartstrings and convinced him to bring her home.

Seth couldn't fault the man.

"Thank you for—" She bit into her bottom lip, her gaze on his chin almost palpable. He scratched at the thin scar that followed his jawline, and her eyes followed his movements. "Thank you for prodding me not to give up."

"You're the one who said we had to make a room around that particular piece."

Her smile flashed especially bright. "And we will." She turned her attention back to the bidding battle over another piece of furniture, content to wait. In fact, she didn't move again until the square table she'd pointed out to him earlier came up. She didn't move enough to signal anyone that she was interested, but her relaxed muscles slowly tensed, and he could sense her anticipation.

This auction seemed to be more about outmaneuvering other players than the actual antiques. And watching Marie play was fun.

Seth crossed his arms and leaned back to enjoy the show.

"Next up is a mahogany table with four chairs. Each seat features a hand-chiseled winter scene across the back. Made in 1937, this piece was owned by the Rosenthal family of Montague for seventy years." The auctioneer looked up from his notes and wiped a white handkerchief across his glistening forehead. "We'll begin the bids at one thousand seven hundred."

The audience sat like statues. All except Seth, who nudged Marie and nodded toward the table. This was her chance. No competition for the table. What was she waiting for?

The shake of her head was almost indistinguishable. And he sat back. *Just watch the show.*

"Will someone bid at one thousand five hundred?"

The audience stirred, looking around to see who would make the first move.

"This item is still steady and includes all original parts. It will make a nice addition to any home. Who will give me twelve hundred dollars?"

The woman wearing the green hat adorned with half a dozen unnaturally colored feathers tipped it to the side, as though she was thinking about throwing her cap in the ring.

Seth chuckled to himself at the mental image of her monstrosity sailing toward the staid man at the microphone, but stopped as pain flashed across the man's face.

Still no one bid. And when the price dropped again, sweat beaded on the back of Seth's neck. He wiped it away, unsure if it was caused by empathy for the auctioneer staring at a silent audience, or the midday sun beating rays onto the canopy that held the heat under it. He lifted the cuffs of his jacket away from his wrists and tugged at the neck of his shirt.

If Marie didn't bid on the table soon, he was going to.

"Surely someone needs this dining room set. The bid is at one thousand one hundred."

Marie raised her hand. She didn't say a word, but the auctioneer targeted in on her in an instant, pointing a finger at her.

"Thank you! Eleven hundred to the young lady there. Going once. Going twice." He whapped his gavel on his lectern. "Sold."

After all the pieces had been bid on and Marie had won a six-chair dining set, Seth followed her to the table to pay for their items. "How'd you get that first table for six hundred less than the opening bid?"

She shrugged, a bounce in her step. "I didn't let anyone else know how much I wanted it."

"Jack would be proud."

She glowed under the praise, the sun highlighting her brown hair with an unexpected halo.

"Well, well." Aretha strolled up to them, her smile pulling taut loose bits of skin in nature's face-lift. "Well done, you two." She stepped between them, patting Marie's shoulder and grabbing Seth's hand. "I had no idea that sideboard would go for so much. But it's worth every penny."

"Marie promised me that we can build a whole room around it," he said.

Aretha's gaze traveled back and forth between them. "She's quite right. Listen to this one. The design genes are strong in her."

"Thank you."

The older woman clapped her wrinkled hands. "Now tell me how things are going at the Red Door Inn. Are you on schedule for a May first opening?"

Seth's eyebrows pinched. It was a valid question, just not one he had an answer to. "I hope so, but Jack's been pretty tight-lipped about how he thinks things are going."

"And he keeps going off on secret errands," Marie chipped in, pinching the skin at her neck several times. "You don't think anything is wrong, do you?"

Seth shook his head. Jack was made of sturdy stock and knew how to run a business. If there was trouble, he'd tell them. "I'm sure he's fine. He's probably just worn out. He's been working on the inn since long before you and I showed up."

Rubbing her hands together, Aretha nodded. "I'm sure you're right. It's a lot of work starting up a business." She raised her eyebrow, then winked at Seth. "Maybe I should stop by later this week with some homemade food. That might boost his spirits a little."

Marie stepped up as the line moved forward. "I think we'd all appreciate it. There isn't much time for making meals."

Aretha snapped to attention, her finger catching under Marie's chin. "Are you not eating?" Then she swooped on

THE RED DOOR INN

Seth, her finger wagging and her tone matching his grand-mother's. "You need to keep your strength up. Why aren't you taking care of yourselves?"

With a gentle touch, Marie pushed the finger down. "We *are* eating. Lots of protein and vegetables. But sometimes we get busy and don't have time to cook a warm meal. That's all."

"That's not all." Like a general commanding troops, she said, "You tell your uncle that I'll be there tomorrow night with dinner, and I'll expect to eat at the table you just bought today."

"Yes, ma'am."

As Aretha marched off, Seth turned back to Marie, whose face exploded with laughter. "I think she means business."

Marie nodded. "Undoubtedly."

After paying for the pieces they'd purchased and lining up a time to load them into his truck, they wandered the stalls, ending up at the one with the handmade quilts.

"Isn't this one beautiful?" She looked at him and he shrugged.

"It's blue."

"It's nautical. It'll go perfectly with the compass we bought at Aretha's. Don't you think?"

He wasn't educated enough in this area to be of any use. Although they had made a pretty decent bidding team.

"Sounds good."

She picked out two others and told the owner which ones she wanted. He was almost finished wrapping them up when she wandered toward the back of the booth, where a black and white stretch of fabric peeked from behind another bed-spread.

"I'm just going to look at this one." She pulled the quilt free, her eyes caressing the black and white pattern and the words stitched about two feet from the top.

"What's it say?" Seth asked as he helped the seller squeeze three quilts into a clear plastic bag.

"'You may tire of reality but you never tire of dreams.'"

The proprietor looked up. "It's a quote from Maud Montgomery. From one of the short stories in her book *The Road to Yesterday*."

Marie beamed. "We have to have this. It'll be perfect in the room with the type—" Her words just stopped, and she stared at Seth as her nostrils slowly flared and her eyes grew large.

Had she suddenly remembered his message on the typewriter? Was she embarrassed by it? Embarrassed for him to know she'd seen it? She wasn't having any trouble maintaining eye contact, but she swallowed several times in a row.

He looked around for something to do, something to distract her, but the salesman beat her to it.

"Are you all right?"

She blinked, emerging from her stupor. "Yes. I just—I must have—excuse me. I just remembered something. I'm sorry."

"So do you want that quilt?"

"Yes." She didn't play coy with this one, so he paid for it. After they wrapped it up, Seth carried all four quilts to the truck. Marie darted across the aisle, pointing to a small table and hollering something about a typing desk. By the time he returned, she'd bought that too, along with an armload of decorations.

"Got enough there?"

"Oh, be quiet." She frowned at him, but her tone was

filled with humor as she held out the small desk under her pile. "Take some of this stuff before I drop three hundred dollars' worth of hominess."

He reached for the lamp on top, but she leaned into him, handing over the whole lot before taking back a small bag of knickknacks. "You got all this for three hundred bucks? Not bad, Carrington." He bumped her shoulder as they strolled from the grass onto the gravel lot and through a maze of trucks and trailers. When they reached his, he opened the passenger door and set her purchases in the backseat next to the quilts. As he stowed the table in the truck's bed, the auction movers approached with the large pieces of furniture.

After half an hour, the furniture was secured, each piece wrapped in padding and tarps.

"Now you'll want to drive slow, Mr. Sloane," one of the young men said.

Seth grinned at him and held out a twenty, biting back the urge to tell him that he knew how to drive a loaded truck. "Thanks, Rob." He turned back to Marie, opening the door for her. Resting a hand on the edge as she crawled in, he said, "I think we've done pretty well for a day, eh?"

"I think so."

He closed her in with a solid thump and walked around the front to his side. Behind the wheel, he checked his obstructed mirror views before slowly backing out of his spot and pulling into the three-vehicle line waiting to get on the road.

As the evergreens turned into rolling fields alongside the road, they sat in amicable silence. It hadn't been like this. Ever. Not even with Reece.

An image of the tall blonde as she'd been the last time he

saw her flashed through his mind. Everything with her had been wild and passionate. Stubborn and exciting. Loud and lively. Nothing about that relationship had just been quiet.

And he'd had no idea how much he'd missed out on until this very moment.

Relationships should have excitement and vibrancy.

But two people should be able to just sit together. Silent and at peace.

"Can I ask you something?"

He glanced away from the road toward Marie, all innocence and perfectly unaware of the irony of her question breaking into his peaceful ponderings. "I guess."

She looked at her folded hands in her lap, then out the window like she was going to ask the trees what she wanted to know. "You said earlier when we were talking with Aretha that Jack had been at this a lot longer than you. And he said something to me on my first day at the inn about you having nowhere else to go . . ."

His fist tightened on the wheel. He didn't want to talk about it. He wanted to go back to the silence. He wanted to enjoy a quiet trip thinking about the great things to come for the inn.

And mostly he did not want to confess Reece's betrayal.

Marie didn't know any of that, so she kept right on. "I thought that you'd been working with Jack since the beginning. But I guess that's not the case."

"Are you going to ask a question in there?"

Her dark hair fell over her shoulder as she leaned forward, twisting to look at him more closely. "Why are you here? What happened?"

He shook his head. He should be asking her the same

questions. Her answers could have serious consequences. His did not.

"It's a long story."

"We only have a few miles, so what's the ten-minute version? Or longer if you follow Rob's advice and go slow."

Her joke provoked a dry chuckle. How did she manage to tease him about the thing that he found most absurd? Maybe she could read him better than he thought.

If he told his history—at least an abridged version—that might prompt her to open up about hers. It couldn't hurt to try.

"I was a builder."

"In San Diego?"

He nodded. "Yes. I owned my own company. Sloane Construction."

"Creative." She shifted again until she was nearly perpendicular in the bucket seat, facing him, one leg pulled up under her.

"It was just me, a couple guys that I trusted, and a few contract crews. We did mostly new construction, custom homes for big-money clients."

She whistled low. "In San Diego? That must have been lucrative."

"It was."

"So what happened?" She twisted a strand of hair around a finger, but stopped as soon as he opened his mouth to continue.

He swallowed, taking time to find the right wording. "We met with a bit of financial difficulty."

"Jack said something about a fiancée. Are you engaged?"

Thank you, Jack. The man had no respect for anyone

else's privacy. "Once. We broke it off about eight months ago." Marie made a sound deep in her throat that said she was sorry to hear it and he should continue. And for some reason, he did.

"Her name is Reece, and we met at the home of one of my clients. He had a party to show off his new house. And he said I could meet potential new clients. His friends were well connected and wealthy. Just my clientele. He said I'd be a fool to miss the chance to sign contracts with them.

"So I showed up at his house and met Reece, who, at the time, was dating one of the other guys at the party. We struck up a conversation around the pool, and I'd never met anyone so beautiful in my life. The way the patio lights reflected off the water and danced across her face. I couldn't look away. She laughed at every one of my jokes—even the really lame ones."

"Interested girls usually do."

He jerked at the sound of her voice. Surprised that he wasn't rehashing the relationship by himself for the ump-teenth time.

Perfect. He'd probably said far too much. "Anyway, we got engaged, but it didn't last."

"Hey. That's not fair."

"What?"

"You can't get me hooked and then give me some abbre-viated version without the details." She lifted her eyebrows twice in quick succession. "How did you get Reece away from that other guy? How'd you win her?"

"Funny. I never—I mean, it didn't—" He paused, putting a hand over his mouth until the words in his mind sorted themselves out. "I never thought of it as winning her. The spark was so strong, I just thought she felt it too and—"

Marie leaned back, the anticipation on her face replaced by uncertainty. "You *thought* she felt it. She didn't?"

He let out a slow breath through his nose. This was not the conversation they were supposed to be having, but he'd just opened up that can of worms on himself. "No."

"How can you be so sure?"

"She made it perfectly clear that she'd never given a flying rat's rear end about me when she cleaned out all of the money from my company's accounts and left me. She'd been with me only for the con." He scrubbed a hand down his face. He hadn't meant to say that. At least not with that much bitterness. It was supposed to be getting easier to deal with. But the sting was still fresh.

Marie's slender fingers touched his sleeve. "I am so sorry, Seth. I didn't realize. I'm sorry that happened. I understand—"

"How could you possibly understand? What about your fairy-tale life makes you think you could possibly understand that kind of betrayal?" The words exploded in his anger at himself for revealing too much, but it was too late to take them back.

He got the silence he'd wanted for the rest of the trip, but this quiet wasn't about peace or contentment. Like her face, it was stony, masking the boiling emotions just below the surface. It grated his nerves and shot pain through his temples.

Of course, his anger was really at himself. He'd let Reece convince him to add her as a partner in his business. Blinded by his own attraction, he'd signed over his entire livelihood. And as their wedding date approached, she'd talked him into a joint banking account too. Better to take care of it before the actual ceremony, right?

How could he have been so stupid? He'd handed her his entire life savings and given up every legal right by signing three little slips of paper.

"This will make things so much easier after we're married," she'd cooed. "This is what's best for us and the business, right? I mean, if anything were to happen to you, who would you want to run things?"

She'd had her hands running through his hair and her lips pursed so close to his that he couldn't possibly have been thinking straight.

A little flick of the wrist and he signed it over.

His own bad judgment had cost him everything.

It still made his stomach hurt, even three thousand miles and eight months away, as he pulled into the Red Door's driveway.

Marie slammed her door open before he could even put the truck in park. She jumped to the ground and marched toward the house without a look over her shoulder.

He hopped out after her, running to catch her before she made it to the stairs leading up to the back door. "Wait. Marie, don't be—" He caught her hand to tug her to a stop.

She flung her arm around, dislodging his grip at her wrist. "Don't *touch* me." Her words slithered like a snake, quiet enough that they wouldn't draw Jack's attention from inside but hard enough to bend rebar.

"I didn't mean to yell—"

"Don't." She cut him off with the flash in her eyes even more than with her words. "I really don't want to hear it."

"Please. Just let me explain." He stabbed a hand through his hair as she turned away. But she stood still for a long moment, and his pulse jumped. This was his chance. "I—"

She shook her head. "You say I don't understand, that I couldn't possibly, but you have no idea about my life. You presume to know about my fairy-tale existence without ever bothering to ask."

His heart wrenched. *Lord, what have I done?* "Will you tell me about it?"

"No." She bounded up the steps, the door slamming behind her. Seth chased her up the stairs, nearly running into her motionless form in the kitchen.

She was staring at Jack, who leaned against the counter with locked elbows and hands that shook, papers scattered before him. Shoulders slumped and head bowed, he didn't move.

"Jack?" She walked up to him, putting a comforting hand on his shoulder, her movements the opposite of what they'd been two minutes before.

The old man jerked up, looking at them. "I didn't even hear you come in. How was the auction?"

"What's wrong?" Seth stepped forward, keeping a wide perimeter around Marie, and pointed to the papers strewn across the counter. "What's all this?"

Jack looked confused for a moment before pulling the pages into a haphazard pile.

"Jack?" Marie's tone had the gentleness of a preschool teacher coaxing a scared student out of his mother's arms. "Are you all right?"

"Sure. Sure. Just fine." His head bobbed with a smile, but the light never made it to his eyes. Marie shook her head, giving him a silent scolding, and his eyes darted to the paper. "Everything's great."

"We can't help if we don't know what's going on." Marie reached for his hand. "We're invested here too. Let us help."

Jack's posture sagged even lower as he leaned his back against the counter. His gaze passed between them, and he hoisted a smile. "Not a big problem. Money's a bit tight, is all."

"Well, I don't need a paycheck," Marie immediately piped up. "And maybe I could help you look over the budget. I have some exp—"

"Nonsense. Get paid as long as you're working here. I promised you." Jack looked at the ground. "Besides, that's a drop in the bucket compared to what we need."

"What about the loan money?"

Jack crossed his arms. "We're going to have to make it stretch."

Marie squeezed Jack's hand, and a pang of something he couldn't name shot to Seth's stomach. "Will they give you some more?" she asked.

"No."

"How can you be so sure?" Seth said.

Jack's chin dropped, and he looked away. "I met with the loan officer at the bank again this morning."

"Again?" Marie straightened until it looked like she'd left a hanger in her shirt. "Why didn't you tell us this was going on? I could have helped you update your business plan."

"I thought they were going to give me another loan." He pasted another smile on his face and straightened his paperwork by tapping the edges against the counter. "Don't worry about this. We're going to make the Red Door a success. We're just going to have to keep an eye on the budget and make the dollars stretch."

So Jack didn't have any more money.

Seth eyed Marie, waiting for any indication that the news

upset her. If she was in this to dupe Jack, she'd gotten a worse deal than she'd counted on. If she was in this for the scam—and more and more he doubted that possibility—she'd jump ship sooner rather than later.

At least she'd go empty-handed.

But if she stayed, they could all wind up where they started. Broke, bitter, and all alone.

14

Jack paced the kitchen, as had become his habit in the
early morning hours after Marie left for her run. The girl
couldn't sleep more than three or four hours a night. If
she wasn't up late painting, she was drawing layout designs
for the bedrooms. Even if she excused herself to her room
early—as she had the night before as soon as Aretha left—
her light didn't turn off until the wee hours of the morning.

And somehow she was still the most pleasant person in
the house.

He rubbed a hand over his hair, the other at his waist as
he stalked the room. The inn was supposed to open the first
of May. Rooms had been booked and guests confirmed. And
they were behind and without money to pay a crew to help
them get back on schedule.

He scrubbed his whiskers with his fingernails.

They had so much more than finishing touches to finalize.
The shower in one of the first-floor bathrooms didn't have
any tile. The outside of the house needed to be painted. All
of the kitchen cabinets needed to be finished.

He shoved at an open drawer, which groaned but didn't move.

And apparently that drawer needed to be fixed.

Then, of course, they hadn't started planting the garden or really gotten into the landscaping. It was too cold to do much yet, but they didn't have a plan in place, and Marie seemed pretty sure that they needed one.

He swung open the refrigerator door, analyzing the breakfast options. Even after Marie's most recent grocery store trip, the shelves seemed bare. Cold cereal and milk it was, despite his craving for something more akin to Caden's sweet rolls—or scrambled eggs and biscuits.

Rose made the best biscuits, light and fluffy layers of heaven.

She'd left a recipe in her tin box. Next to the shortbread and pie crust cards.

He'd tried to make them. Once.

After she'd gotten sick.

He scratched his chin, covering his mouth and wishing the taste of strawberry preserves over oven-fresh biscuits wasn't on the tip of his tongue.

He slammed the stainless steel fridge door closed, but the rubber seal bounced, swinging it wide again.

"Jack? Are you okay?"

Whipping around at the sound of Marie's voice, he tried not to look too embarrassed. This was his home, after all. And if he missed his wife's biscuits, then he was entitled to slam a door.

But the concern deep in Marie's eyes couldn't be missed. Even her rosy cheeks and wind-tossed ponytail didn't detract from the very real unease.

Jack sagged against the counter next to the sink. "I'm fine."

She nodded, but the creases in her forehead told him she wasn't quite convinced. What did she want him to say? That he missed Rose? True. That he had started thinking he'd made the biggest mistake of his life trying to open a bed-and-breakfast? Also true. That he couldn't stop as long as he remembered Rose?

He'd sat beside her hospital bed and promised her. He'd sworn that he'd find a home and open her inn on Prince Edward Island.

Failure wasn't an option.

But success was out of reach.

"I'm sorry, honey." He and Rose had never had any kids, but somehow it seemed right to soothe her with kind words. "I didn't mean to upset you. I was just . . ."

"Are you worried about the money? I think I can help. I'm pretty good at putting together a business plan. And I can help with marketing." When he shook his head and waved off her offer, she simply plowed forward. "And in the short term, you don't have to pay me. Really. I don't need it. I'm all right." She looked away as she said the last words. She'd said them often in the three weeks he'd known her, but no matter how often she did, it was clear she wasn't all right.

Rose had dreamed and prayed for this old house. She'd prayed that the broken would find healing under its roof. Long before the house had an address or an image in their minds, she had petitioned God for a place of healing.

She'd have liked Marie. And Aretha too. Rose would have liked North Rustico in general.

The thought of her smiling and standing in this kitchen brought a grin to his face.

Ignoring Marie's words, he pulled a mug from an overhead cabinet and filled it with coffee. He held it out to her, but she shook her head. Taking a sip himself, he sighed. "Marie, I loved my Rose more than anyone else in this world. She was kind, and she always smelled like peppermints. And not just at Christmas. All year long. How do you think a body gets to smell like peppermint?"

Marie filled up a glass with tap water but stopped with it halfway to her mouth. "I'm not sure. Lotion maybe. Didn't you ever ask her?"

He squinted as he stared at the opposite wall, not really seeing the trim around the plant shelves above the cupboards. "I guess not." He took another sip, the bitter liquid stinging the inside of his lip. "Sometimes a little mystery in life is good. It keeps you wondering. Keeps you thinking."

"About what?"

"I don't know. Life. Dreams."

She gulped down half of the water in her glass in one chug. "Jack, can I ask you a question?"

"Shoot."

"You're opening the Red Door for Rose, right? Because it was her dream. It's what she wanted."

He nodded slowly. The girl's question wasn't quite complete. "Yes."

"I don't mean to be disrespectful, but I'm curious. What's *your* dream?"

Jack opened his mouth to tell her his dream was the inn too. But his trap snapped shut with sudden realization.

He didn't love the old walls or creaking floor. He didn't

care if the bathroom tile was white or taupe. And he couldn't pick an attractive paint color to save his life. Opening the inn wasn't *his* dream.

"Jack?"

He couldn't quite make the words come out of his mouth. He couldn't even pinpoint them in his mind.

The pathetic thunk of the doorbell saved him from having to answer. "Let me see who that is." He scuttled to the front door and opened it with more energy than was required. Marie's friend from church, the one who made all those tasty sweet breads, stood on the porch, a white paper bag in her hands.

"Mr. Sloane. I'm Caden. Holt."

He nodded, stepping aside to let her enter. "Marie's friend."

"Yes, sir." Her short blonde hair bounced around her round cheeks, and her pretty blue eyes glowed.

"Caden." Marie slipped out of the kitchen, a complete opposite to her friend, petite and reserved where Caden was solid and bubbly. "I wasn't expecting you."

Caden shot a tentative glance in his direction. "Mom and Aretha wanted to make sure you're eating well enough." Her chuckle masked the uncertainty in her words.

Jack suffered from no such modesty. "So did they send us something to eat?"

She nodded, holding out her bag. He took it and poked his head inside. The perfume of heaven floated out. Fresh bread and tart apples. And something citrusy, like an orange grove in a bag. "What is this?"

"Um . . ." She peeked over the edge of the sack and pointed. "Those are orange scones with an orange cream glaze. That's a loaf of raisin cinnamon bread. And those are apple turnovers."

He nodded his approval and took another sniff. "Do I have to share?"

Caden's gaze leapt to Marie and back to him. "Only if you want happy employees."

He shrugged. "They've been cranky before. I think I could handle that again if I can keep this all for myself."

Her smile was all teeth and charm.

"What are you doing today?" Marie asked.

"I have the day off." She opened her coat to reveal a bleach-stained T-shirt. "I thought I might be of some help."

◆◆◆◆

Marie twisted the screw in the back of a cupboard door until the handle popped off. Then she sanded around the edges of the hole, smoothing down the splinters.

"These are beautiful." Caden stood next to the stainless steel double oven affixed to the wall. Her fingers brushed the metal handles with a reverence that Marie hadn't ever seen in a kitchen before.

She shrugged. "I guess. I never thought about it."

"Try learning to cook in an oven older than you are that has a habit of burning both the tops and bottoms of your cakes." She winked from behind an unruly swipe of blonde bangs. "You'll gain an appreciation for fine appliances. And Jack has very good taste."

"Try never learning to cook at all." Marie caught her thumb on a rough patch of wood and cringed, popping it into her mouth.

"Never?"

Staring at the tip of her finger until the redness subsided, Marie said, "Nope. We had a—umm, I guess I just never had to. And I didn't really want to either. But my mom's best friend Georgiana was an interior designer, and she took me under her wing when she worked on our house." No need for Caden to know it had been their beach house.

Of course, most houses on the island were on the beach. But the Red Door Inn—although right off the bay—was just half the size of her father's place on the Cape and intended to house three times as many people.

Caden looked down at her empty hands. "I feel like I should be doing something. What can I do?"

"Well, I almost have the handles off the cabinets. Then we'll give them a quick sanding before we paint them. Do you want to sand the ones I've already done?"

"Sure." She picked up a sheet of sandpaper and swiped it in a straight line down the front of a cupboard door. "Like this?"

Marie held up a flat palm facing away from her, making small circles in the air. "Make loose, round motions. You're not trying to smooth it out, just give it enough texture so the paint will stick to it."

"Paint doesn't stick to stuff naturally? I mean, it doesn't seem to be sliding off the wall or anything."

She waited to see if Caden was serious, so when the blonde turned, her eyebrows pulled together and a pleasant frown in place, Marie nodded slowly. "It does naturally stick to surfaces, but sometimes, if there's a glossy coat or smooth surface on the bottom, you have to give it a little extra something to grab on to."

Caden followed her directions, the scratching stiff and

disjointed. "So you learned all of this from your mom's friend? Did you work for her?"

The loose metal handles and screws clanked together as she swept them off the counter into a baggie. "Not exactly."

"An internship?"

"I loved design, so I took any excuse I could to spend time with Georgiana." Marie looked up at the ceiling, searching for the right word. "It was probably more like stalking."

Caden chuckled, then abruptly stopped as a fine cloud of dust reached her nose. Her sneeze rattled the cabinets, sending them both into a bout of laughter. After rubbing her nose, Caden said, "Did you go to university for design then?"

Marie pressed a hand to her chest as a dull ache settled in. Even after ten years, the memory stung of turning down the invitation to attend Parsons The New School for Design in New York. "No. My dad didn't think design was a prestigious enough career path."

The words felt strange as they came out. Like she'd never said them before. Maybe she hadn't. She'd sure thought it enough times, but no one disagreed with Elliot Carrington, especially not his only child.

"Really?"

"Really." She sighed, the memories close, the regrets closer. She hadn't stood up to her dad then. In fact, she'd only stood up to him once. Well, running to PEI just to get away from him wasn't exactly standing up to him. But at least she hadn't become his pawn.

Caden's sanding slowed as she turned to stare over her shoulder at Marie. "So did you go to university?"

"Sure. I went into the family business."

"I didn't know your family had a business. What is it?"

Money.

Well, that wasn't exactly a business. But her father was an expert at making money. Investing in property, building condos, and leveraging assets. He'd leverage anything he could to make a sweet million.

She pinched her eyes closed against the image of her dad's face on that morning in early January. After a week in hiding, a week trying to scrub the filth off her skin, she'd emerged from her suite. He'd acted bored with her, telling her she was overly dramatic. Of course, she wouldn't go to the police right that minute. She'd wait until the right time.

He put his foot down, and she let him. She stayed away from the truth because it hurt just to think about it. Because every breath in Boston was like sucking air through plastic. Because she was sure she was truly alone for the first time in her life.

After her mother died and her father —jealous of Georgiana's influence on Marie—told Georgiana she wasn't welcome in the Carrington home, Marie had clung to her mother's last words of hope. She'd spoken with such conviction of a God who cared for his children.

But how could a good God, a loving Father, leave her to the devices of a man who would barter her pain for a deal on the property he wanted?

"Marie?" Caden's voice was low, concerned. "Are you all right?"

She shook off the memories and the pain that accompanied them. "Yes. Sorry. Just zoned out for a second."

"Are you sure?" She didn't sound very sure, and her eyes were wary as her sanding stopped altogether.

"Absolutely." She plastered a smile in place, hoping it

resembled something real, not the grimace that always accompanied the memories. Best to think about something else. Quickly. "Are you about done?"

"Yep." Holding up a hand covered in white dust, Caden smiled. "All set for painting, I think."

Marie tossed her a wet rag. "Just one more step. We've got to clean the cabinets off so there isn't loose dust."

"Okay."

In no time at all, they were ready to start painting, and as she poured eggshell-white paint into a tray, Caden said, "I like this white against the brick red of the walls. It stands out from the steel appliances and feels somehow modern and classic."

"I was thinking the same thing when I picked these colors."

Caden lifted a hand to her forehead and wiped away a bead of sweat before picking up her glass of water.

"You might want fresh water." Marie pointed to the floating particles that danced in a rhythm all their own, hovering and bobbing. "Let me get you a new one."

As she pulled two water bottles from the fridge, Jack joined them. He leaned against the door frame, crossing his legs at the ankles of his blue jeans. "Having fun?"

They all chuckled. Preparing to paint wasn't nearly as fun as actually painting, but it was worth it for a quality finished project. As long as they didn't end up with multiple hues like the bedroom upstairs had. Of course, they only needed one can of paint for this job, and she'd stirred it. Thoroughly.

"What do you think of our kitchen, Caden?"

"It's beautiful. I was just telling Marie how much I like the colors. It has such a homey feel that I think your guests are going to want to spend more time in here than in the dining room." She took a quick breath before barreling on. "Maybe you should put in a permanent island with stools so that visitors can eat in here too. I mean, I'd have an island, but not so that people can eat at it. There's just never enough counter space in these old houses, so you have to—"

She slapped a hand over her mouth and shook her head. "I'm really sorry. My mom says I talk too much, and Aretha tells me I give my opinions too often when no one's asked for them. I just can't help it. They sneak out sometimes."

Jack's laugh burst out without caution. "Opinions are welcome. What do you think of the room? As a professional?"

"Oh, I'm not a professional."

Marie spoke in her defense. "What do you call those bites of heaven I keep buying from you? Unprofessional?"

Caden's round cheeks flushed red, and she looked at the paintbrush in her hand. Swiping a thumb over the clean bristles, she shrugged. "I'm not trained far beyond my dad's kitchen. My grandma taught me most of what she knows, and I cook for the whole family—all fifteen of us—when we get together. But I always just thought of it as dabbling in the kitchen."

"Well, your dabbling is a far cry better than anything anyone else in this house is doing. So tell us what you think." Marie gave her an encouraging nod.

"True." Jack hit the nail on the head.

"I might change a few things."

"Like?" He stuck his thumbs into his pockets.

Her hair fell into her face, and Caden brushed it behind her ears and pointed toward the dark stone countertops. "To start with, I would find a way to add more counter space. Baking isn't for small areas. And any baker is going to have canisters and cookbooks lining the counter. Also, most of the counter area that you do have is far away from the fridge and the oven. If you were cooking a breakfast casserole and prepped it over there"—she pointed at the counter closest to the laundry room door—"then you'd have to carry it all the way over to the oven. That's at least ten steps, ten chances that you'll drop it. But if you had a stable island, you could prep it all there, and it's not even a step to slide it into the oven."

Jack tapped his chin as she spoke, his eyes narrowing in concentration.

Caden didn't seem to notice Jack's change in expression. "And then I'd add a hanging rack for your pots and pans. Sure, you've got plenty of lower cabinet space, but serving a fast-paced breakfast is all about having the tools you need at hand but out of your way until you need them." She mimed pulling a pan from over her head. "If I'm going to make a berry compote for my French toast, that has to simmer while I prep the toast. So if I can pull my saucepan and my skillet down just when I need them, that's perfect."

Jack pulled a notepad from his back pocket and scribbled a note on it. "Good idea."

"Then if you built in a spice rack on the wall right there next to the refrigerator, you have easy access to the flavors you need most. And most importantly, you need a good trash can."

Everything she'd said made perfect sense until that last statement. "How many kinds of trash cans are there?" Marie said. "As long as it doesn't have a hole in it, isn't it a good one?"

"It's not good enough. You need one with a lid that opens without having to touch it. We have one at the bakery that has a sensor on it. When you wave your hand over it, the lid opens, and you never have to touch it. It keeps you clean and keeps your kitchen tidy even during a rush. At least, that's what my dad always says."

"Smart guy." Jack kept scribbling.

"Will you be cooking breakfasts yourself?"

"Not unless cold cereal has become acceptable fare."

Caden shook her head. "I don't think so. Have you hired your chef yet? If not, there's a good school in Charlotte-town. At Holland College. You might be able to hire a recent graduate."

"Thanks. We're all set. I've hired an executive chef from New York."

Marie waited for a twinge of recognition to cross Jack's face as her stomach lurched. But he didn't seem to realize that the chef's arrival would mean her departure. Or he didn't care.

Jack just continued writing with his stub of a pencil, nodding as Caden offered him another thought on the types of plates they'd need to look for. Dishwasher-safe didn't look as classic or homey, but they would save endless hours of hand-washing the china that Aretha sold.

Marie watched them, even as their conversation faded away.

Did Jack not remember that he'd promised her room to someone else and he hadn't even told her? Except it wasn't really her room. She was just temporary help. Jack would send her packing as soon as the chef arrived.

Marie took a deep breath and swiped her paintbrush down the inside of a cabinet door. He couldn't ask her to leave if she was already gone.

15

Two Sundays later, Marie woke up later than usual. Rolling over on her bed, she stared at the red numbers on the little clock. She never used to wake up before the alarm jerked her from her sleep on the weekends. But ever since New Year's Eve, she'd been more eager to get out of bed every morning.

But today she'd slept until well after seven. A little sore from helping Jack lay paving stones in the backyard the day before, she scooted from under a thick blanket, grabbed her only pair of clean pants and a thick sweater, and hugged them to her chest to ward off the basement chill as she ran for the bathroom.

When she emerged from the steam-filled room half an hour later, the bone-chilling cold was a distant memory. She pulled on thick socks and padded up the stairs, careful not to hit the creaky step. Jack or Seth might still be asleep. She didn't really know what time they got up. It was usually while she was on her morning run, and that was all she needed to know.

She also needed to find something to fill the gnawing in her stomach.

Tiptoeing into the kitchen, she pulled a box of cereal from the cupboard and poured a generous helping into a plastic bowl. She topped it off with a long splash of milk. The granola made a loud crunch as she chewed slowly, surveying the room. The white cupboards had turned out just as she'd envisioned, and the hanging rack that Jack had asked Seth to install at Caden's suggestion glimmered in the light of the sunrise.

"So you decided to join us this morning?"

She jumped at Seth's voice, sloshing milk down the front of her sweater. Frowning at the damp trail, she took the washcloth next to the sink and tried to mop it up. It only succeeded in leaving a wider path.

Oh well. There was no helping it now. She'd just have to wait for it to air dry.

She shrugged. "Don't I always?"

His gaze roamed from the top of her head to her shoulders and back up, his face void of emotion. "I wasn't sure you were going to make it on time today."

"Well, I did." She held up her bowl and shoveled the cereal into her mouth, never taking her eyes off him. After too long, she swallowed a painful bite. "Can I help you with something?"

One side of his mouth angled up. "I don't think I've ever seen your hair down like that."

"My hair?" She ran her fingers through the still-damp strands hanging over her shoulders, suddenly wishing she'd pulled it back before leaving the safety of her room.

"You should wear it like that more often." He turned up his smile from half-mast to full-blown.

She held her breath as her stomach performed a complete barrel roll. Hugging her bowl just below her chin and squinting at him, she asked, "Why?"

"It's pretty."

A war waged in her chest, and she tightened her features to keep it from showing on her face. It had been months since anyone had offered such a simple, sweet compliment, and she longed to accept it. Longed to believe it.

But the part of her that carried the memories of another man who had said she was beautiful cried out in fear. She couldn't trust any man who offered such flippant comments. She couldn't believe he said them for anything but his own benefit.

Except there was a twinkle in Seth's eye that suggested he meant it.

And as she scooped another bite into her mouth, his face turned serious, and his eyebrows pulled together. "I'm sorry for what I said when we were coming back from the auction." His voice low and insistent, he leaned toward her as though proximity equaled sincerity. "I shouldn't have been such a jerk."

Her stomach clenched, putting a pause on her breakfast. This kind of genuine apology was new to her. Her mom had never done a thing requiring an apology—at least from Marie. And her dad had certainly never offered one for anything—despite his numerous offenses.

Just when she compared Seth to the men of her past, he surprised her.

He stood there, the pain in his eyes testifying to his true remorse, even as he fidgeted with a screwdriver that had been left on the counter. Owning up to his mistake. This was what real men did. Not perfect ones. Just ones who recognized their shortcomings and tried to make things right.

He attempted a grin, which fell flat, then added, "I didn't mean to tell you so much about Reece. It just sort of came out. And sometimes what she did is still a little too fresh. You know what I mean?"

Marie nodded around the mouthful she was slowly chewing.

"Anyway, I just—" He stabbed a hand through his hair before flattening a black eyebrow with a finger. "Well, I'm glad we could finally talk alone. Seems like Jack has stuck to you closer than glue."

Her swallow was so loud she was sure he'd go deaf.

The truth wasn't that Jack had been sticking to her side. It was the exact opposite. In the almost two weeks since the auction, she'd made it a point not to be left alone with Seth. The easiest way to do that was to stay by Jack. He always had a project, and she liked talking to him, hearing stories about his courtship with Rose. At least that was what Jack called it.

Working with him kept her entertained *and* safe from another run-in with Seth. Listening to Jack and Rose's love story made her forget—if just for a few minutes—why she was even on the island. Why she'd left Boston in the first place.

And it gave her a glimmer of hope.

She wasn't quite sure what she hoped for. But maybe it was a future.

Seth heaved a sigh from somewhere deep in his stomach and pressed a thumb and forefinger against his eyes. "I really am sorry, Marie. I had a good time at the auction."

She licked her lips, steeling herself to tell the truth. "I did too."

"Maybe we should do it again sometime."

"Another auction?" She sidestepped his suggestion, anything to keep from having to respond to it.

He shook his head. "Not an auction necessarily. There are plenty of other projects we could work on together. Or we could go for a walk and get ice cream. I could show you my favorite spot on the beach."

Her tongue stuck to the roof of her mouth, which had turned into a desert. Ice cream. He'd just suggested they get her favorite thing on earth. Like, on a date. Or maybe not a date, but definitely alone. Just the two of them. Eating her favorite thing.

Did he know that ice cream was her worst weakness?

Her stomach shot into her throat. She'd left her mini diary in the typewriter. She'd confessed to wishing she'd gone to get ice cream and left it there for anyone—including Seth Sloane—to find.

And then she'd promptly forgotten about it. Twice.

She was such a birdbrain. What a stupid mistake.

Biting her cheeks, she tried to find enough moisture in her mouth to respond to him, but instead her tongue seemed to swell. Her throat felt like sandpaper as she tried to swallow.

She grimaced against the pain.

"Are you all right?" Seth asked.

Nodding with forced enthusiasm, she backed away. "I just forgot something." She set down her bowl and pointed over her shoulder, then ran down the hall. She hoped she didn't sound like a herd of island cows stampeding over the hardwood, but she couldn't get to the room at the end of the hall fast enough.

She closed the door behind her, at the last minute turning the knob to silence the sound of the click. As she wove her way between stacks of newly purchased antiques, she found the original piles. And there was her beautiful black Underwood.

The sheet of white paper she'd left there nearly glowed on its curved perch.

She grabbed the edge of it, intent on pulling it free, until she saw that a second line had been boldly typed below her original confession.

I wish you had too. Next time?
S

She stared at the letters, unable to make sense of their meaning. "Next time?" She said the words aloud, hoping that would help them sink in.

The knot in her stomach pulled taut, and she pressed a hand to her belly.

This was the third time he'd asked. Or maybe it was the second. She had no idea when he'd typed this note. It could have been before the auction.

But did that make any difference? All it really meant was that he had asked again. That he really did want to spend time with her. But that could be just to ask more prodding questions about her past.

She tightened her grip on the paper, ready to pull it free.
What if it's not?

She harrumphed at the voice in her head. What did it know?

That you're lonely. That you miss having a friend who's not twice your age. That you like being told your hair is pretty.

She frowned at the paper but left her hand in place. "I don't have to, you know. I can turn down ice cream."

Yes, but do you want to? Or are you just scared?

"What do I have to be scared of?" Even as she whispered the words, her voice shook. She had plenty to be scared of. Haunting memories. Losing her breath to another panic attack. Being coerced into returning to Boston.

Taking a wavering breath, she released the paper and knelt to sit in front of the typewriter. Resting on her heels, she stared at the blank area below Seth's message until her eyes crossed. She had to give him an answer. And leaving it here was easier than saying her piece in person.

Except she wasn't quite sure what her answer was.

She pinched her eyes closed and clasped her hands in her lap. "Oh, God, what am I going to do?" The prayer passed over her lips before she even realized what she was doing. Somehow it felt natural, like it hadn't been three months since she'd talked to him.

Letting a slow breath out through tight lips, she pressed one of the keys. Then another. The reports picked up speed, echoing against crates and boxes.

Quick footsteps down the hall outside the door announced Jack's imminent arrival. "Marie? Ready to go?"

"I'll be right there." She lifted her voice to carry through the closed door, pounding out the last word in careful measure. As she pushed to her feet and scurried toward the door, she gave her note one last glance.

As long as next time is soon.
M

◆◆◆◆◆

The pews were empty. The parishioners had long since fled the indoors, prompted by the unusually warm midday. Their voices—faint but lively—carried from the front lawn through the open door.

Jack welcomed the solitude, leaning his arms against the back of the bench before him and folding his hands. His gaze followed the outline of the wooden cross hanging behind the podium, where Father Chuck had dismissed the congregation more than fifteen minutes before.

As he closed his eyes, numbers and columns flashed before him. From black to red they danced, leaving only dread in their wake.

"God?" He lifted his eyes toward the rough-hewn beams above, his voice falling far short of the vaulted ceiling. "I'm in a bit of trouble, and I could use your help here. I'm just trying to do what Rose wanted, but the numbers aren't adding up. And the bank says I'm not a good investment anymore. But I can't pay back the loans I've already taken out if the Red Door doesn't open."

He bowed his head, staring at the swollen knuckles and broken fingernails. He was working hard—they all were—but it wasn't going to be enough.

Soft steps approached, and he turned to find Aretha making a slow path up the center aisle. "I'm sorry to interrupt you." She pointed to the bench behind him. "I forgot my hat."

He nodded, doing his best to give her a smile. "No problem. Just talking with God for a bit."

Her floppy pink hat flourished as she picked it up and waved it under her round chin. Green eyes—so different from Rose's deep brown—squinted at him. "May I ask you a question?"

Jack nodded.

"You seem troubled. Is there something I can do?" Though they were a different color, the compassion in Aretha's eyes was exactly like Rose's.

He shook his head, looking down again, his chin touching his chest, his shoulders falling. A sigh escaped pinched lips from somewhere deep inside.

Her skirt swished as she slid into the pew beside him and rested a silky-smooth hand on his outstretched forearm. "There's something weighing heavy on you. Will it help if you talk about it?"

"No." He patted her hand. "Thank you for offering."

She bobbed her head slowly, scooting a little closer until her shoulder brushed his. They sat in silence for several minutes as he prayed for a way to solve his money dilemma.

"Is this about Marie?"

He jumped at the sound of her voice. "Not so much. But I've certainly pulled her into my problems."

"What do you mean?"

He scratched behind his ear. "I thought I could help her. Thought she needed a safe place to stay. She was just so sad."

Aretha rearranged her skirt as she crossed her legs and took a soft breath. "How did you meet her?"

"On the Wood Islands ferry." Had it only been a month since he'd spotted her in the terminal, so alone? "She was hugging her bag like it was a matter of life and death, and I'd never seen a grown-up curl into a ball like that. Everything about her screamed that she wanted to be left alone, but when I saw her counting the change in her pocket and staring at the lunch specials, I knew she didn't have two nickels to rub together, and I couldn't stay where I was. My Rose and I didn't have any children. God never saw fit to give us any. But when I saw Marie . . . guess my fatherly instincts kicked in. Lord knows I never wanted a daughter. Too much to worry about. Too many emotions."

Aretha chuckled, her eyes glistening and her lip trembling. But she remained silent, nodding for him to go on.

"I didn't know what else to do with her, so I sat down next to her and said the first thing that popped into my mind—the only thing I thought about. I asked her what color I should paint my inn. She actually answered me. Once she got to talking about colors and flowers, I didn't want her to stop. By the time we were on the ferry, I thought, 'Well, this girl could be the answer to my prayers.' We needed a woman's touch, so I talked her into taking a job. Nearly had to force her into it."

"Jack, that's wonderful."

He swallowed the lump in his throat. "Sure. Sounds nice. But now I've got her counting on me, relying on me for a roof over her head and a weekly paycheck, and the Red Door is bleeding money."

Aretha's eyes grew wide, her hand at her throat. "How?"

He had to look away, so he studied the crevices in the ceiling beams. Saying the truth was harder than he'd imagined. And he knew that Aretha would be disappointed by his failures. Just as Rose would have been.

"It started with having to replace the pipes in all the bathrooms. They were corroded and below grade. Seth worked with a local plumber and replaced them in record time. But it was an unexpected cost. I made an adjustment, taking from elsewhere in the budget. Then the materials for the two bath-rooms that needed to be completely remodeled were much more than the original quote. More money from another part of my budget. I'm stealing from Peter to feed Paul. And in a month, I'll add the salary for an executive chef."

"Well, that shouldn't be too much. The island is full of young, talented chefs looking for jobs."

He shook his head, covering his face with his hands, his elbows leaning on the pew in front of him. "I've already con-tracted a trained chef from New York City. I'll just be able to make his salary. If one more thing goes wrong or costs more than it should, I'll . . . I don't know where I'll be. In trouble, I suppose. Bankrupt and on the road back to Chicago."

He held his breath for a lecture. Or a look of pity.

He got neither.

"Is that all?" Her bright red lips pursed as she crossed her arms. "My, my, Jack Sloane. I expected more. Seems we may need to toughen you up a little bit. You're borrowing worry from tomorrow. For today, right this minute, Marie has a safe place to stay and a little spending money in her pocket. You have an inn and a plan and two people who are willing to work their trim little rear ends off for you." She scoffed. "Sounds to me like you've got it pretty good."

She pulled herself up and held out her hand. "You have friends, and two kids who couldn't love you more if you were their biological father. The good Lord may not have seen fit to give you children to raise, but he certainly hasn't left you alone."

The words sank in slowly, their warmth spreading from the center of his chest to the tips of his fingers.

"Jack, are you about ready?" Marie said, peeking around

the edge of the door. "Seth is getting hungry. And you know how grumpy he gets when he isn't fed."

He laughed. "I'll be right there."

Aretha was right. Marie wasn't a liability. She was an asset with a soft heart and an eye for design unlike anyone he'd ever met. She completed the team, and he needed her at least as much as she needed him. He'd offer her everything he had until he didn't have anything left to give. God would just have to take care of the rest.

"Thank you, Aretha."

"You're quite welcome." She straightened her hat, and he jumped to his feet, then offered her an elbow as they strolled toward the double wooden doors. "Now, let this friend bring you lunch today. We can eat at one of your fabulous new tables and wonder about all the delightful guests who will find their way to your inn when the doors open on time and within budget."

He prayed she was right.

This was his only shot at fulfilling Rose's dream.

And maybe then finding his own.

16

After Aretha's impromptu lunch of cold lobster quiche, Seth left her and Jack at the antique table Marie had bought at the auction and carried a stack of paper plates into the kitchen. Marie closed the dishwasher as he dumped the plates into the trash can. When he stood, she was watching him with an intense focus that made him stand up straighter.

"It's a beautiful day today."

She nodded. "Do you think it'll stay this way?"

He shrugged. "I hope so. But Father Chuck seemed to think that we're bound for another cold snap." She shivered at just the mention of another front. But he wasn't going to be held captive by the thought of cold. He'd enjoy what was before him. The warmth of the shining sun and a gentle breeze off the water. And maybe even an opportunity to take Marie up on her last note. He'd had a feeling she'd seen his message that morning, so he'd checked as soon as they were back from church and found her response. "I was thinking about going for a walk. Maybe down the boardwalk for some ice cream. Want to come with me?"

He held his breath as she nibbled on the corner of her bottom lip, her face a war zone. She opened her mouth with a smile, then snapped it closed with a shake of her head. Rubbing her cheeks with swift movements of her flat palms, she looked at the floor between them.

She'd said she wanted to go. And sooner was better than later. He was giving her the chance she'd asked for.

So why was she hesitating?

Watching her internal battle made his skin crawl and his heart pound.

Maybe there was a more important question. Why did he want her to go with him so badly? Oh, he had a ready answer for that. He still knew almost nothing about her past, or what had brought her to the soon-to-be red door of Jack's bed-and-breakfast.

But an annoying pest in the back of his mind suggested that he just liked spending time with her. That he wanted to see her smile again because when she did, her whole face lit up.

He searched around for something to do with his hands in an effort to silence that voice.

Grabbing the drawer that was jammed about halfway open, he yanked on it until it broke free with a terrible screech, blank white paper flying into his face.

"What are you doing?" Her giggle took the edge off the nuisance in the back of his brain.

"Nothing. Just thought I could fix this drawer before I go for that walk."

He set the drawer on the counter and squatted down next

to Marie, who was already shuffling the strewn papers into a pile. From under her bangs, she glanced up at him, her smile warm. Not brilliant. Just kind.

He nodded toward the papers in her hands. "Thanks." When he held out his hand to take them from her, she handed the pages over, and their fingers touched.

And she didn't pull back like he disgusted her.

His gaze shot to where her trembling hand still rested on his. The tremors were invisible, but the vibrations made his whole hand tingle.

"All right?"

She nodded, her eyes trained on the exact point where their hands met. Long lashes fluttered to a stop on her pink cheeks, her lips nearly disappearing as she squeezed them together. A cascade of waves fell over her far shoulder, and he reached to brush the hair behind her ear before he consciously made the movement. It felt like individual strands of brown silk, and he had to fight every urge to rub it between his fingers.

She jumped when he touched her hair, but she didn't pull away.

That was a victory in his book.

He leaned in just enough to catch the full scent of her shampoo—something clean and subtly flowery. She smelled like a garden on the beach. She smelled like a woman should.

She cupped a hand around the smooth skin of her cheek and licked her lips with the tip of her tongue until they were sleek and glossy. All the moisture in his mouth vanished. His gut clenched like a clamp had been twisted on it.

Dear God.

He wanted to kiss her.

Wherever the urge had come from, he beat it down, grasping for something—anything—else to think about. But a man couldn't be expected to focus so close to her perfectly pale features, silky skin, and heavenly scent.

He managed an audible swallow, leaning back just enough to inhale fresh air, clean air.

He had to think of something to say. He had to get his mind off kissing those perfectly shaped lips she pursed as she lifted her eyelids to meet his stare.

Was she taunting him? Inviting him to press his mouth to hers?

Nope. He was still thinking about her lips. And his. Together.

And that would be a recipe for disaster.

His attraction wasn't to be trusted. He'd proved that with Reece.

And he'd never be able to forgive himself if he let this bumbling, uncertain attraction to Marie get in the way of protecting Jack. If she was anything but who she appeared to be, he'd miss it being this close to her.

Still, he couldn't pull his hand away from hers without saying something. "I got your note."

"I thought maybe you did." Finally she pulled away, and he could suck in a whole breath, the fog around his mind slowly rolling away. "Is that why you asked me to go with you?"

"Of course. Did you change your mind?"

She stuck her tongue out between her teeth. "It may be a woman's prerogative to change her mind, but she'll never change it about ice cream."

"Fine. Fine." He held out a hand to help her stand, but she was already getting to her feet. "I'll never say such a thing again."

She waggled her eyebrows and pasted a crooked smile into place. "I just thought you might have wanted to give Jack and Aretha some alone time."

He turned his head in the direction of her gaze, wondering if Jack had walked into the room. But the dining room door was still firmly closed. Squinting at her, he tried to read between the lines of what she was saying. The message didn't translate, so he shook his head. "Why would I give them time alone?"

"Oh, I don't know." She covered a secret smile with her fingers. She'd gotten into the catbird seat and was in no rush to let him in on the mystery.

With a riddle sparkling behind her sapphire-blue eyes and slender fingers hiding a girlish smile, she was beyond pretty. She was absolutely stunning.

He grabbed the broken drawer from the counter and banged at the dented hardware on its side with the palm of his hand.

Anything to keep his mind off her.

At least her, meaning *her*.

He wasn't making any sense.

Marie, the mildly antagonistic, always enigmatic housemate, was fine. He could think about her and her plot to swindle Jack. But *Marie*, the beautiful woman with a smart tongue and kissable lips, was off-limits. She was bound to be trouble, and he had to keep his mind as far away from that version of her as possible.

He stretched to pick up a hammer and beat the dent until it resembled the metal strip on the opposite side. He slid the drawer back into place. It wobbled but closed all the way. He opened it and shoved the paper back inside, then closed it again.

"There. That's done. What's next?"

"Ice cream."

He hadn't really been asking her. He'd been trying to forget she was even in the room, actually. But he had invited her.

"All right. Let me just tell Jack we're going." He ducked into the other room, where Aretha sat with perfect posture, mesmerized by one of Jack's stories. Clearing his throat, he waited for them to look his way. "We're going to get some dessert. Would you like anything?"

"None for me." Jack patted the plaid flannel shirt over his flat belly. "That lobster and egg deal was something else. I'm not sure I'll need to eat again until next week."

"You kids have a good time," Aretha said. Immediately her eyes returned to Jack, who launched back into a story of how he'd gotten caught during a storm on Lake Michigan in a kayak. Seth had heard that tale a few times, and this version was bigger, more grandiose, than ever before. Was Jack trying to impress Aretha?

He frowned at Marie as he turned back into the kitchen. She just smiled that cat-who-ate-the-canary grin.

"What do you know that I don't?"

"Enough."

He scowled as he pulled a jacket over his T-shirt. Jack had sworn he wasn't interested in Aretha as anything other than a friend. But Marie seemed to suspect something different.

Her levity added a bounce to her step as she traipsed through the mudroom and down the back stairs.

"Don't worry about it," she said as he caught up to her.

But that's what he did. He worried about Jack. He worried about the inn. If he didn't, who would?

And something was definitely going on between Jack and Aretha.

Whether Jack was aware of it remained to be seen.

◆◆◆◆

Marie's pulse slowed down, her breathing unfettered as she stepped onto the planks of the boardwalk. She drew the warm afternoon air into her lungs, full and whole. What was it about this place that made breathing so much easier than it had been in Boston?

"Do you think there's magic in the air here?"

Seth looked at her like she'd lost her mind, his forehead a sea of wrinkles.

"Don't you feel it? It's like the ocean is calling and good ol' St. Lawrence wants us to go for a swim."

"St. Lawrence?"

"Well, the gulf was named after someone, wasn't it?"

His nod was as slow as his steps. "I suppose."

"You're hopeless, Seth."

His head jerked. "What's that supposed to mean?"

"Only that there's something incredible about this place, and you're missing it." She spun in a slow circle, lifting her face to the sun. Pine trees lent their scent and gulls their song to the day's delights.

"I'm not missing it. I'm not missing anything." He marched on, ignoring her, save for his monologue. "It's a Sunday afternoon. It's a nice day. But it'll be better with ice cream."

"Everything's better with ice cream."

"What's gotten into you?"

She pulled off her jacket and pushed the sleeves of her

sweater up to her elbows, the sun on her skin taking the sting out of the wind. "I don't know." And she truly didn't.

Maybe it was the way Jack and Aretha had sat so close during lunch, exchanging stories and secret smiles. Maybe it was the local lobster in their lunch. Or simply the smell of spring winning the fight against winter's freezing rain.

Maybe it was that for the first time in three months, she'd had butterflies.

Innocent. Unexpected. Thrilling butterflies.

When Seth had brushed his thumb across her cheek, pushing her hair out of her face, her stomach had erupted like a swarm of monarchs. Their wings had fluttered and flickered, both calling for further contact and terrified of the same.

He'd pulled away just before she flew apart.

And beyond all of that, her body had remembered how to respond to a man's touch.

For months her only reaction to physical contact had been gasping for breath and incapacitating dizziness. But maybe this island was changing her.

She couldn't turn down her smile.

When they reached the fishing village at the end of the path, they veered toward a weather-beaten shack, red paint peeling off the wood siding. In bold letters it proclaimed the treat they'd trekked almost a mile for.

"Ladies first." Seth offered a slight bow, and Marie didn't need him to offer twice.

At the window, she smiled at the teenager behind the counter. He was less enthusiastic about having to work on such a beautiful day. "How can I help you?" His words were as flat as his metal scooper was round.

Put a smile on your face and be thankful that you're giving

215

out the world's sweetest gift. "I'll have a double scoop of mint chocolate chip."

"We're all out of that."

She glared at Seth, who shrugged. This was clearly a second-rate establishment. "Two scoops of strawberry on a cone."

"Waffle or sugar?"

"Waffle."

Despite the kid's flagrant disregard for the joy that all ice cream scoopers should display, his portions were generous, and her smile was firmly back in place by the time he handed her the cone. Seth ordered two scoops of vanilla, in spite of her harrumph.

Shrugging, he said, "What? I'm a purist. Chocolate or vanilla."

She licked at the frozen delight as Seth led the way toward the walkway. But instead of continuing toward the Red Door, he nodded his head in the direction of the beach. "Want to see something?"

"On the beach?"

He nodded.

"All right."

If she'd thought her day couldn't get better than a tongue coated in strawberry cream, she changed her mind the minute they crested the little hill. The water, so secretive during her morning visits, shone like a diamond under a spotlight in the noon sun.

"I'm not missing out on anything," he said.

"You're not?"

They strolled past a couple holding hands, drawing nearer to the rock jetty. Her attention shifted between the beauty of the scene before her and the cone in her hand so that she missed the hole in the sand. Her knee buckled as she lurched forward.

Seth grabbed her arm, righting her by the sheer force of his grip. "Are you going to watch where you're going now?"

Kicking sand out of the cuff of her pants, she said, "Where *are* we going?"

"To my absolute favorite spot on the island."

"You have a favorite spot?"

He cocked his head to the side. "Just because I don't dance down boardwalks or ramble about the guy they named the gulf after, doesn't mean I don't appreciate it."

When they reached the jetty, he climbed onto the rocks, holding his cone high in the air with one hand and using the other to climb the uneven steps. Glancing over his shoulder, he wrinkled his brows. "Watch your step."

"I'm more worried about my ice cream." She licked a melting drop that slid toward her finger.

"Come on." He held out his free hand, and when she tucked hers into it, he pulled her up with a strength that his earlier save had only hinted at. Several yards out over the water, he pointed to two rocks that formed a perfect bench. "There."

"This is your favorite spot? On the whole island?"

"Try it out."

She shrugged, dropping to her knees before sitting down facing the water. The catch in her breath had nothing to do with his proximity and everything to do with the view of the village. From their vantage point, she could just make out the beach beside a big yellow barn-like building. There waves clapped against the island's famous red dirt with breathtaking ease. The little white lighthouse shone brightly even in the sun, and a few wildflowers were braving their way back, reaching for the sun.

After nearly five minutes of silence, she whispered, "Thank you."

"Why?" He smiled around a bite of waffle cone.

"You know why." She used her melting treat to motion across the water.

"You're welcome." He licked around the edge of his ice cream. "This makes me wish I still had my surfboard."

"You surfed?"

He shrugged.

"I figured as much. San Diego guys always do."

"Well, not all of us. We moved there when I was twelve, and I was obsessed with the water. Not very good at surfing, but I didn't care."

She nodded toward the rolling waves. "I don't think these would make for good surfing either."

"Nope. But I'd give just about anything to paddle out past the break and just sit there, letting the surf float me back to shore."

She crunched on a piece of the crispy waffle, knowing exactly what he meant.

When her cone was gone and her stomach so full she could pop, she leaned elbows on her knees and rocked in motion with the waves. Closing her eyes, she let the water lull her almost to sleep. "Wake me up when it's time to go back."

"All right." He leaned back on his hands.

The rhythmic lapping of the waves was the only mark of time, so when he nudged her, she nearly fell off her seat.

"Maybe we should head back. I've got to get the mirror hung in the upstairs bathroom."

She nodded, taking his hand as he helped her up and then back down the rocks. They walked side by side in silence all the way back to the inn. Whether he was trying to avoid more dancing or afraid that she'd begin rattling on again, he kept his mouth closed, a small grin in place.

Seth held open the back door as she walked inside.

"Thanks for the ice cream."

He followed her closely into the house. "I didn't pay for the ice cream."

"You didn't?" She whipped around, almost running into the middle of his chest. Her hands rose to fend off the bump, her fingers grazing the front of his T-shirt.

His forehead wrinkled, his eyes narrowing. "I thought you did."

"I didn't. He didn't tell me how much it was." She pointed in the general direction of the beach. "But he didn't call after us. Did he?"

She tried to replay the scene in her mind, but everything before strawberry on the beach was a blur.

Seth's chest rumbled, his laughter building from deep within. When it finally exploded, he had to put his hand on his side as the guffaws shook him. "I owe him some money. And if I don't pay him, I might be labeled persona non grata."

Between her own giggles, she said, "Yes, I'm sure they'll post your picture next to the window and tell their whole staff to refuse you service."

With quick backward steps that matched the rhythm of his laughter, he reached the door. "I'll be right back." He

219

disappeared around the side of the house, his chuckles still ringing in the room.

Marie wandered into the dining room, a skip in her step to match Seth's laughter. The table was empty, and Jack and Aretha had disappeared. "Jack?" she called down the hall, wandering to the foyer. At the front door, she spied two figures walking down the road toward Aretha's shop.

She pressed her face as close to the window as she could without leaving a smudge. Jack's white hair fluttered in the wind, and Aretha clasped her hands around his elbow as she looked into his face.

This was very, very good.

If anyone was right for Jack, it was Aretha, with her warm heart and bright smile. Jack needed that after his loss. Even if he didn't realize it.

Marie wandered back to the kitchen, put a few more glasses into the dishwasher, and wiped off the counters. There were still plenty of walls to paint, but maybe if she waited for Seth, she could help him hang the mirror and he'd help her paint.

Jack's *New York Times* sat in a haphazard array on the corner of the counter, and she shuffled the pages together, automatically scanning the business section for anything of interest. The Dow was down, but that wasn't new.

She flipped the page over and nearly crumpled it up to throw into the recycling bin. But her hand stopped at the edge of the page. She blinked several times, trying to focus on the tiny script and praying she'd misread the name in the article.

She hadn't.

As the words came into focus, she scanned the lines as fast as she could, mumbling the words. "Boston area real estate group Carrington Commercial hit a snag in the purchase of two and a half acres of land . . . Current property owner Derek Summerville Sr. is asking the National Register of Historic Places to preserve the buildings on his land and halt the purchase of the land, which Carrington Commercial owner Elliot Carrington says . . ."

Her voice trailed off as her breath vanished. Leaning an elbow on the counter, she covered her face.

The land where her dad planned to put multimillion-dollar condos was still in limbo, still of more import than his daughter.

She tried to swallow the lump that lodged in her throat, but it stayed put.

Her father had tried to use her, but he wasn't getting what he wanted. While he might be able to pressure Derek Summerville Sr. into selling, the land was worthless if it couldn't be developed. Mr. Summerville knew that and was using it to fight back the only way he could.

The lines on the page blurred, and she knuckled away the wetness on her cheeks until she could make out the rest of the story. It was mostly financial jargon, except for the last line, a quote from Elliot Carrington.

"We believe there's an expert who can clear up any confusion about this property, and we're making every effort to locate her immediately."

She sagged against the counter and covered her face with both hands. Tears splashed into her palms as she swallowed a sob.

It could only have been clearer if he'd used her name. He was coming for her, because without her, his bite was toothless. Without her, he could prove nothing. And Derek Sr. knew it.

17

Marie counted the money in her stash for the fifth time in as many days. There wasn't any more than there had been the night before, and she folded it twice before tucking it into the hidden zipper of her backpack. Pressing her fists into her eyes, she pulled her knees up to her chin.

Was it enough? Was the meager stash enough for her to move on? To keep her father guessing at her whereabouts?

The lingering questions left her head pounding.

Not yet. But she had to go. And soon.

Jack and Seth hadn't signed up to face down her father. When they met him, they might not initially intend to send her packing. But after he coerced and cajoled them in the same voice he used in the boardroom, they'd wish she would go. They might even encourage her to go back to Boston with him. And she couldn't do that.

She wouldn't do it.

No matter how much she might want to stay with them— or how much they could use another hard worker—it wasn't an option. Her father would find her. His private investigator was almost certainly tracking her. It wouldn't have taken him long to find whatever security video the bus station in Boston had recorded. And someone at the Wood Islands ferry terminal had most likely remembered a lonely woman. At just two inches over five feet tall, she was noticeable. Memorable. The PI might still be stuck there if he hadn't yet connected her with Jack. But the island wasn't very big. It wouldn't take long to track down a new resident, especially outside of tourist season.

She didn't have much more time.

Two solid thumps on her door jerked her from her position on top of the bedcovers, and she scurried to answer it. Seth leaned one shoulder into the other side of the frame, his grin cocked to the side and a wink at the ready.

"Morning, sunshine."

She put both hands on her hips. "What do you want?" The words tasted like sour grapes, and she wrinkled her nose at her own surly tone. "I'm sorry."

"Wake up on the wrong side of the bed?" He pushed his long sleeves up to his elbows. The pale blue of the shirt made his hair even darker where it curled over the back of his neckline, and she had a sudden urge to run her fingers through it. He pushed a lock off his forehead, but it refused to stay behind his ear.

"You need a haircut."

"I'll take that as a yes."

She scowled at him. "What can I do for you?" Although she'd changed the words, her tone was still not convincingly pleasant. She cleared her throat and plastered a smile in place. "How can I help you today?"

His grin ratcheted up, the corners of his eyes crinkling as his shoulders shook in silent humor. "Before I knew about your stellar attitude this morning, I thought I'd ask you to help me hang up a closet rack. It's a two-person job." He squinted at her. "But now I'm thinking I might try to do it by myself."

"I'm sorry." She shook her head and pressed her fingers to the throbbing at her temple. "I didn't sleep very well last night, and I wasn't . . . Never mind. I'm sorry."

"Apology accepted. So you'll help me."

He was halfway up the stairs before she could even reply. "You're pretty sure I'm going to, aren't you?"

Facing straight ahead, he nodded. "Hey. You can't resist the chance to spend some more time with me."

She massaged the bridge of her nose with a thumb and forefinger.

She hated when he was right.

And she hated that she really did want to spend the day with him.

After their ice cream and beach trip, things had been different between them. More playful, less intense. More open, less congested. More fun. Period.

"Why are you such an easy target?" she asked herself as she stomped up the steps behind him.

"You say something?"

"No."

His lips pursed to the side as he waited for her at the landing. He didn't believe her, but that didn't keep him from moving along. "Want to carry my toolbox or the rack?" He motioned to the giant metal box the size of a large cat carrier. Beside it sat what looked like fifty pounds of wire pieces cut into odd shapes and sizes.

"You want me to carry one of those?"

"Well, I'm not going to do your work for you." He blinked twice, his mouth straight and delivery completely solemn.

"How about you tell me which tools you'll need for this job and I'll just take those."

He scratched his chin. "I'm not quite sure yet exactly which we'll need. I might need them all."

"A pipe wrench? You're going to need a pipe wrench to hang these shelves?"

He shrugged. "You never know. They look pretty complicated to me. But Jack told me you said something about wanting to put racks into the closet in the room next to the green one. Really, I think this is more your project than mine. But I've decided to give you a hand."

She narrowed her eyes and wrinkled her nose. "I don't think Jack would agree. Care to ask him?"

"I'm happy to. He's off on an errand—which he promised me was not another trip to the bank—so we'll waste the whole morning waiting on his decision if you're not willing to carry your own weight."

"Literally." She pressed the toe of her shoe to his metal box. "That thing has to weigh almost as much as I do."

He shrugged in an "oh well" movement, and she shoved his bicep, the muscle firm beneath the lightweight cotton of his shirt. Her push did nothing to budge him. In fact, he only leaned in closer, his voice dropping to a whisper. "Well, maybe we should find out."

"What—"

He grabbed her waist, throwing her over his shoulder as she screamed and smacked at his back.

"Put me down, you jerk." But the laughter in her voice left her words impotent.

He scooped up his toolbox and the shelves in one hand and ran up the main staircase, his breathing never labored. She grabbed at his waist to keep from toppling off his broad shoulder, the muscles in his back flexing and bunching beneath her hands. He walked into the room and dropped his cargo on the floor in one stoop.

Back on her feet, Marie straightened her clothes, her shoulders still shaking with laughter.

Kneeling in front of the gray kit, he glanced up at her. "You definitely weigh more than my toolbox."

"Watch it, Sloane."

He winked at her, pulling a screwdriver, tape measure, and pencil from the top tray. "I'm only teasing. Now help me measure and mark the height of this thing."

The closet wasn't intended to be a walk-in, so when they both squeezed into it, the air vanished. If Seth had seemed big when she was slung over his shoulder, he positively dwarfed her in the confines of the closet. The muscles of his neck flexed as he turned toward her, holding out the end of the yellow measuring tape.

He pressed the lip of it to the corner as he squatted to the floor. Looking at the ceiling, she tried to find anything more interesting than the way his hair flopped to one side. Or the way the light shimmered off it.

Her fingers were inches from touching the sleek strands when she jerked away. She couldn't just run her fingers through his hair.

Well, he just snatched you up and hauled you upstairs. Surely you're free to touch him.

That was a good point.

She bit the corner of her bottom lip and held her breath as she reached for the top of his head. Just. A. Touch.

She trailed one finger along an errant lock. It was thick and sturdy, like Seth.

Suddenly his hand zipped up to hers, his callused fingers twining around her wrist. Her scream caught in her throat as he tilted his head and met her gaze with narrowed eyes. Pushing off the floor, he rose slowly before her, just inches away. Every moment was an eternity, his eyes never blinking as his face drew even with hers, their lips a breath apart. He kept going until he towered above her. Forced to crane her neck, she refused to lose eye contact, to let him win whatever unspoken contest she'd started.

Never looking away, he twisted his hand until his fingers pressed against her open palm, then between her fingers. Their hands flush, he squeezed ever so gently, his eyes flashing at the same moment.

The touch was so much more intimate than she'd imagined after months of avoiding any kind of contact. Sparks flew up her arm, stealing her breath. But she hadn't been breathing anyway.

After dropping the measure into his pocket, he lifted his free hand to her cheek, trailing a finger around the edge of her ear until her rebellious hair stayed in place. His touch left a trail of fire as he dragged his finger along her jawline, achingly slow. His Adam's apple bobbed.

He felt it too.

The pull was too strong, and she suddenly couldn't keep her eyelids all the way open. They dropped to half-mast, leaving her only a view of the pointed line of his jaw and mouth.

Training her gaze on the little scar near his chin, she readied herself for what was coming. Oh, how she wanted him to kiss her. To feel safe in the arms of a man. To be protected from the world, even if only for a moment.

He licked his lips, his pink tongue darting from right to left as a muscle in his jaw jumped.

And then he leaned forward, his face hovering above hers.

This was her chance to escape. Her chance to say she wasn't ready or didn't want this. Her chance to run away before her feelings galloped out of control. If she ran now, leaving later would be easier. If she ran now, hearts didn't have to be wounded and her memories of this home would be happy.

Instead she pressed onto her toes, steadying herself with a hand on his chest. His breath hitched, and she fisted her hand into his shirt, the warmth of his body surrounding her.

◆◆◆◆◆

Seth paused just a fraction of an inch from completing the motion, suspending the kiss. In his hand Marie's face angled even closer to him. The scent of minty toothpaste lingered on her breath, mingling with the aroma of shampoo still clinging to her damp hair.

Her satin skin set him on fire, his stomach burning with a need that he hadn't thought he'd ever feel again. He wanted to make her laugh, to make every dark shadow in her sapphire eyes disappear.

But that wasn't right.

If he let the flames consume his mind, he'd never be able to be objective. He couldn't protect Jack if he let her seduce him too.

228

He pressed his forehead against hers. Her eyelashes fluttered, and she twisted her hand in his shirt, pulling him closer.

It couldn't hurt.

Just one little kiss.

But one would never be enough. His gut promised he'd need just one more. And then another. And another.

He'd set himself up for a Reece repeat. Whatever Marie wanted from Jack was on the line, and Seth wasn't about to be the cause of his uncle's pain.

It took every ounce of his strength to tear his hand away from her cheek and set it on her shoulder, gently pressing her back to the floor. She fought him for a brief moment, uncertainty splashing across her face as she leaned away.

Space to breathe.

He gasped for oxygen, needing a clear head. But his hands weren't willing to fully release her. Even as he stepped back in the confines of the closet, he wrapped both hands around her upper arms.

She blinked in quick succession, her lips parting and arms wrapping around her middle.

He let out a slow breath and jammed a hand through his hair, nearly yanking out the piece that had started this whole thing. When she'd put her hand on his hair, it had been everything he'd thought it might be. Everything he'd worried it could be. It was a jolt of lightning and a crashing wave in the same moment.

How easy it would be to get swept away.

But he couldn't let himself.

"I'm sorry."

She nodded, her front teeth biting into her lip and turning it cherry red.

THE RED DOOR INN

He couldn't drag his gaze away from her mouth, wondering what it would feel like to share just one kiss.

Shaking his head, he wiped away every thought in that ballpark. He couldn't do that. He wasn't strong enough to stop a second time.

She tried for a smile, but it wavered, leaving only a grimace in its wake. Her eyes filled with tears, the light from the bedroom fixture making them shine.

"Listen, this is just a bad idea. You're amazing." He meant to keep going, but the words evaporated.

Her lips pinching together, she nodded frantically but said nothing.

His arms ached to pull her to his chest, but it would only mean confusing the situation further. "I am sorry, Marie. I shouldn't have let it get this far."

She swallowed, the sound filling the cramped space. "You're right. Of course. It was a bad idea. Excuse me."

She ran from the room, her steps echoing down the stairs and out the front door. She'd be on the boardwalk. He could go to her and say something. Except there were no words that would fix what he'd just done.

He thumped the back of his head against the wall, the ache a welcome distraction.

"Just brilliant, Sloane." He deserved every bit of his own derision. Marie didn't deserve to be led on. He shouldn't have made her think he wanted more.

Even though, of course, he did.

He just shouldn't have made her think he was going to act on it.

As he wrestled the new shelves into place—alone in what should definitely have been a two-person job—he played the scene over and over in his mind. And every time he reached the same conclusion. He wanted to protect her, but he'd added to her pain in order to guard Jack. He wanted to make her happy, but he couldn't do that and watch Jack's back.

He leaned against the wall and scrubbed his face with an open palm.

It smelled like her lotion.

If that was all he could think about, the shelves were going to go in crooked, and he was going to smash his thumb with a hammer. He probably deserved it.

◆◆◆◆◆

Marie avoided Seth the rest of the day, which wasn't too difficult. He was dodging her too. When she was potting a plant in the mudroom, he'd walked in the back door. His eyes had blazed with something she couldn't name. He'd immediately turned around, the door slamming behind him.

Jack was picking up on the tension.

"You kids okay?" he said as he forked a bite of Aretha's leftover roast beef into his mouth that evening. His gaze went to Marie across from him then to Seth on his other side. "Haven't said more than three words between the two of you."

Marie nodded, unable to look in Seth's direction without her face bursting into flames. Her hand still tingled where his calluses had brushed her palm. And every time she closed her eyes, she could feel his finger tracing the edge of her face, smell the coffee he'd sipped that morning.

She couldn't close her eyes without her body reacting to those memories.

Just being in the same room set her skin tingling and her

head spinning. It wasn't the familiar feeling of one of her attacks. This was different, painful on a deeper level.

She hadn't thought of her first kiss post-Derek. She hadn't considered anything about it, really. But whatever hopes and dreams had worked their way into her subconscious, they didn't involve being snubbed.

Or the awkwardness after.

She hadn't known what to say after kissing her first boyfriend in high school. He hadn't either. So they'd sat in silence for ten long minutes before running their separate ways to first-period classes on opposite sides of campus.

This thing with Seth was so much worse.

She couldn't just run away to the other side of campus.

But she could go.

Snapping her head up, she stared at Jack, who had given up on getting a response to his question. Could she leave him? Could she go now and save them all this horrible discomfort? It would save both Jack and Seth the distress of her father's imminent arrival, and Jack the task of sending her on her way when the chef arrived.

Her stomach lurched, and she set her fork on her plate next to a lump of barely tasted beef and two potato halves.

"Getting cold out there today." Jack chewed another piece of meat. "Good thing we haven't put the flowers in yet."

"You think it'll freeze tonight?" Seth sucked on the tip of his thumb, the nail newly black and blue. He cleared his throat loudly, giving a valiant effort to engage Jack. "Father Chuck didn't seem to think it would get that cold."

Jack shrugged. "Don't know. The weatherman said we're in for a cold one. Some front coming off the Atlantic. Supposed to hit Nova Scotia and PEI pretty hard."

Marie tuned their words out, thinking about what she would need to do before taking off. She'd have to wait until they were both asleep, or they'd try to stop her. If she left about the same time as her typical morning run, they wouldn't think anything was out of the norm. Then she'd have a couple hours to get to her next stop. But where was that? Someplace with a bus or a cab.

A city big enough that she could blend in.

On the island, Charlottetown and Summerside were her only options. And Summerside was well out of the way of anywhere.

She'd take her backpack and as much as she could stuff in it. Jack had insisted on buying her jeans to replace the ones speckled with paint. She could leave the old pairs behind.

Moving through North Rustico would be no problem that early in the morning. With only the cows for company, she could probably make it to Rusticoville before dawn. From there she might be able to hitchhike south.

As her plan formed piece by piece, she steeled herself against having to say goodbye. Even to Seth. But it was time. The right time. They'd make do without her. All the paint for the exterior and what was left to do in the interior had been purchased. The room of antiques was nearly overflowing, and linens had been picked out and paid for.

There were still plenty of finishing touches to put on the house—including painting the front door red. But they'd be all right without her.

And with one less salary and mouth to feed, Jack could put his money where it needed to go.

She chanted those words to herself as she washed up their dinner dishes and wiped down the counter for the last time.

"Going to hit the sack early," Jack said, handing her a plate. "Been a long day."

"Sure." She took the plate and dunked it in the sudsy water, swallowing the lump in her throat. The back of her eyes burned and her voice cracked. "Sleep well."

He nodded and shuffled toward the door, and her heart seized. She'd never see him again, this man who'd cared for her better than any other man had ever tried to. Blinking against streaming eyes, she swiped her arm across her face.

She couldn't let him walk out of the room without a good-bye.

"Jack?"

"Hmm?"

He stopped halfway across the room, his white hair ruffled and his dear face sagging under the worries of the inn.

With hands still dripping wet, she ran to him, throwing her arms around his neck and holding him tight. Both of his arms stayed at his side for several long seconds as she buried her face into his shoulder.

Stiff and slow, he reached around her and patted her back with solid thumps. "Everything all right?"

She sniffed, blinking hard against the rush of tears. "Yes. Everything's going to be fine."

He leaned away, looking directly into her eyes. "Is this about Seth?"

Clamping her lips together to keep them from quivering, she shook her head.

His face pinched like he was eating a lemon as he asked, "Want to talk about it?"

"No." The word floated on a chuckle as relief washed over his face.

"Then take care. Things will look better in the morning."

She nodded, letting him go.

Releasing him from her hug was a lot easier than letting him go completely. Her tears were just as troublesome as she packed her bag later, stuffing each corner until the zipper strained to close.

And then she waited.

Knees tucked under her chin. Arms wrapped around her legs. Head bent until she nearly disappeared.

She knuckled away the tears again, but one slipped through, making its way along her nose before dripping off the tip. The mark that it left on the top of her shoe taunted her. But she was making the right decision. This was the best time to leave. Jack would save money. Seth would be saved any lingering embarrassment.

And she would be saved a further broken heart.

The hours dragged on, marked only by her occasional sniffles and shivers. In her basement the temperature dropped until she had to get up and move or risk freezing in place.

The alarm clock glared 4:26. As good a time as any to find her next step.

She slipped up the stairs, skipping the squeaking board, and waited on the landing. Silence filled the hallway to Jack's and Seth's rooms, but somewhere near the dining room the old house groaned.

Marie patted the kitchen door as she crept through the darkness. "I don't like the cold either." The words were more breath than sound, but the old home whined in response. Her outstretched hands brushed the counter on her way to the mudroom.

A sound like a wrench hitting a pipe made her jump, and

she stared hard into the darkness. But there was no one there. She held her breath, waiting for any sound from down the hallway. Jack and Seth hadn't woken up, so she twisted the door handle. But when she picked up her foot, her shoe was heavy and wet.

She flicked the light switch, blinded for a moment before she could make out the deluge from beneath the kitchen sink.

18

Seth jerked from a deep sleep at the sound of Marie screaming his name. Rubbing the heels of his hands into his eyes, he rolled out of bed. As he stood, the world tilted, and he grabbed at the wall to hold it still. He yanked a T-shirt over his head and shoved his arms through the sleeves as he slammed into the door. Shaking his head, he grabbed the handle again and got it far enough open to barrel down the hall.

"Seth! Jack!" Marie's pitch rose, the words steeped in panic. "Help!"

The hardwood floor shot ice through his bare feet, but he didn't slow down as he neared the sound of her voice, which was coming from the kitchen.

In the dark, he ran into one of the new dining room tables, grunting as the corner branded his thigh. "I'm coming. What's wrong?"

Light beneath the swinging door shimmered, dancing like a swaying chandelier.

Barging in, he nearly tripped over Marie on all fours,

sopping towels in her hands. She looked up at him, tears in her eyes matching the ever-growing flood.

The wooden cabinets were already waterlogged, and the water would reach the appliances if he didn't get it turned off. There wasn't time to check if the water was coming from directly under the sink or spurting from somewhere within the wall. He had to get the main water valve shut off.

Jumping over Marie, he raced through the mudroom and sailed down the back stairs. Frozen grass crunched under his feet, and he tried not to think about the searing pain in his bare toes. He raced around the side of the house to the hidden knob next to the spigot. By the time he reached it, his fingers were so numb he could barely grip it enough to turn it off.

"Come on. Come on." His words rose in puffs of white, chills making his hands shake. The main line refused to turn, and he looked around for anything to give him enough leverage to close it. "God, a little help here?"

There. A trowel that Marie had been using to prepare the flower beds. He snatched it up and pressed the blade into a rivet on the handle, cranking it hard.

Once it was moving, Seth turned it the rest of the way, breathing a prayer of thanks that he'd found just what he needed. Now to find out how much damage had been done.

As he bounded back into the kitchen, Jack grunted at him from the floor beside Marie. Bags hung beneath his eyes, and his hair was a mess. But he looked almost like a child wrapped in a thick terrycloth robe.

"I'm going to turn on a faucet to empty the pipe faster." Seth slipped as he hurried past Marie and caught himself on the door. His trail to the bathroom was marked by wet footprints, and as he reached the warmest part of the house, the shivers settled in.

He fought them as he ran the shower and the faucet full blast and scooped every towel he could find from the linen closet. His hands trembled as he entered the kitchen, but at least the rush of water from the blown pipe had slowed to a trickle.

From her knees Marie pulled two dry towels from him and added them to her terrycloth fortress in front of the refrigerator. He tossed one to Jack, who snatched it out of the air.

"Seth?" He turned toward Marie, her tone a warm coat to his freezing body. "You're shivering. Go put on something warm and dry."

He shook his head and pointed toward the backyard. "The wet/dry vac." He swallowed the tremor in his voice and tried again. "Let me just help get this cleaned up." He stepped around her, but his foot caught on a pink backpack. He shook it off, his brain trying to figure out why it was sitting there.

"Seth." She stood. Placing her hand on his forearm, she nodded slowly. Where she touched him, his skin burned. She was nearly on fire. "You'll get sick if you don't take care of yourself."

He blinked hard several times. Her words jumbled in his brain, and all he could focus on was the outline of her hand on his arm.

"Do what she says, boy." Jack's words sounded like gravel scraping against gravel. "I'll get the vac."

Seth scrunched his eyes closed, running a hand down his face, except he could only feel the touch on his cheeks. His nose and hand were too numb to register the contact.

Marie pointed to the pool and pulled the last two towels

from his grasp. "Look. It's not growing. You can go. We'll take care of it."

He nodded and backed out of the room, following the trail of footprints past his room and down the stairs into Marie's apartment. There he found just what he feared, water dripping from the ceiling and down the side wall directly beneath the kitchen sink. The leak was somewhere in the wall behind the cabinets and leaving a trail of spongy drywall.

This could ruin Jack.

◆ ◆ ◆ ◆ ◆

Marie wiped her forearm across her face, pushing her hair out of the way and leaning on the mop handle with the other arm. Jack had gotten most of the water with the vacuum but had taken it outside to empty it and call the insurance company, leaving her to touch up the trails from the towels.

As the sun rose, illuminating the room through the window over the sink, she bent over to wring the mop into the bucket. The water just kept coming up from the wooden floors—the pool was gone, but a water mark that spanned the entire width of the room remained.

She cried right along with the floorboards for all the work that had gone into the now-ruined room. She cried for the misery etched into every line of Jack's face as he paced, the phone pressed to his ear.

And she cried because it could have, would have, been so much worse.

If she'd left ten minutes earlier.

Jack took a deep breath from his spot along the far wall of the dining room, and she peeked at him through the open door as her mop swung in his direction. "This is Jack Sloane. I need to make a claim."

"He still on the phone?"

Seth's voice in her ear sent tremors to her toes, warming every inch of her. "Yes. He's been on hold for more than half an hour."

Seth's frown pinched his features, wrinkling the straight line of his nose.

"What do you think they're going to say?"

He shook his head. "I don't know. They'll send an assessor to see how much damage has been done. But I don't know how fast they can get someone out here. I doubt the insurance company has a large office on the island."

"How soon do you think they'd pay out his claim?"

Seth shook his head. "I don't know. But it might not be soon enough."

He hadn't bothered to step back, and the warmth of his body called to her in the still-frigid morning. Or maybe it was the aching reality of the Red Door that made her teeth chatter. Either way, she stepped toward him, keeping her voice low as Jack continued his conversation. "Did you find any other frozen pipes?"

"No. Most of the pipes inside are insulated enough just by the house. And when the plumber and I put in new pipes in the bathrooms a few months back, we protected all the new ones along the outer walls." He tugged at the cuffs of his sweatshirt and stared at Jack, following the older man's stilted movements with dogged determination. "There must have been a weak joint under the sink." He clenched his hands into fists and shook his head, a low sigh escaping.

"You were working under the sink a few weeks ago. You don't think it was that pipe, do you?"

"I hope not." When he looked at her for a moment, fear flashed in his eyes, sending a kick to her chest. Her breath disappeared at the pain in his features, her stomach tying itself into a knot.

She pressed her hand to his. "I'm sure it wasn't."

"We'll find out as soon as the assessor gets here and we can dig around under there." Uncertainty covered his words. If only there was something she could do to reassure him. Instead she could only distract him.

"Are you feeling warmer?"

His gaze jerked from following Jack's stilted paces to her face. Slowly it dropped to the space between them. Then her knees. Then their toes, which were almost touching. A little smile tugged at the corner of his mouth. "Yes."

Pushing his shoulder, she laughed out loud. His chuckle mingled with hers, a welcome noise after four tense hours. Shivers completely unrelated to the cold ran down her spine.

She clung to that sensation, to the simple pleasure of his presence.

Jack trudged toward them, his footfalls painful to her ears. He cleared his throat, and Marie swallowed the lump that jumped into her own. "They're going to send out an assessor on Monday. Until then, we can't touch anything."

"What are we supposed to do?" Her words came out more of a cry than a question, so she tried again. "What can we do until then?"

"Check for other damage. Get some fans blowing to dry out wet spots. Need to report all areas affected." Jack shoved his hands into the pockets of his pants.

"I've checked the laundry area, bathrooms, and any place with pipes in the walls, but it wouldn't hurt to do another walk through," Seth said.

"Good." Jack's shoulders drooped. "And then we'll have to find a place to stay, I guess."

Marie rubbed his shoulder with her free hand. "It'll be okay."

He stared at her, and she knew the truth. She had no right to say such a thing. She'd made a promise that she couldn't keep. If the insurance company failed to give Jack the money he needed, he would have an inn he couldn't run and a loan he couldn't repay.

He needed money.

She had money. More than enough to save the Red Door. Nearly a quarter of a million.

Her mother's will had been generous and explicit. Marie was to get everything that Claudia Carrington had brought into the marriage.

But the strings attached to that money were too heavy.

Her father's name was on the bank account. And if she accessed that money in any way, he'd know. He'd track her down. His PI wouldn't need more than an hour to find her, even in North Rustico, Prince Edward Island—population 637 residents, one drifter, and a herd of cows.

Maybe the insurance company would come through with the money they needed in time.

Dear Lord, let them give Jack enough money.

Marie closed her eyes on the prayer, recognizing it for what it was. Her only hope.

"Check the back bedroom?" Jack pointed to her. He didn't expound on his direction, but their eyes grew wide at the same moment. All of the antiques were in that room. Thousands of dollars' worth of furnishings and decorations would be ruined if a pipe had burst in there.

Her mop splashed into the half-full bucket of water as she slid it out of the way. She ran down the hall, her stomach somersaulting. She slammed the door open and dipped and jumped to get a look around the stacks and crates.

"How's it look?" Seth sounded close, probably investigating in his own bedroom.

"Good so far. I'm going to have to move some of these boxes to get a good look."

"Need help?"

"I've got it." There wasn't really room for more than one person at a time. Especially someone Seth's size. They'd have no choice but to touch. In spite of his flirtatious smile and her unruly butterflies, space was an appreciated commodity.

Especially if she didn't want to be rejected again.

After nearly two hours, she'd looked behind every crate and moved every antique until sweat poured down her back and her hands stuck to every piece. All of it was safe. The walls were solid and intact, the floors dry.

She took a breath, deep and filling. So unlike those first days on the island.

Setting down the last box, she surveyed the room. Like a white flag, the paper still in the typewriter caught her eye, and she slipped between the stacks to reach it. As she bent to pull the page free, she bumped the lid of another box, sending it skittering across the floor.

"Great," she mumbled as she twisted to reach the errant piece of cardboard. Stretching her fingers until they couldn't reach any farther, she caught the edge of the lid and yanked it back over the box. Before it fell into place, a flash of color caught her eye.

The black and white photograph of the Red Door before she had a name. But when she did have a crimson entrance.

A slow smile crept into place. Marie had almost forgotten about this second gift from Aretha. And she'd never shown it to Jack.

Too bad guests wouldn't be able to see how much work Jack and Seth had put into this home to make it shine even brighter than it had when it was first built. The original house should be on display.

An idea, complete and clear, popped into her mind, and she jumped toward the door, calling for Seth.

He stepped out of Jack's bedroom, Jack trailing slowly behind him. "Did you find something?"

Yes. But not what he was asking about. "No."

His eyebrows formed a V, his hands on his hips. "What do you need?"

"Um . . ." Her gaze danced between Jack and Seth, worry sweeping over their faces. "Nothing. It was nothing."

"You sure?"

Jack could use a surprise, and not one like he'd gotten that morning. She'd wait and speak to Seth privately. If she could just get him alone.

Nodding, she backed away. "Everything's fine in here. No damage."

Jack heaved a sigh, a small weight removed from his shoulders.

The two men walked away, and she tiptoed back through the maze to her Underwood. She squeezed into place before it and scrolled the paper past her last message to Seth, memories of sweet strawberry ice cream and his favorite spot on the island swelling in her chest.

After a long moment, she pressed the keys, glancing over her shoulder every few seconds to make sure that no one had wandered into her haven.

I have an idea. But it's a surprise, and I need your help. Meet me at your favorite spot?
M

The far right line on the last letter faded into almost nothing, and she ran a hand over the old machine. "Hang in there, girl. I just need a few more notes out of you."

She sought out Seth in the dining room. When Jack's head was bent over a copy of his insurance policy, she tugged on Seth's arm and whispered, "I left you a note."

Two lines appeared between his brows, and he shook his head.

"A note. Not about ice cream this time."

Seth's mouth dropped open, but he nodded slowly, scratching at the scar on his chin.

"What?" Jack looked up

"Nothing." Seth and Marie said it at the same time. Their gazes caught and held, until he looked down, and her eyes followed his to her hand. Which still rested on his arm. She jerked it back, but her smile didn't flicker as his blossomed.

Later that morning, Seth motioned to her to follow him to the antique room, but Jack asked her for help. Seth nodded toward the room and behind Jack's back lifted his hands to mime typing with two fingers.

She nodded and stole away from Jack as soon as she could.

The message from Seth was succinct, the letters paler than the line above, but readable.

What time?
S

She bit on her lip, steepling her fingers under her chin. When could they get away? When would Jack not notice them missing?

A yawn cracked her jaw. They had to get some rest and find a place to spend the night. Preferably a place with running water.

Aretha might take pity on them. It couldn't hurt to ask. Marie could meet Seth after talking with Aretha.

Today at 4. Bring hot coffee.

The long line on the number was still faded, but the machine hung in there. And it made it through one more message from Seth right after lunch.

Bossy much?

And one final note before she left to beg Aretha for a dry place to stay.

Yes.

◆◆◆◆◆

As he crossed the beach, balancing two cups of hot coffee and a bag of sweet scones from Caden's bakery, Seth stumbled in the uneven sand.

"Whoa there, Sloane."

He spun at Marie's voice, handed her a coffee, and wrapped his shivering fingers around his own paper cup. She smiled, hunching over the steam rising from the java and pressing her lips to the lid before tilting it back.

He looked away, battling with himself over even agreeing to meet her out here. It was colder than a penguin's playground. The afternoon sun even seemed to understand and had tucked itself away under a blanket of gray clouds.

And he had no business spending any more time alone with her. Not after the debacle in the closet the day before.

He'd been doing a good enough job of avoiding her. Except for a little flirting that morning. But he hadn't been able to help it. The way her cheeks turned rosy and her lips parted when she smiled made him want to make her smile every day.

And she'd kept her distance too. Something important had her willing to brave not only alone time with him but also the weather.

He took the lid off his coffee and blew into the black liquid. Steam bounced back and warmed his nose for an instant. Pulling up his scarf and hunkering into his jacket, he frowned. "What's this about?"

She motioned to the rocks. "Want to sit down?"

"They'll be freezing, but we can sit on the sand."

She nodded, lowering herself to the ground and reaching for the white bag in his hand. "What's that?"

"Tell me what I'm doing out here first."

She scowled, but he held the bakery items over his head, out of her reach. She leaned in toward him, stretched out and close enough to touch. His skin lit on fire at her nearness, and he hated himself for craving her touch and knowing it would only lead to blinded eyes.

When he dropped the bag in her lap, she backed off and dug in. "Strawberry and cream scones." Her smile flashed, instant and brilliant. For a moment, the sun shone from her face. With her nose still in the bag, she said, "They smell like happiness."

Pulling one out and popping the end into her mouth, she handed the bag back to him. "Thanks." The word was garbled around her scone.

He took slow bites of his, the creamy icing melting in his mouth, the bread soft and not at all like Reece's onetime attempt. Hers had resembled rocks more than clouds. But Caden's handiwork tasted like a sunrise, light and fluffy and pink.

When her treat was gone and she had only her coffee to distract her, Marie stared at the crashing waves. After a long sip of joe, she looked in his direction. She opened her mouth, then closed it, repeating the motion several times before wrinkling her nose. "I don't know where to start."

"You want to tell me where you were planning on going this morning?"

Her shoulders jerked, her posture suddenly straight as rebar. She licked the corner of her mouth and twisted a hand into the edge of her jacket. "How'd you know?"

"You didn't remember to hide your bag."

She sighed, running her hand through her hair. "I thought it would be better if I left."

He grunted. What was a guy supposed to say to that? He didn't have a response, so he waited. Maybe if he let the silence hang long enough, she'd reveal her plans.

"You don't need me anymore. I'm an expense that Jack can't afford. I've told him not to pay me, but he insists."

"So this is just about the money?"

She wrinkled her nose and pursed her lips, her profile perfectly aggravated. "And you know . . . there are other things." She looked about ready to stay more, but whatever was on the tip of her tongue stayed there.

He stole a swig from his cup, the java turning lukewarm in the cold spring conditions. Time to get talking and get moving back to the house. "I am sorry about that. The other things, I mean. I shouldn't have—um . . ." He jabbed at his hair, scratching behind his ear, hoping the words would spring free. But they didn't. "I'm just sorry."

When she turned toward him, her eyes were filled with questions, the biggest and boldest clear. Why? Why hadn't he kissed her? Why had he backed away?

He couldn't answer those unspoken queries without admitting that he sometimes still suspected her motives weren't entirely altruistic. After all, her timing was perfect. She'd chosen to leave without telling a soul when it was clear that Jack's money was running out.

Less clear was why she'd stayed and stopped the water.

So he asked a question in return. "Why didn't you leave?"

Her forehead wrinkled, her bottom lip disappearing as she chewed on it. With a shrug she shook her head. "I'm not sure. When I saw the water rushing out from under the sink, I knew you would still need me."

She meant that both he and Jack needed her, of course. But the simple use of the word *you* made his heart stop, completely unrelated to the icicles he inhaled.

Her long lashes fluttered against her cheeks, and she took

a long breath. "I don't understand why these things happen. Jack is a good man." The corner of her mouth rose, her eyes still closed. "He's the kindest man I've ever met and more of a father than I've ever had."

The biting wind carried her words, jerking him upright. "What do you mean by that?"

"Nothing. I mean, I guess . . ." She shook her head as she pulled her knees into her chest. The fabric of her jeans pulled tight over her legs, and she flicked at a piece of sand stuck to them. "My dad is about the opposite of Jack. He's never met a deal he couldn't make or a situation he wouldn't leverage." She curled into a ball, her head bent and smile gone.

He needed to comfort her. He'd been prodding and pushing for the details of her past, and now that they were coming out, he couldn't stand to see the strain on her face or hear the quiver in her voice. Wrapping an arm around her shoulders, he pulled her into his embrace. She held fast at first and then let him guide her into his side. Her warmth made him forget about the cold and the reason for hurrying back to the inn. He could sit with his arms around her and her head tucked under his chin for hours.

She leaned into him, her shoulder resting over his heart, which picked up its pace with each passing second.

"Is that why you left Boston?"

"Yes."

"Want to tell me more?"

"It's a long story." Her fist clenched, then relaxed, then tightened again. And she shifted like she was uncomfortable. But maybe she was just trying to decide how much she would tell him. Maybe she was trying to figure out how much she trusted him. He nodded gently, prodding her on. "Before I left, my father made it very clear that his priority was a real estate deal. Not me. He—" Her voice caught, but she cleared her throat and continued. "He tried to use some information that I had told him to blackmail the landowner."

"What did—"

"Jack's so different from my dad." She cut him off, and at the rate she was talking, she had no intention of answering his half-formed question. "Jack really only wanted me to be safe and happy. He didn't have a clue about me, and without questions he gave me a home and work that I love. Because of him I met Caden and Aretha." She elbowed him gently in the stomach. "And you too. But I don't understand why such bad things can happen to such a wonderful man. What did he do to deserve this?"

Seth knew that question well. He'd asked—sometimes yelled—it at God time and again after Reece. Was he being punished? Or did God just not care? His conclusion hadn't been hopeful at first.

"I'm not sure. I asked Father Chuck something like that when I got here. I guess I had some pent-up anger after my business was stolen out from under me."

She turned her head, her hair catching on two-day-old stubble that he couldn't shave. "What'd he say?"

"Something about it raining on the just and the unjust." He moved his arm, and she leaned further back against him. "In this case I guess it floods on the just and the unjust. We all have hard times."

She nodded slowly. "Father Chuck talks about God as a father, and up until I met Jack I thought I knew what that meant."

"How so?"

"My dad was distant. He didn't care. He didn't hear me when I needed him. God didn't either." Her shoulders lifted as she faced the ocean. "But if I'd had a father like Jack, well, I'd have had a different picture."

He sighed. He didn't have many answers either. He knew about being angry with God. Even months after Reece's betrayal, it snuck up on him at times. "I wish I had some great wisdom to offer. But I wonder, if you had had a dad like Jack, would you see more of the good gifts that God the Father gives because that's what Jack gives you?"

She stayed silent and motionless for at least a minute, the only sounds the wind's whistle and the waves cresting on the sand. When she finally spoke, her words were soft. "I want to give Jack a gift of my own. I have an idea, but I need your help."

"All right. Whatever I can do."

19

Jack paced outside the doorway of the kitchen, his arms crossed and his gaze never leaving the middle-aged man with the clipboard standing in the center of the water-logged mess. Aretha stepped into his path, holding out a steaming paper cup.

"Take a deep breath and have some coffee." Her eyes were soft but the line of her mouth firm. "You can't make him work any faster."

The man in the kitchen looked under the sink and scribbled something on his clipboard.

Jack nodded, taking the coffee and a quick sip. It burned his tongue, but the warmth pushed some of the dread out of his chest. "Thank you." He ran a hand through his freshly washed hair. Aretha had been right that assessing the damage was easier after a hot shower and warm breakfast. "And thank you for letting us stay at your place this weekend."

"Oh, I'm happy to help. When Marie asked, I couldn't refuse her."

"I know what you mean."

"You have a place to stay as long as you want it." Her cheeks flushed, the fine lines and wrinkles near glowing. She looked away, and her tone dropped like the phrase might add up to more than the value of each word.

But he didn't have time to do the math before the assessor joined them.

"Well, I've looked it over and taken pictures." He tapped his pen on his chin as his eyes ran down the form on his clipboard. "You were pretty lucky to catch the leak when you did, but the water damage inside the walls could be excessive. The cabinets will have to be removed and the drywall cut out and replaced."

That wasn't new information. He and Seth had known that from the moment they'd seen the leak.

"How much will the check be?" He let out a slow breath, clenching and unclenching his hand at his side.

"I'm not sure." The man's eyes were gray as stone, his response about that helpful. "I'll have to run some numbers, look at your policy, and consult with your agent."

Jack nodded, rubbing a hand over his hair. "We're scheduled to open up in three weeks. What are the chances we can get a check in time to get this fixed?"

The other man pursed his lips and squinted at his writing as though the answers to all the world's questions were written there. "I'm not sure. I'll ask the accounting department, but I can't make any promises."

It seemed to be the guy's favorite line, but it wasn't very helpful.

Jack's only hope of paying off the loans he'd taken out to open this place was to actually get it open. A few of his rooms were already booked for after the first of May. But he couldn't open without a kitchen. And he couldn't redo the kitchen in a few weeks without a check.

Jack stuck out his hand, and the other man's grip was looser than a limp fish.

"We'll be in touch."

He showed the guy to the front door and closed it after him. Then he pressed his forehead against the cool wood.

A warm hand snaked its way into his and squeezed. "It'll be all right."

He shook his head, not even looking at Aretha. But he clung to her hand, the only stable point in this day. "The deductible is going to nearly wipe me out. And I have an overpriced French chef on his way with no kitchen for him to cook in and no place for him to stay."

"Where was he going to stay?"

"The basement apartment. It was part of his compensation, a private apartment. But that's Marie's room now. I'm not going to take it from her."

"You're a good man, Jack Sloane." She brushed some hair from his cheek. "How can I help?"

Still pressed against the door, he turned his head until he caught sight of her glowing green eyes. "I suppose prayer is about our only hope at this point."

She slipped an arm around him, pulling him close. When she hugged him tight, some of the pressure on his shoulders fell away. He knew he'd still have to deal with the issues at hand, but it was almost as if she'd taken some of the weight on herself.

As she tucked her face into his shoulder, he rested his chin on top of her head, inhaling the sweet berry scent that clung to her hair like a halo.

He'd almost forgotten what it felt like to hold a woman like this, to be comforted by a gentle embrace and calmed by soft words.

One of God's sweetest gifts.

◆◆◆◆◆

"I can't believe how hot it is today." Marie dumped a load of splintered wood into the back of Seth's truck and wiped the sweat off her forehead. Only five days after the midnight freeze, the sun had returned and true spring weather had descended on the island. It was almost as if that night had never happened.

Except for the gutted kitchen.

As she trudged back inside for another armful of the remnants of the cabinets, she pulled off the leather work gloves Seth had loaned her and used them to fan her face. But the meager breeze barely registered against her steaming skin.

Where the lower cabinets had been, Seth lay sprawled, his head halfway between two exposed beams in the wall. He must have heard the gloves clapping together, because he looked in her direction, pointing the flashlight in his mouth directly at her.

Holding up a hand to protect her eyes, she said, "Did you find the leak?"

"Yep."

That might not be a good thing. He'd been stewing about the point in the pipe that had leaked, worried that the section he'd replaced had failed under the pressure of the freezing water. Slipping her gloves back on and picking up a piece of wood from the pile on the floor, she prodded him. "So?"

He pulled the flashlight from his mouth. "It was the joint in the pipe right behind the one I fixed."

"Well, that's good." Shooting for an appropriate level of enthusiasm, she grinned.

He grunted.

"It's not?"

"I should have seen it. I should have checked it."

"I don't see how you could have had any idea that the pipe was weak."

He was silent a long time, so she just kept stacking damp wood in her arms. Finally he sighed. "There are water stains on this pipe, like it'd been leaking for a while. Not a lot. But enough. I should have looked for this kind of damage. It could have saved us all of this." He sat up, sweeping his hand around the littered room.

Balancing her chin on the stack in her arms, through tight lips she teased, "And then what would we do for the last few weeks before the grand opening?"

As she'd hoped, his chuckle followed her all the way through the laundry room. They both knew there had been more to do than time to do it before the inn was ready to officially open its doors. And that had been before the pipe burst.

When she returned, he was sitting in the same spot, his elbow resting on a bent knee. Paint spots adorned his long, powerful legs, and his gray T-shirt stretched across his shoulders. The bands around his biceps stretched under the cut muscles. He stared at her, following her path across the room. A wave of heat completely unrelated to the weather shot through her, stealing her breath in a most pleasant way.

Why did he insist on stirring things in her that made her

dream of a real future and a forgotten past? Her therapist had told her that eventually she'd meet someone she could envision a healthy relationship with. That eventually the hope for her future would begin to help the old wounds heal. But Seth? He'd been so sour, so angry. Until he hadn't been. And always he'd protected Jack, loved and cared for his uncle in a way she didn't know men could.

Swallowing quickly, she fought to break the silence. "Have you seen Jack?"

"He and Aretha went to fix us some lunch. They'll be back soon." The lid of his toolbox closed with a metallic clang, but she refused to look at him. When she stared into his eyes, she wanted nothing more than to stay there forever. When he smiled, she remembered being a breath away from his lips. And his three-day stubble only made her miss the little scar on his chin.

She had to think about something else. Anything else.

"Jack and Aretha have been spending a lot of time together this week."

"I guess." He drew out the last word as though stumbling and tumbling over the thought.

"Don't you think they make a cute couple?"

"I don't think Jack's interested."

She glared at him over her shoulder. It was just quick enough for him to see. But also quick enough for her to take in his stance. He'd pushed himself to his feet, his legs shoulder-width apart and arms crossed over his chest.

She hadn't had a panic attack in weeks, but the rhythm of her heart picked up and her vision narrowed. He had the power to affect her like no one else.

"You're kidding, right?"

He rubbed a hand across his wrinkled eyebrows. "They're not . . . Aretha's just a friend, and Jack still loves Rose. He told me so."

"Of course he still loves Rose. But that doesn't mean there isn't room in his heart for someone else. He's still young—" She paused for a moment, ticked her head to the side, and held up a rocking hand. "Well, young-ish. He's got lots of life left, and I get the feeling he's a little less lonely when she's around."

"Why would he be lonely? He's got us, doesn't he?"

She scoffed in his direction—this time careful to only look at his boots, which did nothing of significance to her breathing or heartbeat. "Are you going to hug him like Aretha did a few days ago?"

He didn't say anything for a long time. He was probably remembering the scene that they'd walked in on after the insurance assessor had left. "Well, I'm not sure that's the point."

"Well, what is then?"

More silence from him, the only sound in the room the scrape of wood against wood.

He sighed. "I don't know. He still loves Rose." His voice went up on the last word.

"Is that a question?"

"No." He stabbed his fingers through his hair. "It's just that Rose hasn't been gone all that long."

"It's been over a year, hasn't it?"

"Yes, but she was the love of his life."

Marie adjusted the boards in her arms, chancing another look into his face. "But that doesn't mean he can't love again." Seth's features twisted as if he didn't like it one bit.

He just didn't have an argument against it either. "It's been a rough week, and in the midst of tearing this room apart, I'm enjoying watching two people that I love find some happiness in spite of it all."

"Point taken."

She turned back to the trash pile, reaching for another handful to carry out to the truck. "When you were cutting out drywall and pulling out insulation, didn't you ever see something good in this fiasco? Wasn't there anything good about that pipe bursting?"

"I'm glad you stayed."

The low baritone of his voice made her hands shake, and she kept her back to him so he couldn't see the blush already creeping up her neck.

He cleared his throat, but the intensity in his words didn't change. "There's nothing good about this mess. It's going to be backbreaking labor to finish before the first of the month. And we don't even know if we have the money to complete the project. Everything about that morning is a nightmare. Except that it made you stay."

The back of her eyes burned and a lump clogged her throat. No man had ever said such kind things about her. Certainly never *to* her.

She didn't turn toward him, even as his boots scraped the floor. His warmth surrounded her as he drew close. His breath stirred the strands of hair that had escaped the knot at the nape of her neck. Closing her eyes, she held every muscle in check, fighting the temptation to fly apart.

His fingers wrapped around her arm, cupping her elbow as he leaned so close that she could feel his lips moving against her ear. "I'm sorry I've been a jerk."

She nodded, unable to offer anything else in response.

"When I look at this mess, I think about how glad I am that you're here. How much I like your smile and your bossy notes." Chills swept down her spine as he swallowed. She took a deep breath but only managed to inhale his scent, the smell of earth and lumber and the island. "The Red Door wouldn't be the same without you. I don't think I'd be the same either."

Eyes still pinched closed, she turned her head in the direction of his voice. The rough pad of his thumb swiped across her cheekbone, and she nearly dropped everything in her arms. Taking a shaky breath, she opened her eyes, then slammed them closed again as his lips pressed to the corner of her mouth. Like silk ribbon in the wind, her stomach danced at his caress. A strong arm slipped around her back, the other hand tucking into the hair above her ear.

He pulled back, a lopsided grin spreading across his face. "It's been a while since I've done this."

"Me too." Her words were hoarse, like they had to fight to make it out of her throat. But she didn't have to say anything else when he swooped down again, pressing his lips against hers.

She dropped the weight from her arms and turned to meet him. His lips were at once soft and urgent. Gentle and persistent. Light and fire. The arm around her waist tugged her closer to him until there was nothing between them but the pounding of her heart. The breadth of his shoulders both dwarfed and protected her.

Blood rushed through her veins, thrumming at her neck, eclipsing every memory from the scene in the closet.

Stretching to her tiptoes, she leaned into his kiss and clung to his shoulders. Without them, she'd have lost all balance.

Even with her hands firmly knotted into his shirt, she was falling onto a cloud.

Then the front door slammed closed and the cloud popped.

She jumped out of Seth's embrace, standing in spite of trembling knees. Rubbing at a raw spot on her chin, she stared at his lips. His perfect, pink lips.

"We brought lunch." Aretha's voice carried through the house, but her footsteps didn't follow.

Seth blinked several times, a Cheshire-cat grin already in place. While he kept a couple feet between them, he rubbed a particularly sore patch on her cheek with his thumb. "You're kind of red." He combed his fingers over his whiskers. "I'll shave next time."

The words rang in her head. A promise, at once terrifying and exhilarating.

Next time.

Dear Lord, let there be a next time.

"You kids coming to eat?" Jack stuck his head into the kitchen. "I'm hungry."

Seth broke from his statued stance first. "Yes. We'll be right there."

Marie slipped off the work gloves and rubbed her palms over her cheeks. "How bad is it?"

Seth put a hand on the small of her back as she stepped past him. "Hey, maybe they'll be so focused on each other they won't notice."

She pushed his arm, eliciting only a laugh. He held open the door for her, and she plastered a smile into place, ignoring Aretha's curious glances and knowing smile.

◆◆◆◆◆

The sun was still an hour from setting as Marie opened a can of paint in the backyard. Candy-apple red dripped from the lid, and she stirred it with a wooden stick until it was smooth and even.

"Where do you want this?" Seth's voice came from the opposite side of the front door, only his hand visible on one side as he balanced the door on a dolly.

"Right here." She pulled a sawhorse up alongside another, and he laid the door in place.

"Why didn't you get Jack to help you?"

Seth brushed his hands together. "He's on the phone again. And I didn't want you to lose the light."

"Thanks." She smiled as she ran a damp rag over the door. "The insurance assessor again?"

With his hands on his trim hips, he squinted back at the house. "I don't think so. But whatever it is, it isn't good news. Jack was stomping and growling."

She hesitated before dipping her brush into the paint can. "What else could it be? Everything that could go wrong already has."

"Not quite." His words were low and filled with dread, and they sent a needle of fear piercing through her stomach.

Pushing it aside, she swiped red paint down the front door in even, smooth strokes. The white disappeared behind the brilliant red, and she smiled.

The inn was getting its namesake.

"You know what Jack told me the first time we talked about the red door?"

She glanced up to find him staring at her, following the movements of her hand as she methodically applied even, clean stripes of paint. "What's that?"

The memory brought a smile to Seth's face, and he dropped his hands from his hips. "He told me red doors are a sign of welcome, an invitation. Years ago during harsh Canadian blizzards, red doors helped stranded travelers find safety and protection from the storm."

Her hand stilled, her lungs forgetting how to breathe. Somehow Jack had known at the very beginning how much she needed protection from her own storm. He'd offered her a red door in every sense of the word. And now he needed her help.

Oh, she'd given him her time and sweat. She'd stayed when she thought she should go.

But could she give him the thing he needed most—the money to get the doors open on time?

She could solve all of his worries. She could fix his problems with one call to her bank. One conversation and Jack wouldn't have to worry about anything but what to serve for breakfast on the first day.

And she'd have to face her father.

But perhaps—with Seth and Jack by her side—she could handle that.

Seth seemed oblivious to the dilemma his words had prompted, so she turned back to her work. She might not have to do anything. If the insurance assessor came back with good news and a fast check, they'd have what they needed to fix all that had been destroyed.

Halfway through her next brushstroke, the back screen door rattled and closed with a crack. Jack marched down the steps, his movements tense and face tight.

"That no-good, lying son of a gun."

Seth looked at her with raised brows, and she could only lift a shoulder and shake her head.

"Jack?" she started cautiously. "What happened?"

He paced the length of the door, head bowed and hands clenched. "I took his word. He said he'd be here. No need for a contract. No need for anything formal. A handshake and his references were good enough. And now this." He swung an angry hand toward the house, his face a mix of pain and fury.

Seth stepped in front of the older man, blocking his path and putting his hands up to calm the angry rant. "What's going on?"

"He's ruined everything."

"Who?" Marie said.

Jack turned to her, the steam escaping from his tirade as his shoulders slumped. His bushy brows hung over his eyes, shadowing the pain there. "Jules Rousseau."

"The chef?"

He nodded.

Seth's face turned into a younger version of Jack's, his features twisted with indignation. "That no-good, arrogant—" When he glanced at her, his words abruptly ended. "What are you smiling at?"

She pushed the corners of her mouth down with a thumb and forefinger, but her lips wouldn't stay put. This wasn't the disaster they thought it was. If only they could see that this freed them up to find someone better.

Someone who knew and loved the island. Someone who could spoil them all with her pastries. Someone already invested in the inn.

"What are you thinking, girl?" Jack said.

"Only that now you don't have to pay an exorbitant salary for a man you never really needed."

"But we don't have a chef." Seth scrubbed a hand down his face. "We can't open a bed-and-breakfast with no breakfast."

"Right. We need a chef who can make breakfast shine. Someone who bakes sweets so intoxicating that your guests can't wait to get out of bed. Someone used to making meals large enough to feed a houseful. Someone with talent and skill and a love of local produce." She nodded slowly, urging them to see the image taking shape in her mind. But they both stared at her like she was trying to get them to understand a foreign language.

"We already know the perfect person for the job."

20

B ut I never went to culinary school."

Marie patted Caden's hand. "What you do in the kitchen is nothing short of miraculous. The first time I ever tasted your cinnamon rolls, I said I was sure that's what an L. M. Montgomery short story would taste like. Remember? Your treats taste like red-dirt roads and jagged red cliffs."

Caden's eyes grew wide, and she looked to Jack, who sat across the table, for help.

He chuckled. "Not like dirt. Think she means your cooking tastes like island food should taste."

Marie nodded, holding on to Caden's arm, her smile growing. "You're an amazing talent, and we love working with you."

"I think you mean my dad. He's the one with the training. He went to school for it."

"We want you. We want your talent and your generosity. Your willingness to experiment. If your dad can spare you from the bakery, we want to hire you as the executive chef at the Red Door."

Caden's lips twitched in an attempted smile, but her eyes were still filled with uncertainty. "There's a big culinary school in Charlottetown. Don't you want someone who knows how to handle a kitchen?"

"Yes. Which is why we want you."

Jack nodded his agreement, really only at the table for official purposes. After all, it was his inn and his future. And he'd told Marie to do whatever it took to get Caden to take the job. He'd negotiate the contract when it was time.

"What about your New York chef? Doesn't he want that double oven?"

Jack harrumphed deep in his throat, and Marie smiled. "He decided to take another job in New York City, which is for the best. I'm pretty sure that his specialty would have been snooty eggs and tiny portions."

Caden cringed. "I don't cook like that."

"I know. That's why we're glad he's not coming." Marie bit into her bottom lip, her mouth watering at the very memory of the first time she'd eaten one of Caden's sweet rolls. "Think about what a bed-and-breakfast is supposed to be. It's a home away from home. A place where your first meal of the day is a special treat, not something that you have to pick at. Guests want something that tastes great and will give them the energy to hike into Prince Edward Island National Park and walk along the beach. And we want something that will keep them coming back to the Red Door year after year. Breakfasts should feel like you're at home. Only better. That's what the food you make tastes like to me."

THE RED DOOR INN

Caden chewed on a fingernail, her usually happy features pinched in thought.

"In fact, I think your cinnamon rolls are the reason that Seth started tolerating my presence."

With a little chuckle, Caden said, "I need to think about it."

◆◆◆◆◆

Seth slid the newly painted red front door into place, angling it until the hinge pieces fit together. A low whistle split the air. He spun to see Jack and Marie walking up the road, and the momentum of the door nearly toppled him.

"Looks great." Jack's voice carried past the neighbors on their front porch, who waved brightly.

"The inn is coming along," the middle-aged man called.

"Sure is." Jack's chest swelled, his shoulders back and head held high despite the gutted kitchen and an uncertain future.

The meeting with Caden must have gone well.

When they reached the front porch, Seth asked, "So? Did she take the job?"

Marie's grin split her face. "She's going to think about it and let us know, but I'd stake good money on her taking it. You should have seen her eyes light up at the offer. She kept saying she wasn't qualified and there had to be someone better, but we know we can trust her. She cares about this place or she wouldn't have helped us paint cabinets and sent over so many goodies to keep us going. Besides, Aretha swears to her skills, and I don't know anyone who would argue with Aretha."

Her words bubbled like an overflowing fountain, her face shining even in the shade.

270

His fingers ached for the feel of her skin, his heart hammering at her nearness. She maintained a safe distance between them, but all he could see were her pink cheeks and the gentle curve of her neck.

And he had to touch her.

He leaned against the door to keep it in place and reached to brush his fingers down the side of her neck into the hollow where it met her shoulder. Her entire body trembled, but she smiled at him.

How was it possible that someone like Marie could feel for him even a fraction of what he felt for her?

His stomach bunched then soared. Writhed then quivered. And he was consumed by the memory of their kiss. Why on earth had he denied himself the acute pleasure of holding her against his chest and inhaling her fragrance even once? She was kind and smart and beautiful.

And he'd never have known her if Reece hadn't taken everything.

She'd emptied his accounts, his wallet, even the pockets of his jeans.

But she couldn't take his future. And with every passing day, he was pretty sure that Marie was going to play a big role in that.

Jack cleared his throat loudly, pointing back and forth between them. "Something going on here that I should know about?"

Marie laughed, and Seth shrugged. "Nothing to worry about."

His narrowed gaze said Jack didn't entirely believe them, and he homed his finger in under Seth's nose. "Be careful, boy."

"Yes, sir."

After he walked away, mumbling something about Aretha being right, Marie grabbed his hand and laughed up at him. "Do you feel sixteen, or is it just me?"

"Oh, it's not just you." He dipped his head to press his lips to hers, but stopped just shy. Were they at this stage? Was he free to kiss her anytime he liked?

That could end up being more often than not.

She leaned in, resting a hand over his speeding heart. But instead of the kiss he hoped for, she whispered against his lips, "Were you able to work on Jack's surprise?"

"Jack's surprise? That's what you're thinking about right now?"

She blushed and looked away. "Well, not the only thing."

The door shifted, and he had to lean away or drop the whole thing. Blasted door. He'd much rather invade her space and watch the inevitable pink seep from under the collar of her sweater, up her neck, and make the apples of her cheeks glow.

"Were you?" she prodded, tugging on his hand. "Able to work on his surprise?"

"Are we in a rush?"

Her smile faded, leaving only remnants of joy where it had been. "I think he could use some good news. I think it's been a hard week, and I want to give him something wonderful, something that reminds him why all of this is worth it."

Why did she care so much? What was it in her heart that melted at the sight of an old man losing a personal battle? He'd wondered the first time she'd mentioned the frame for the old black and white picture of the Red Door.

Reece wouldn't have cared a lick about a man's failing business. Marie worked night and day to help save it.

For the life of him, he couldn't figure out what he had thought was so special about Reece.

He pushed the door back into place and pulled one of the hinge pivots from his pocket. "Will you put this in the barrel of the bottom hinge there?"

She knelt down and slipped it in place. Then took the top one and slid that into place too. She stepped inside as he swung the door all the way closed.

"I finished the frame while you were talking with Caden. And I ordered the glass from a guy I know who's also going to do the brass plaque like you asked for. Just write down what you want it to say, and we can have it in plenty of time for the grand opening party."

When he spoke the words, he felt so much more certain that they would have a grand opening. That the insurance company would pay out and the kitchen would be fixed, the doors would open, and Jack's venture would be a success.

"Thank you." She grabbed his shoulders and pulled him down until she could reach his lips with her own. She smelled of berries and cinnamon, like Caden's kitchen. And she tasted like heaven, warm and pliant in his arms.

He'd build her a hundred picture frames if that was his reward.

◆ ◆ ◆ ◆ ◆

Marie was elbow deep in dirt and flowers, her shins and knees caked with mud, when the phone rang that afternoon. She jerked out of the muck, stumbling up the steps and leaving dirt clods in her wake.

As soon as she was inside the door, she called out, "Is it Caden? Did she call about the job?" But no one answered her.

The house felt empty as the phone rang again. She snatched it up. "Hello?"

"May I speak with Jack Sloane?"

The grouchy voice did not belong to Caden.

"I'm not quite sure where he is right now. Can I have him call you back?"

"This is Jeff Tate."

From the insurance company. She scribbled his name and number onto a piece of paper on the kitchen counter, her hand shaking. This call was the difference between triumph and collapse.

"I work for Jack. Can you tell me what the decision is?"

"No. Have him call me immediately."

"I will." The other end of the line clicked in her ear, and she set the handset back in its cradle.

She called for Jack but still received no answer. A quick circle of the house confirmed she was all alone. The truck was still there, but Jack and Seth had disappeared. They'd mentioned picking up a few supplies in town. They'd probably walked to the grocery store. Or to see Aretha.

She didn't try to squelch her smile as she settled back on the dirt, planting the rich peonies and colorful irises that Jack had brought back from a nursery on the east side of the island. Aretha hadn't said anything about going on the drive with him, but the minute he invited her along, she'd closed up her empty shop, poured a little more food into Chapter's bowl, scratched behind the cat's ears, and hurried to meet him.

Jack deserved to be happy. He'd been on his own for a long time. Marie knew the feeling, and he'd rescued her. He might have been lonely too. But she'd been desperate for affection. She hadn't even realized how much she missed it until he took her under his roof and opened his heart to her.

She'd wondered if it was the island's special brand of magic that had healed her heart and cured her attacks, but maybe it wasn't the island at all. Maybe it was just the love of a father. Maybe feeling safe was a by-product of being loved.

He'd offered her everything he could give and trusted her to help him with his dream.

And she could help him. If Jeff Tate had called with bad news, she could step in.

A vision of her father—red-faced and yelling, as he'd been the last time she'd seen him—danced across her mind's eye.

"Do you know what your son did to my daughter? Do you know what would happen to your precious reputation if that became public knowledge?" He'd held the phone away from his ear, glaring at it like the little piece of plastic itself was his enemy. "I'm offering you a fair price for land that you're not even using. What's that land going to be worth when your name is dragged through a long court case and splashed across every tabloid in New England?" He had paused, letting a seething breath out between tight lips. "Agree to a deal now, and I'll convince her not to press charges."

The memory made her stomach ache, and she heaved just as she had that evening when she peeked through the narrow opening into her father's study.

What Derek had done was inexcusable.

What her father had done was worse.

She'd run away, afraid to stand up to him. Afraid to face him down. Afraid to tell him that she wouldn't let him use her like that.

Could she do it now? With Jack and Seth beside her, could

she tell him what he'd done was wrong and she wasn't going to be party to his blackmail schemes?

If she gave Jack the money that her mother had left, she'd have to.

"Marie." Caden's voice singsonged from across the street as she climbed the stairs from the boardwalk.

Marie wiped the back of a dirty hand across her eyes, swiping away any wayward tears, and swallowed the lump in her throat. "Caden." It was more of a croak than a greeting, but the other woman was still crossing the street and far enough away that she might not have noticed.

"I was hoping you'd be here."

"Really?" Marie leaned back on her heels, nodding toward the whitewashed step. As she rubbed her hands together, the scent of earth wafted around her. "What's going on?"

Caden plopped down on a step, hugging herself and leaning forward. "I need to talk to you about this job."

"Do you want it?"

"No—yes—I don't know." She squeezed her eyes closed and pressed a palm to her forehead. Her blond bob hung in a loose curtain over her round cheeks, and Marie jumped up to sit by her friend.

"Tell me what's going on."

She shrugged. "I'm not sure I'm the person for this job. I really appreciate the offer, but I don't have the experience that you're looking for."

"This inn doesn't need experience. It needs you. We want you." She reached out a muddy hand but pulled it back before she left dirty handprints on Caden's arm.

"It's just that I'm supposed to take over the bakery from my dad someday."

"Oh. If he needs you, that's all right. Is he retiring soon?"

"Not for another ten years or more, probably."

"Then I don't understand."

Caden turned her head, her pale blue eyes filled with the pain of uncertainty.

Marie sighed, folding her hands over her lap. "It's okay if you don't want the job."

"Yes, but I do want it." She stared toward the row of pine trees and the sun-kissed inlet beyond. "I want to take it, but I don't want to disappoint you. What if I don't have enough recipes or enough knowledge? What would happen if I couldn't live up to your hopes or people didn't like my food?"

"I don't think there's much chance of that."

"But I couldn't let Jack down. If I take it and fail, then I'm not just letting him down. I'm letting down my mom and Aretha, who believe in me and want me to succeed. And moreover, I'd be letting my dad down. He's taught me everything he knows about baking. If I fail at this, then I'll fail him. How could I hold my head up if I fail at the only thing he's ever wanted for me?"

Marie shook her head. "What is it with fathers and daughters? Even as adults we can't help but want their approval. Why is that?"

Caden shrugged. "I don't know." Cradling her chin in her hand, she leaned her elbow on her knee. "Maybe we're just wired to want that affection, to want that affirmation."

"But it seems like your dad really loves you."

She jerked her head up. "Oh, he does. My dad's the best. But it doesn't mean I don't crave his blessing. You know how Father Chuck always talks about God as a father. It's the same thing."

"What do you mean? The same what?"

She pursed her lips to the left and wrinkled her nose. "We all want the gifts, right? The good things that God has for us. We want God's blessing. His approval. Maybe we want the same things from our dads. Their approval and their blessing, because we know that good things come with those."

"Maybe with *your* dad. Not so much with mine." She hadn't meant to sound so acidic, but the words rang with years of anger and pain.

"What do you mean?"

Marie dismissed the comment with a wave of her mud-stained hand. "Nothing."

But Caden wasn't buying the brush-off. "What happened with your dad? You never talk about your parents. I guess I assumed they were gone."

"My mom is. She passed away when I was seventeen. But my dad is alive and well and causing trouble wherever he goes."

"I'm sorry. I didn't realize."

She forced a smile. "It's all right. How could you have?" Brushing mud from her pants leg and trying for all the world to think about anything other than her father, she said, "So, what did your dad say when you told him about Jack's job offer?"

She pinched her lips together. "He said he'd support me no matter what, and that if I really wanted it, I should take the job."

"You have his approval no matter what, but you're still afraid of disappointing him."

Caden's head bobbed. "Stupid. I know."

Why did Caden insist on beating herself up? "It's not

stupid." She swallowed, stalling for time and praying for anything to say to encourage her friend. But there was only one thing she could say. "At least your father is worth trying to impress. What's stupid is knowing that your father is an underhanded liar and still wanting to impress him." Her throat tried to close, but she fought through it until the words could come again. "I left Boston because I'd been trying to please my dad for years. After my mom died, I craved his attention, longed to meet his approval. And then I overheard him on the phone with a business associate, leveraging what was best for me into a deal on some land he wanted to develop."

Pale blue eyes narrowed in on her as Caden laid a hand on her arm. "What happened to you?"

Marie looked away, blinking at the tears that seemed intent on moving in. "It's not really important right now. But trust me when I tell you that I know how much we daughters want to please our dads. And if I had a dad like yours or Jack, I would still be trying to make him happy."

"I'm glad you left. I'm glad you came here." Caden bumped her shoulder and winked. "I think Seth is too."

Time to change the subject. "So, what about this job? What if it started on a temporary basis? What if you could give it a test drive and decide if you even like doing it? You have plenty of time to try out recipes and plan a schedule before we open."

If we open.

She banished the thought as soon as it popped into her mind. They would open. On time. They wouldn't leave travelers stranded or guests hungry. She couldn't leave Jack to flounder. They'd open. Whatever she had to do.

"And if it doesn't work, you'll look for someone from the culinary school?"

"Sure. No contracts. No pressure."

"All right then. You have a deal." Caden stuck out her hand to shake, but Marie held up muddy messes.

They were still smiling from their perch on the front steps as Jack and Seth plodded up the street, Jack with his hands in his pockets and shoulders slumped. When the men reached the end of the walkway, Marie called out to them, "We have a chef."

Jack lifted his head, looking between the two women. "We don't have money for a kitchen."

Her stomach hit the ground, her ears ringing.

Jeff Tate hadn't come through.

And now the money from her mother's trust—and facing down her father—was the only way to save the Red Door.

21

Seth paced the perimeter of the dining room the next evening, his arms crossed and head down. He couldn't look at Marie or Jack, who sat across one of the tables from her.

She leaned toward the old man, her hands outstretched and face pleading. "Jack, let me loan you the money. It's the only way. And you can pay me back. It'll just be an interest-free loan. I'll be an investor or a partner or whatever you want me to be. Just let me give you the money."

Seth had heard the same thing over and over all afternoon until it rang in his head like a mantra. It made him sick to his stomach. She wanted part ownership in the inn. She wanted to become an investor.

And she wanted to eventually take over everything that he and Jack had worked for.

She hadn't said it in quite those terms, but that didn't change the facts. It was too much like Reece. She was weaseling her way into the paperwork, adding her name to documents. All the things that had left him vulnerable to Reece's schemes.

A flashing blue gaze caught his as Marie looked for help, but he shook his head. He couldn't seem to separate the two women, so different yet so similar.

Jack covered her hands with his gnarled ones. "It's not going to do any good. A couple thousand dollars isn't going to be enough. The insurance company isn't going to pay out for at least thirty days, and the check won't cover the entire cost of the kitchen. By then it'll be too little too late."

"You're not hearing me. I have money. Lots of it."

Seth paused his march to stare at her. What was her game? What did she think she could gain through this charade? And why hadn't he figured it out sooner?

She couldn't have any money. She'd come to the house penniless. Jack had said she didn't even have enough to buy a ferry ticket onto the island. So why claim to have a secret stash of money now?

"Jack, please hear me out. My mother left me a trust fund when she passed away. She came from a family of means in Boston, and when she died, she left all of her money to me. I have more than enough money to fix the kitchen. We can pay to have a crew fix it instead of breaking our backs to get it done in time for the grand opening."

Her words jumbled together until he couldn't make any sense of them.

Jack seemed to be struggling to understand too. "What do you mean?"

"You need help. You're bleeding, and I have a cure."

"It should come from family." Bitterness laced the words Seth hadn't even meant to speak.

She took a long breath through her nose and let it out slowly. "Then call me family. I want to help you open the Red

Door. And I have money to loan you. I love this place, and I want others to love it too. If it doesn't open, it's a loss for the island. You deserve to see it open. For Rose."

Okay, that was true. The inn needed to open. But the rest of it, the recurring bit about the money, didn't compute.

"Seth, will you please tell him to just accept the money?"

"I'm not sure I can. We don't know what strings might be attached."

Her face jerked as though she'd been slapped, her eyes shining in the chandelier light. His arms reached for her, but he pushed his hands into his pockets. If what she said was true, she'd been lying to them all along. And if that was the case, he couldn't believe anything she'd said or done.

The kindness in her eyes. The gentleness in her touch. The passion in her kiss.

If some of it was untrue, all of it was.

And he'd been duped again.

Like an idiot, he'd let down his guard and fallen for a pretty face. Again.

He resumed his journey around the room, glancing at her as he turned every corner. "So you're saying that you've had loads of money the whole time you've been with us."

"Well . . . yes." Barely a whisper, her words hung in the air.

"And you didn't bother to mention it. You just thought you'd take Jack's charity."

Her eyes sprang open. "No. I mean, I didn't want his money or his charity. I wasn't trying to take anything. I just needed a safe place to stay."

"Why not use some of this money you claim to have to rent a room somewhere?"

She cowered under his glare, and he hated himself for

doing it. But he couldn't stop until he knew all of it, the entire terrible truth. This was the past she'd hidden so carefully. But there had to be a reason for all the secrecy.

Tears welled in her eyes, but she wiped them away without breaking eye contact. "I couldn't get to it before."

"So just in the nick of time, you suddenly have access to it? Very convenient." He rubbed his temples, praying for relief from the pounding there. He wanted to believe her, but everything she'd said and done had been duplicitous. She was a con woman. An artist trying to stake a claim in Jack and Rose's dream.

And she'd waited until the most opportune moment. Out of money and out of options, Jack could hardly be blamed for considering the offer at this point. Seth was the only thing standing between him and the worst mistake of his life.

He wouldn't let his uncle make the same mistake he had.

"What I meant—" Her voice trembled, so she cleared her throat and carried on. "What I mean is that I wasn't ready to face the consequences of using that money."

"And you are now?"

"Enough." Jack held up a hand to him and patted Marie's arm with the other. "Why on earth would you want to invest in a business that's on its last leg before it's even open?"

"I don't. I want to give my money to you, and you can do whatever you like with it."

Seth scoffed, but held his tongue as Jack raised his hand again.

"Why?"

Her gaze locked on Jack's wrinkled face. She wore a mask of sincerity like she'd been born with it. "You took me in when I had nowhere to go. How can I sit back and let Rose's legacy end like this? I'd do anything for you. I love you like I always wanted to love my own father."

Every word sliced him like a knife. She played it all so true, so real. But no stage talent made it any less of an act.

Jack's face broke, tears welling in the corners of his eyes. "I never wished for a daughter until I met you."

"You're not actually buying this line, are you, Jack?"

She looked at Seth, her face a mirror image of Jack's. Except confusion etched into the lines of her forehead, hurt painting each of her features. "I don't understand. I'm giving you everything you need to open the door."

"At what cost?"

"No cost. No strings." Her voice was jagged, aching. "I just want the Red Door to open. I want you to be happy here."

Seth leaned into her, placing one hand on the table in front of her and one on the back of her chair. His breath stirred the long, chestnut strands of hair at her shoulder. This close, he could see the dark smudge across her cheek, a leftover from the garden. "I've been through this before."

"Reece?" She blinked those sapphires at him, her lips parting on a sob, and his gut clenched.

She'd wiggled her way into his arms, dug herself a place in his heart. He'd held her, promising shelter from the world.

But he couldn't stop the words from coming out. "You're *just* like her."

He'd never loathed himself more.

She licked her lips, swallowing several times before whispering, "I think I need to go."

He couldn't stop one final jab as she slithered out beneath his arm, scurrying for the door. "We don't want your money and the conditions that go with it."

Just inside the red door that she'd painted—in the exact spot where he'd hoped to be free to kiss her whenever he liked—she turned watery eyes on Jack. "Take it or leave it. I've already called the bank. More than enough money will be wired in your name to the credit union by the bakery tomorrow morning. Please, please, take it."

"What about the consequences you mentioned?" Jack's voice was gravel as he reached out to her across the room.

"It's too late to worry about those. They're in motion already."

◆◆◆◆◆

Marie couldn't wipe away the tears as fast as they flooded her eyes, so she ran blindly to the only friend she could count on. With trembling hands, she banged on Caden's door until it opened.

"Marie? What's wrong? Is it something at the inn?"

She hiccupped, and biting her lip didn't do much to stem the trembling there.

"Come on in." Caden swung open the door and held out her arm toward the living room of her quaint bungalow. She guided Marie into a fluffy chair and plopped down on the couch across from her. "Tell me what's going on."

Marie rubbed her hands over her face, and they came away sticky with tears and streaks of leftover mud. She must look a mess.

Caden seemed to understand. "Why don't you go wash up, and I'll find us a snack. Something sweet."

Nodding, Marie headed down the hall. In the little bathroom, she refused to look into the mirror. She didn't need a firsthand view of her red, puffy eyes or mud-streaked cheeks.

She scooped cool water into her hand and splashed it over her face, drops running down her neck, trailing the places that Seth had once touched with such tenderness.

Did he really think everything she'd done was an act? Or that she was anything like Reece?

As she wiped away the water, she tried to do the same to the memories. But they weren't so easily dispatched. His caress. His embrace. His kiss. They swarmed in on her, surrounding her lungs until breathing became a distant memory. Dark spots danced in the corners of her eyes, and she sank to the floor, praying to be delivered. From what, she wasn't quite sure.

After what felt like an hour on the cold tile floor, a soft knock at the door was followed by Caden's voice. "Are you all right? Can I get you something?"

Marie snatched at whatever breath she could find. "Yes. I'll be right there." With all the strength she could muster, she pulled herself up by the lip of the sink onto shaking legs. After a long minute, she managed a shaky breath and a tentative step. As she slipped back into the hall to the smell of chocolate and peanut butter, her stomach rolled.

The chair and couch seemed to fill the entire living room, but Caden had made a small dinner tray appear and set two steaming mugs of tea and a plate of brownies on the server.

She smiled up from her seat on the couch, hugging a pillow close to her chest. "Feeling better?"

"A little."

Caden motioned to the heaping dessert plate. "These are my specialty. Peanut butter fudge brownies. Have one. And then tell me what happened."

With rolling insides, Marie didn't really want it, but she couldn't refuse. She broke off a corner and put it in her

streets, and watch the midnight fireworks. So I went." She stared at her hands, swallowing the urge to change topics or gloss over the facts.

"But we didn't look at the lights. He threw me on his bed, held me down, and took what he wanted." Her throat ached and her stomach burned. She pressed her hands over her face, wishing she could hide from the truth of the memories. "He took everything."

Tears streamed down Caden's cheeks. "I am so sorry." She seemed to know there was nothing else she could say. There weren't words deep enough for one woman to say to another when she'd been broken like that.

But somehow it hurt a little less to know she wasn't crying alone.

"It took me a week to tell my dad." She hiccuped on a sob but pushed forward. "And he told me not to tell anyone. He said it wouldn't do any good, and it would hurt me more to have to testify. I let him talk me into staying silent for almost two months before I overheard him on the phone with Derek's dad. My father threatened to have me swear out a warrant against Derek if his dad didn't sell some land."

"So you left?"

"I couldn't be a pawn in a deal like that. I couldn't let him use what had happened to me for his profit."

When Marie didn't pick back up with the story, Caden filled in a few holes. "And that's when you met Jack, who took you to the Red Door and gave you a home."

"And a family. I didn't even know I didn't have one until I met them." She took a deep breath, the last vestiges of the bonds around her lungs that had given her countless panic attacks falling away.

THE RED DOOR INN

"So what happened today?"

"Today I offered Jack the money from my trust fund."

"Your what?"

She picked up the lukewarm mug of tea, sipping it more for something to do than because she wanted to drink it. "My mother left me money when she passed away. Not enough to put me in with the Boston elite on my own, but more than enough to fix the kitchen and get the inn open on time."

"What did Jack say?"

Marie shrugged. "It wasn't what Jack said, it was what Seth did. He accused me of trying to worm my way in so that I could steal the inn. He said I was lying to them and had waited until they needed my money to offer it so I'd have the upper hand."

"He what?" Caden's quiet vehemence filled the room as she slammed her mug on the tray, warming Marie from the inside out. Family got indignant for each other.

She couldn't help the half smile that worked its way across her face. "I don't want to take the inn. I just want to see it open."

"I know. And so would any man with half a brain."

Seth's words repeated in her mind, striking a blow with each replay. "He's been hurt before, and he thinks I set out to do the same."

Caden mumbled something behind her mug about men who don't know how to treat a lady. It was true. And some women didn't treat men well.

Seth had been hurt just enough to leave him too wounded to try again. Marie had been hurt too. One too many times.

It was better for everyone if she left. It would save both her and Seth from wondering if they could try again.

She'd face her dad, and then she'd find a new home.

Finding a new family, though . . . That would be more difficult.

"Aretha's hinted that Jack's been having money trouble for a while. She'd never tell us something he said in confidence, but she's been worried about him. Why did you wait until now to offer him the money?"

"Because Derek's dad is refusing to sell the land that my father wants. And my father's name is on my bank account. Accessing that money meant revealing my location."

Caden's jaw dropped. "How long until he's here?"

"Knowing my dad, I'd say tomorrow."

◆◆◆◆◆

For the first time in six weeks, Marie knocked on the red door. The morning sun had nearly crested, but the paint was cool and clean beneath her knuckles. Pride swelled within her. She'd done a good job on this home.

And she'd done a good thing giving Jack the money.

Butterflies assaulted her stomach, diving and swooping as she waited for someone to answer the door. She couldn't tell if they anticipated Seth's greeting or her father's imminent arrival. Either way, she'd be thankful when they were gone and she could move on.

The footfalls on the other side of the door didn't belong to Seth, and she let out a quick sigh.

Jack's face registered surprise and then a glowing smile. "Marie, girl. Come in. You don't have to knock."

She stepped inside and he closed the door behind her. "Thank you."

His smile faded as he reached for her hands and squeezed

them. "I'm so sorry about the other day. Seth shouldn't have said any of those things. He feels awful. And he doesn't really believe any of what he said."

She looked down and to the side. "Yes, he does. But that's all right. I didn't come here looking for an apology."

"He cares for you. I know he does." The wrinkles around his mouth grew more pronounced as he frowned. "He's scared."

Bitterness rose in her throat like a wave of bile, but she pushed it down, refusing to cling to past memories. This day was about facing her present and figuring out her future. She couldn't do that and be angry at what Seth had said.

"It could never work between us."

"Why not? It's not too late."

"Because he can't ever see past my lie. I'll always be another Reece to him. Just someone else who lied to him." The truth sat like a stone in the pit of her stomach, but she ignored the pain. She squeezed his hands, giving him a tremulous smile. "Now. Did you go to the bank? Did you get your check?"

The corners of his eyes angled down. "It's too much. Fifty thousand. I can't accept it."

"It's enough to get your doors open, and I have more left over."

"Leaving the island?"

A memory from the first time she met Caden popped into her mind. "Caden warned me that the island gets under your skin so that you never want to leave. I don't know where I'm going yet. But I hope not far. I can't imagine never coming back here."

"Don't go. You could stay. You have a job here as long as you want it."

"I appreciate that, but I just came back to pick up a few things I left in the basement. I'm staying with Caden for a few days."

"Won't leave before the grand opening party, will you?"

She shook her head. "Of course not. I'll stay at least that long."

Three sharp taps sounded on the door, followed immediately by the pathetic thunk of the doorbell. Her stomach dropped to her toes.

"Who could that be? Haven't had so many visitors in months."

He twisted the handle of the door and opened it to reveal a fit man in his fifties. A Burberry leather jacket matched his stylishly cut brown hair and blazing blue eyes.

Marie pinched her eyes closed, squared her shoulders, and asked for some sort of help from above. "Hello, Dad."

22

arie." Elliot Carrington's voice never changed, always cold, always businesslike.

"It didn't take you long to get here."

His gaze swept over Jack, his frown announcing that he'd clearly found something lacking in the other man's mild manner and relaxed attire. "Are we going to talk on the porch, or is there somewhere private"—again he stared at Jack—"we can speak?"

"Can use the parlor if you like. We moved in the furniture last night. It's just missing the finishing touches you already picked out."

"Thank you." Marie touched his arm, wishing for all she was worth that this man, with his wrinkled features and wide smile, had been her real dad.

Instead she walked into the parlor off the entryway. The antique burgundy love seat she'd found at Aretha's sat along one wall. Adjacent to it was a gray wingback chair and matching ottoman. The end tables and hutches were all in place.

What the room needed were those personal touches. The lamps and antique books she'd so carefully selected.

And, of course, guests to enjoy the space.

She sat in the chair, but immediately stood back up when her dad began to pace the room. He towered over her, nearly as tall as Seth, and she wasn't going to give up any more height than she had to.

"I hope you've had fun. I've been worried to death about you."

"Were you?" The tone of her voice matched his, so cold that it could have burst a few pipes on its own.

"What kind of question is that? Of course I was. You ran off without a note or any way to contact you. I called your cell and filled up the voice mail. You never returned my calls."

"That's because I dropped the phone in a trash can at the bus terminal in Bangor. But I'm sure you already knew that. You probably had it tracked within hours." She crossed her arms over her stomach and stared at her tennis shoes. They weren't the only piece of her clothing stained with paint and dirt. She was surprised he'd even recognized her without her designer labels.

"Of course I knew," he snapped, pausing to glower at her. "I did everything I could to track you down, but instead I had almost two months of silence. Two months of worrying about you. If your mother were alive she'd be horrified."

"Maybe. But she never would have let you try to use me to get a better deal with Derek Summerville."

"I never!" His voice rose. "Where did you come up with such a ridiculous story? Is that why you ran away? Well, forget it. It's a lie."

"I didn't run away. Twenty-eight-year-olds don't run away. I left when I overheard you trying to use me to make your deal."

His stony exterior cracked but went back up almost immediately. He resumed his marching, shaking his head. "I don't know what you think you heard, but it was never cause for this. I'm not even trying to do a deal with Summerville."

Had she misheard him? Was it possible that this was all a misunderstanding and she'd left Boston for no good reason?

No.

This was his ploy and his plan. Always, always, he made her doubt her decisions.

"Then what about the *Times* article?"

He snapped to attention, his eyes narrowed and turned hard as steel. "What article?"

"I read it." The words felt like acid on her tongue. "It said you were still looking for an expert for your case against the historical significance of whatever's on his property. That expert was me. You were looking for me. Because when I left, you couldn't lord me over his head and force him to sell. And you couldn't promise him that I wouldn't press charges if you didn't have me under your thumb."

Her stomach ached, and she would have given the entire sum of her trust fund to have Seth standing by her side. Facing her father had seemed so much more manageable when she'd pictured Seth's broad shoulders to lean on.

She hadn't known it when she left Boston, but what she'd needed was more than an escape from her father. What she'd needed—what she'd been missing for most of her life—was family. All she'd wanted was family. Someone to love and someone who loved her.

The man standing on the other side of the room didn't know how to love her. She wouldn't let him talk her into thinking he did.

Elliot waved off her comment like it was a bad call in baseball. "Don't be silly. Our company does hundreds of deals in a year. Anyone at the firm could be working with Summerville."

"You were quoted in the article."

Another dismissive wave and toss of his head. His perfectly styled hair didn't budge. "It could have been about anything."

"But it wasn't." She ran her hands down the front of her shirt.

At a stalemate, they stared at each other, neither willing to give up the high ground. He glowered at her, apparently expecting her to back down. Clearly she'd learned stubbornness from him. And he wasn't pleased that she was using it against him now.

"What do you want, Dad? Why did you come here?"

With furrowed eyebrows he shook his head. "What do I want? I want my only daughter to come home. I want to have my family close."

"We're not a family." Prickles along her scalp made the hair on the back of her neck stand up. She wrapped her arms around herself to ward off the following chills.

"Don't be ridiculous." His roar, while not louder than normal, was lethal. "Of course we are a family."

"Not since Mom died. And maybe not really before then."

He spun around and walked to the door, his hand resting on the handle. "You're coming with me. Don't argue anymore. You sound like a child."

She closed her eyes and inhaled the scent of fresh paint and antique furniture. "Maybe so, but I'm not a kid anymore. And I'm not going back to Boston."

"And I suppose you're going to make this rinky-dink town your home? Is that it?" He spit the words out like they tasted bad. "You're going to find a use for your Wharton MBA here?"

"Probably not." It hurt to say the words more than she expected. Not that she couldn't find a use for her degree, but that she wouldn't be in North Rustico to look for one. "I'll go where I need to. And I can do that now. I needed a safe place, and I found it here. Now I can face whatever I need to. But I'm not going back to Boston with you."

He cursed low and long, finally yanking on the hem of his jacket and straightening the lapels. "Obviously we need some time to relax. You've been thinking something terrible for a long time, and it's gotten to your head. I'll take a room here for the night, and we'll talk again tomorrow."

"You can't. The inn's not open yet."

"Fine. I'll find another in town."

"Don't bother looking. There aren't any other bed-and-breakfasts in North Rustico."

His eyes flashed as his face turned red. "What kind of place is this?"

"It's my kind of place." A little smile worked its way across her lips, and she pressed her fingers over her mouth. This was her kind of town. With people like Jack and Aretha and Caden. Even Father Chuck and Caden's slew of nieces and nephews. They were her kind of people. And that made this home.

Maybe she didn't have to leave.

Maybe she didn't have to keep running or keep searching for something she'd already found.

She nodded, pulling her fingers from where they'd twisted into the bottom of her sweatshirt. She had found it. She'd been about to leave, but she didn't want to anymore. She'd never really wanted to.

Now she didn't have to.

Her own fears, her dad's conniving, even Seth's response, couldn't drive her away from the home that she'd found.

"Thank you, Dad."

His glare could cut through platinum. "For what?"

"I just realized that I don't have to go. I can stay here, where I want to." She walked toward him with open arms, almost as if to hug him, although she couldn't remember the last time they'd touched. Instead, she opened the door and ushered him into the empty foyer. "And now you can go. You know where I am, and I'm staying put."

He bent at the waist, his fists balled in front of him. "You're not willing to help me out with a deal? You'd let me lose out on a multimillion-dollar investment deal for this?"

And there it was. His motivation for everything.

"Yes. I would. Now I want you to go."

"You're throwing away everything. Everything. And for what? For some indiscretion by Summerville's son?" He'd dropped all pretenses, the fury in his eyes clearly caused by what he'd patently denied just minutes before.

"It wasn't some little indiscretion. Don't trivialize it like that." Heart pounding, she forced out the word she hated most. "He raped me. Do you not get that?"

"It's over now, but you can still use it to help our company."

"It's not my company." Her hands shook with pent-up rage as she hurled the words at him. "I won't do it. I won't be party to that. He deserves to be in prison for what he did, and I won't give up my right to see that happen just for your deal."

He'd never struck her before, so his unexpected movement caught her off guard. She flinched before his hand could strike her face. And then suddenly it was gone, wrenched behind his back as Seth hauled him to the front door.

"I believe the lady asked you to leave. You're not welcome here unless she invites you back. Do you understand?"

"Let go of me." He wiggled and writhed, but Seth didn't let him go until he was firmly planted next to her flower beds. "I'll have all your money for this."

"By all means." Seth dug into his pocket, found a loonie one-dollar coin, and flicked it at Elliot. "That's all I've got to my name."

As he marched up the stairs, Seth eyed her like a starving man spying a fresh steak. "That made my day."

She nodded in appreciation and offered a half smile. "Thank you."

He nodded in return, his smile more in his eyes than on his mouth. "I'll be right inside if you need me."

She stopped him with a hand on his arm, those telltale butterflies taking another spin around her insides. Heat washed over her as he stared at the place where their skin touched. Always the instant, undeniable reaction to him.

And this time more than ever, as he'd saved her from a red cheek and probably a black eye.

He'd heard it all, and he'd still come to her rescue.

Seth left the door open, and she took an extra breath for courage as she faced down her father's sputtering curses.

"You should leave the island now. Go back to Boston and tell Mr. Summerville that I'll be there soon."

Her father's head perked up.

"To swear out a warrant against his son."

◆◆◆◆◆

Aretha knocked on the red door and arranged the table-cloth over her picnic basket as she waited. She tapped her toe and hummed the fiddle reel that had been playing in the store that afternoon. The warm evening breeze swept over her. She hadn't been this content in years. Not since her husband had left, really.

Seth answered the door, a hopeful smile falling away from his face. "Aretha, it's good to see you." He didn't exactly sound like he meant that, but she let it go for the moment.

"I brought dinner." She held up her basket and he motioned her in.

"I hope not a pork and jerk."

She touched a finger to her nose and smiled all the way up at him. Goodness, his head nearly touched the top of the door frame. "You're quite right. Where are Jack and Marie? I haven't seen you hardly at all since you moved back in here. My house is awful quiet. I didn't even realize how quiet until it was noisy again. Chapter and I just don't make enough of a racket, I suppose." She looked around, hoping to spot Jack's broad grin. "So, the dining room?"

"Sure. The dining room is great." He led the way into the house and disappeared behind the swinging kitchen door. When he emerged a moment later, he had a stack of plates in his hands. "The dishes and flatware came in, so we can actually eat on real plates."

"Wonderful. Marie must be so excited."

He set the dishes down and put a hand on his waist

before plunging the other one through his hair, which was already a disheveled mess. Actually, all of him was a mess. From his rumpled T-shirt to his stained pants. Even the dingy socks that he plodded around in were hanging off his toes.

"Seth, are you all right?"

"Sure. Great."

"Seth . . . tell me the truth."

He kept his head down but glanced up, misery in his eyes.

She put her hands on her hips and frowned at him. "Where is Jack?"

"He's out back checking on the new garden. He'll be in here in a minute, I'm sure. We just planted squash and green beans. And Jack has a tomato plant he's trying to get to bud. He figured now that the weather is warmer they won't freeze. Might be pretty good, even."

The boy's tongue flapped like it was attached with a hinge. Like he was intent on keeping her from having a chance to ask any more questions. That had never stopped her in all her sixty-seven years.

"Where's Marie?"

He cleared his throat just as Jack slammed the back door. "Something smells wonderful! I know that's not Seth. Must be my favorite girl." He strode through the kitchen without stopping to wash his hands and leaned in to hug her.

She put her hands up and stepped out of his reach. "Where's Marie?"

He stopped and rubbed black hands together. Shooting a glance at Seth, he shrugged. "She's staying with Caden for a bit."

"Why?" But she already knew. These fool men. They'd

run her off. The best thing that had ever happened to them, and they'd chased her away.

Seth dipped his head, more grade-schooler than grown man. "There was a misunderstanding."

"So why didn't you go after her and explain? Apologize if you need to. That's what grown-ups do."

Jack cleared his throat and nodded. "That's what I've been telling him. He's got to go after her and apologize."

She shot him a stern look, and he quieted down. "You're in no position to give the boy advice about going after what he wants. We'll come back to you in a minute." Turning her attention back to the younger Sloane, she stepped into his space, staring hard into his puppy-dog eyes. "Nothing's so bad that you can't ask for forgiveness. She cares about you too, you know."

He stood up a little straighter. Maybe he just needed to be reminded that he wasn't the only one with a hurting heart. But his face didn't brighten and his words were laced with anger. "It's not that easy. I said something terrible." So that anger was directed at himself.

"What did you say?"

He looked at Jack as though begging for him to step in. But his uncle had the good sense to stay where he was. No need to get mixed up in this. She'd have a few choice words for him in a moment.

With no help coming, Seth cleared his throat. "I said that she was just like my ex-fiancée."

"Who did what?"

"Swindled me out of my business and life savings."

Aretha couldn't stop herself. She smacked his arm, which didn't budge. In fact, she was pretty sure it hurt her hand more than him, but the grief registering on his face melted her heart. "That was an awful thing to do. You've run her off just to spite your own self."

He looked up at the ceiling, running both hands over his face. "She was offering a loan, offering to be a partner with Jack. Reece wanted to be my partner too. That's how she got on all of my accounts, cleaned me out, and left the country."

"You do realize how stupid that is. Marie is not this Reece girl."

"I know. It was stupid."

"Good. We're on the same page. Now go talk with her. Make it right."

"I don't think she wants to talk with me right now. She was here this morning, and she left as fast as she could after her dad took off." Seth's shoulders, those big broad shoulders that had rebuilt the house in which they stood, slumped.

"Her father was here? At the Red Door?" What else weren't these men telling her?

They both nodded mutely. Perfect.

She sighed, giving him a firm pat on his rather muscular arm. "So, what? She walked out of this house, but she didn't go home with her dad, right? You're just going to let her go? That is not how a man treats the woman he loves."

"Whoa." His hands shot up as if he was defending himself. "Who said anything about being in love with her? We're friends. We get along."

He wouldn't even see the nose on his own face if someone didn't point it out. "It doesn't even take both eyes to see how much you care about each other. I've seen the glances you give her when you think no one is watching. Well, I'm watching. I've seen them. So set it right. Now."

"I've been telling him the same thing."

"Oh, don't get me started, Jack Sloane." Her voice jumped at least an octave, but she was rolling too fast to stop now. Wagging a finger at him, she said, "You've been perfectly content to create an inn for your late wife, who I think I would have loved being friends with, while building a relationship with another woman." She waved her finger in the air, her heart beating fast enough to steal her breath. "You don't get to give love advice. Not until you figure out what you want and decide to do something about it."

She snatched up her picnic basket, ignoring the stunned looks on their faces, and swung around. "There won't be any more free meals from me until then either."

23

Seth straightened his polo shirt, tucking a loose tail into the waistband of his khakis and making sure his collar laid flat. He hadn't been this cleaned up and put together all week. After all, there'd been no time between painting the front porch, touching up the blue exterior, setting up the guest rooms, and overseeing the remodeling crew in the kitchen. Actually, Caden had done a fair amount of that—telling them exactly where she wanted her permanent island, showing them how high she wanted the shelves.

And with her help, they were going to open on time.

Well, with Caden's help and Marie's money.

Which had come with no strings. Just as she'd promised. She hadn't asked for her name on the deed or a percentage of the profits. They'd only had to worry about the finishing details. And there had been plenty.

But no matter how busy they'd been, Seth had found more than enough time to think about Marie, to imagine what she was doing, to wonder if she was missing him as much as he missed her. And he'd thought about what Aretha said.

She'd been right, of course. Even if it had taken him almost a week to come to terms with it. Whether or not he wanted to admit it, he'd fallen in love with Marie. But instead of treating her like the woman he cared about, he'd acted like a wounded rhinoceros, stampeding over her heart.

Now he only had one option—try to make up for it.

Licking his lips and taking a deep breath, he knocked on the door of Caden's bungalow. It was more guesthouse than stand-alone, but Jack had assured him that this was where she lived. And where he could find Marie. The porch light flickered on, breaking the evening darkness.

After a short pause, the blinds in the window next to the front door flicked, showing just a glimpse of Caden's blonde hair. It took another ten seconds for her to open the door, and instead of inviting him in, she stepped onto the cement stoop, crowding his space.

"Hi, Seth."

She didn't play coy, pretending she didn't know why he was there. But she wasn't going to make this easy on him either. He tugged at the top button on his shirt and swallowed, his mouth as dry as Palm Desert.

"Is Marie here?"

"She's sleeping right now."

It was only eight o'clock. The sun had disappeared for the night as he'd strolled down the road, playing out what he would say when he saw her. He wasn't any closer to scripting his words, but he wasn't sure time was going to be much help.

"Is that code for she doesn't want to see me?"

Caden looked away and pulled on the sleeves of her sweater. "She's hurting right now. But she told me what you said to her dad."

THE RED DOOR INN

He raised his eyebrows.

"I think that was awesome."

"The guy's a jerk. He doesn't realize what an amazing woman she is. Take it from someone who's been stupid enough to do the same. He's going to regret it someday."

Caden nodded, putting a hand on the doorknob behind her.

"All right." He shoved his hands into his pockets. "I guess I'll try to catch her another time."

As he turned to go, she tapped his arm. When he turned back, she whispered, "Church. Tomorrow."

"She'll be there?" Marie hadn't made an appearance at the service the week before. He knew. He'd watched and waited for her.

Caden nodded and winked before dashing back inside.

Thirteen hours. He had just thirteen hours to figure out what he was going to say to her and how he would say it. That was more than enough time to drive himself crazy.

He stabbed his fingers through his hair and yanked on it as he walked up the inn's front steps. Falling into one of the red Adirondack chairs Jack had put on the porch, he crossed an ankle over his knee.

"That you, Seth?"

"Yes."

Jack appeared behind the screen door and leaned on the frame. "How'd it go?"

"She was sleeping."

"At eight o'clock?" The timbre of Jack's words echoed Seth's own hunch.

"I know. But she's going to be at church in the morning. She can't avoid me there."

"Good for you."

"When are you going to talk to Aretha?"

Jack hung his head, the light of the early moon making his white hair glisten. "I don't know yet." He looked in Seth's direction. "We're quite a pair, me and you. You came to the island running from love troubles. I think I was hoping to forget how lonely I've been since your aunt Rose passed. And now look at us."

"You feel as lonely as you were back then? Right after Rose died?"

Jack hummed from somewhere deep in his throat. "I guess not. But it's probably because of you and Marie."

"Are you sure about that?" He'd never been one to analyze someone else's feelings, but Marie had been right. Jack was ten times happier since meeting Aretha than he'd been when Seth arrived. And it wasn't just because Seth had been so sour.

Jack stared at the nearly full moon as if it had answers that couldn't be found on earth. "I never figured I'd meet anyone I liked as well as Rose. Never figured I'd meet anyone like Aretha. She's not your aunt. She's different." He scratched his cheek, his whiskers rasping beneath his fingernails. "She has so much life, always bouncing around getting things done. You know her husband left her almost forty years ago?"

"I didn't."

"She told me that's why she opened the antique store. She needed something to keep her from thinking about him all the time, and she'd always liked vintage things. See, something like that could break a woman. Her husband leaving her like he did. Shoot, I knew the cancer was taking Rose from me, and it still almost broke me." Jack ruffled his hair, scratching behind his ear, never leaving the support of the door frame. "I've been doing this all for Rose. Made a clean mess of it too."

Seth chuckled. The old man wasn't lying. He didn't have a head for the hospitality business or much knowledge of the market. He didn't even have the construction skills or the eye for design to put the finishing touches on the house. But he'd barreled forward because this inn was Rose's dream.

"What is it that you want, Jack?"

Jack smacked his lips together, the noise reverberating off the porch's white support beams and ceiling.

"I guess I want to know that my life isn't over. I thought maybe it was, but it's not. I've got more to offer than just my memories of Rose. And I want to share this next phase with someone else."

Seth pushed out of his chair. This was all getting a little touchy-feely for him, so he slapped Jack on the back as he entered the house. "Go get her."

Jack frowned, nodded, and stalked off the front porch and down the street, his form disappearing between streetlights and picking up speed as he approached the three-way stop and Aretha's house just beyond.

In his room, Seth changed into something more comfortable before picking up a brown paper–wrapped package on the foot of his bed. He opened it to find the finished gift for Jack, the glass and brass plaque in place. The old image of the house nearly glowed in the mahogany frame, and he ran a finger over the plaque, Marie's idea.

She would love it. The perfect gift for Jack, and they'd hang it in the dining room. Somewhere that everyone would see it. He needed to show it to her. But first he had to apologize.

If she wouldn't speak to him, would she read a note? Maybe the old typewriter had one more letter in it.

He moved a stack of boxes to make room to sit in front of the black machine. As he scrolled a fresh sheet of paper into place, he closed his eyes and waited for the words to come. But they didn't.

He'd been afraid to trust again. The scars had been too deep for him to see how God could give him another shot at love. But he had, and Seth wouldn't waste it. "God, I need your help. Don't let me blow it again."

And then the words came in sharp, rhythmic beats against the page, each filling the sheet with his deepest hope. With every fading black line, he prayed that the typewriter would hold out. Just long enough to tell her the truth.

He loved her.

Dear M,

I read in a book once about a man who wrote a letter of apology. And the girl took him back.

I wish I had his words. But somehow I can't find them. So I'll give you the only ones I have.

When I met Reece, I thought I'd met the woman I would marry. She was everything I'd ever hoped to find. And when she left me, I realized that everything about her had been a lie. She'd constructed a pretense so perfect that within weeks I couldn't imagine my life without her.

When you first arrived, I thought I was protecting Jack from the same fate by pushing you away. Except I couldn't ignore how you cared about him. And when I realized that my feelings for you were

*beginning to resemble what I'd felt for Reece, I feared
the same deception. I wanted to kiss you so much
that day in the closet. But you were already finding a
place in my life that I couldn't imagine filling again.*

*I was terrified. And I was angry with myself.
I should have been the one to help Jack when he
needed it. He's my uncle, but because of my own stupidity, I don't have a nickel to give him.*

*At the first hint of what I thought to be a betrayal
of my trust, I turned on you.*

*I have been a fool and the worst kind of man. I
should have protected you. Instead, I left you to fend
for yourself because I was so caught up in the pain of
my own memories and anger at my own mistakes.*

*I don't want to be that man. I want to be deserving
of you.*

Will you let me try?

Yours,
S

*P.S. The frame is finished. Meet me at my spot? I'll
show it to you. I'll be there until the sun goes down. I
promise I'll pay for the ice cream this time.*

◆ ◆ ◆ ◆ ◆

Aretha smiled when her doorbell rang.

She stood from the chair in front of her television, and
Chapter jumped down, flicking her tail as if to say she wasn't
very happy about losing her seat. "Get used to it, girl." She
chuckled as she opened the door.

Jack didn't even wait to be welcomed in. He just stepped past her and began pacing the living room, scratching his head and mumbling to himself.

"Please. Won't you come in?"

He looked up in confusion and promptly resumed his shuffled steps. "There's something I need to say to you, Aretha Franklin."

She turned off the news that she'd been watching and sat on the edge of her seat, smoothing the wrinkles from her skirt with flat palms. "What is it, Jack Sloane?"

He pointed toward the Red Door, never stopping his pace. "We don't just invite you over to bring us food." His words were benign, but his voice shook, almost as if he were angry.

"I know that. I volunteered to bring you meals."

"Right." He stopped, clearly confused that they were already in agreement.

"Right. So that's one thing."

Now she was confused. "What is?"

He pinched his eyes closed and rubbed his forehead, the lines around his mouth growing even deeper. "Here's the other thing. It's just that I'm not usually someone who likes to talk a lot."

"You could have fooled me."

He shot her a look, and she stemmed her smile with pursed lips, thankful she'd just put on a touch of lipstick. She smoothed a hand over her hair, making sure the ends curled under just as they were supposed to.

"I don't usually talk so much. Don't usually have that much on my mind. But ever since I met you, I can't seem to stop. Between you and Marie, you've got me thinking about things and wondering what my life is supposed to be like.

I only had a plan to get the inn open. Now that's about to happen, and I don't know what's next. Running a bed-and-breakfast? I don't have a clue about how to do that."

"Because it was Rose's dream."

"Right. It was all her idea, and she would have loved the inn, but she's gone. And I'm in that big house."

"You have Seth." She shrugged. "And if he plays his cards right, you might have Marie too. Plus it'll be full of visitors soon enough."

"That's not enough." He stopped pacing, his shoulders rising and falling, but his gaze level on her face.

She sat up a little straighter, trying to breathe and pushing all the hopes that this man had stirred in her somewhere deep inside. She'd said her piece, and he'd taken his sweet time to think about it. It was time for him to step up or walk away.

She'd been through that once, and she prayed that Jack was a better man than her husband had been.

"The thing is, you're alone too."

"Well, I have Chapter."

He dropped his head toward the gray tabby winding its way through his legs. "Right. A cat. But you don't have anyone to talk with. Anyone to share ideas and laugh with. And truth is, we've been doing a lot of that these last couple months."

"That's true. We have been."

He rubbed flat palms together before making fists. They were big hands. Strong and callused from years of manual labor. A mechanic who opened his own shop. Aged with spots and little white hairs at his knuckles, his hands were still capable.

"Do you hear what I'm saying?"

She shook her head, pulling back from an image of those

hands holding hers, caressing her face. "I'm sorry. What is it that you're trying to say?"

He paced a little more. Sat in the chair opposite her. Stood again. Marched. Then sat back down.

"I wasn't this nervous at twenty-five."

His words surprised her, and she took pity on him. She pushed herself to her feet, stepped in front of him, and held out her hands. He grabbed them like a lifeline, squeezing until she smiled.

"Jack, don't be nervous. Just tell me what's on your heart."

"You are."

She gasped. How was she supposed to respond to such a simple declaration? But she didn't have to. He wasn't done.

"For as foolhardy as those kids can be, Seth and Marie have both asked me what I want. And I realized tonight that what I want most is a second chance at life. Didn't even realize it until I was halfway in love with you. But I guess God knew what I needed."

"And Rose?"

He put a hand over his heart and took a loud breath. "She's always going to be here. But that doesn't mean she's going to be here." He motioned back and forth between them with his finger. "I asked God to help me honor her, and I do that by living. You're my answer to prayer."

Tears filled her eyes, and his face turned blurry. She reached out anyway, finding his cheek despite her temporary blindness. She smoothed a thumb over his wrinkles, and he leaned into her hand.

"That's the kindest thing anyone has ever said to me. I like being an answer to prayer."

"I like you."

She blinked, setting the tears in her eyes loose. As they ran down her cheeks, he leaned in, kissing them away. His lips were soft and warm, filling her heart with a need she'd thought long since forgotten.

"Please don't cry. I'm sorry it took me so long to realize what was right in front of me."

"I'll stop." She swallowed the lump in her throat. "On one condition."

"What's that?"

"Kiss me for real."

He met her condition with flying colors, pulling her close and sealing their deal in one easy motion.

◆◆◆◆◆

Marie jumped as Ruby Holt poked her in the ribs. "Turn the page," she whispered.

This was becoming far too much of a habit, and if she didn't start paying attention to the hymn singing, Ruby would take the book away. At least she hadn't torn a page in the hymnal yet that morning. Which was quite a feat given the set of eyes that had been staring at the back of her head the entire service.

At least it felt like he'd been staring.

She'd have been staring if she were sitting behind *him*.

As it was, the tingles going down her spine the entire service and the letter tucked into her pocket had been more than enough to distract her in her weekly hymnal-holding duties, and Caden's little niece had learned nothing about patience and understanding since they first shared a pew nearly two months before.

Marie had barely had a chance to read the letter after Seth

slipped it in her hand as he passed her on the lawn beneath the giant tree dressed in purple leaves. No words, no explanation. Just a gentle smile, his hand on hers, and an envelope tucked into her fingers.

She followed him with her gaze until he disappeared into the church behind Jack and Aretha, who were holding hands like they were on their way to the prom.

She'd had to hurry to make it into her place on the Holt family pew before Father Chuck began the service. And when she sat down, Seth had sat directly behind her.

It hadn't taken more than a quick scan of the letter—typed out on the trusty Underwood—to know exactly what it meant. What Seth wanted.

He wanted a second chance.

All she wanted was a chance to think things through without the weight of his gaze on her shoulders.

From his place at the front of the room, Father Chuck finished leading the hymn, and her duties were paused for a brief moment.

"Before we close the service with one of my favorite hymns, I want to remind you of a wonderful promise from the book of Matthew, chapter seven, verse eleven. 'If you then, being evil, know how to give good gifts to your children, how much more will your Father who is in heaven give good things to those who ask Him!' God isn't a vending machine to ask for the things that we want. Rather, he gives us what is best. He works the things of this world for the good of those who love him. He's the fountain of every blessing, the loving Father who longs to give us sweet gifts.

"Turn in your hymnals to number 273 as we close the service."

She began flipping pages as fast as she could, automatically curling into the inevitable jab if she didn't get there fast enough. At least the hymn had made it onto one page.

The pianist hammered out a quick introduction, and the church took a collective breath before launching into the first lines. "Come, Thou Fount of every blessing, tune my heart to sing Thy grace." The rest of the church continued on, but her voice fell silent. The first line rolled around in her mind over and over again until she could see the words on the backs of her eyelids. The fount of every blessing. Like the blessings fathers longed to give their daughters.

Her entire life she'd only been able to see God as distant and uncaring. If he was her heavenly Father, he must be like Elliot Carrington.

But what if he was like Jack Sloane? Intent on loving and blessing her, even when she had nothing to give him in return.

She swept a glance down the row to Caden, who gave her a quick smile. And then there were Aretha and Jack, snuggled together sharing a hymnal across the aisle. And Seth, his rich tenor joining in the chorus that swelled until it seemed the sanctuary's windowpanes would burst.

All of the terrible times had brought her here. To the island she loved, the home she'd hoped for, the blessings of a family she'd always wanted.

And a love she'd never expected.

On the third verse, the pianist stomped his foot and pounded the keys, and she joined in as the words rang through the ceiling beams.

"O to grace how great a debtor
Daily I'm constrained to be!

Let Thy goodness, like a fetter,
Bind my wandering heart to Thee."

Her voice trailed off, tears coming to her eyes. She didn't have a clue what a "fetter" was, but the goodness they sang about—she knew a thing or two about that. And it would keep her coming back to him over and over.

24

Marie forced herself to walk the path along the bay, wrinkling the paper in her hand as she strolled. It didn't matter—she'd memorized every word in Seth's letter by the fourth read, and she hadn't stopped there.

Like a confirmation of the good gifts God was pouring over her, the letter sealed her heart until it couldn't contain any more. She had to talk with him. Tell him everything.

Her pace picked up, feet pounding like they had the first time she'd run these boards. Except this time she wasn't broken by her past. Her future stood before her, and if his note was any indication, Seth was going to be an important part of it.

She crossed the street to the deserted beach, her steps slowing only to accommodate the give of the sand. But as she rounded the corner, eyes trained on Seth's spot, her motion stopped. The jetty was empty.

She looked at the envelope in her hands, then back at the rocks reaching into the clear blue water. He'd said his spot. He'd said he'd be there until dark. It was barely noon.

She'd rushed to change out of her church clothes and run to meet him.

And he wasn't there.

Tears tingled the corners of her eyes, but she rubbed them away, refusing to give in to the emotional letdown. White puffs dotted the sky's blue expanse, and she followed a particularly fast one. "God, I don't understand. What's going on?"

The sea-salt breeze carried her whisper to the heavens, but the rest of the world was silent save for the clapping waves and a stray seagull. She knelt on the sand, sat back on her heels, and bowed her head as the island's lullaby rocked her back and forth.

She could do nothing but wait for an answer.

If God was the fount of every blessing, then he heard her needs, knew the breaking of her heart and the insecurities that still lingered in the shadows there. He wouldn't leave her to face another disappointment alone, would he?

He'd never stopped caring for her before. Real fathers never did.

It brought a smile to her face as she rubbed her hands over her cheeks.

"Gosh, you're fast."

She whipped around at Seth's voice, nearly falling into the sand, but he beat her to it, dropping down beside her, his long limbs splayed.

"I've been chasing you since the Red Door. I was calling you, but you got to the fishing village and took off running." He panted, staring up at the sky from his flat position. "You should definitely look into running in a race."

Her heart galloped and her mouth dropped open, but the only response she could manage was a loud hiccup.

He jerked up, looking right into her eyes. "Hey. What's wrong?" He wiped a sandy hand across the leg of his jeans before brushing a crooked finger under her eye where a tear had gotten loose. "Why are you crying?"

"I'm not."

His smile grew with each moment, his eyes burning with something she couldn't name, but it called to her. "You're a bad liar. Especially when your perfect cheeks have tear tracks down them."

Her stomach swooped, and she had to look away, but he used that same finger to tilt her chin back up.

His smile waned, the line of his mouth turning serious, but the fire in his eyes never dimmed. "Tell me what's going on in that head of yours."

She shook her head. She couldn't tell him the whole truth.

You need to.

She tried to shush the voice in her head, but it was right. She couldn't deal in half truths and partial lies and expect to earn Seth's trust. If she forgave him, she had to act like it.

Taking a deep breath, she let it out in a deluge. "I was afraid you weren't going to show up. When you weren't here, I was worried that you'd changed your mind or forgotten or . . . I don't know."

He licked his lips, squinting at her like she was a piece of furniture up for auction. "You don't have to worry about that. I don't think I'll ever forget about you. And I'm not going to change my mind."

She swallowed as the hand that had been cupping her ear traveled down her neck, his fingertips brushing into the hair at her nape. Fire shot through her, every nerve in flames, every extremity blazing.

"Are you sure?" She closed her eyes as she took a deep breath, and opened them just before continuing. "You heard what I said to my dad, right?"

Anger flashed through his hazel eyes, and she leaned away. At least she tried to. But the tender hand under her chin held her still as compassion filled the crevices of his face. "I did." His Adam's apple bobbed. "And I am so sorry. I can't imagine how terrible that was—is." His lips pinched tight for a moment, little lines forming around the corners. The cleft in his chin quivered for a moment, and he blinked hard, but he never looked away. "I'll do whatever you want. I'll support you however you need to deal with this."

Her pulse thrummed, especially under his palm at her neck. "It took me a week to leave my house afterward. And I was in counseling for two months after that. But none of that was as good for me as just being here. Learning to feel safe around a man." And she did feel safe with him. Now.

"I scared you at first, didn't I?"

"Maybe. A little."

He lifted his eyebrows.

"All right. A lot." She pushed his shoulder. "You're just so big. But it's not so bad when you have your arms around me." Heat rushed up her neck.

Oh, she hadn't meant to say that out loud.

He chuckled. "I'm okay with that." Slipping an arm around her shoulders, he tugged her against his chest, a wall of muscle beneath her head and the steady beats of his heart under her ear.

It was easier to talk to him when she didn't have to look into his eyes, and she let herself open up about the things that she'd never admitted to another soul. Some things she'd barely acknowledged to herself. "After everything that happened in Boston, I convinced myself that God was like my dad. It was easier to picture a God who didn't hear my prayers than a God who had heard and let it happen anyway. I wanted to be angry. And I had this uncontrollable reminder of that night with every panic attack."

His muscles tensed against her back. "For a while there at the beginning when you had attacks, I thought you were dying," he said.

"For a while, so did I." She closed her eyes as his heartbeat slowed to a more normal rhythm. "I hated them. I felt so weak, so defeated. Like it was God's cruel reminder that Derek had won. Over and over. So I kept telling myself that God didn't hear me, but I still called out for him to rescue me with every attack. Because even though I told myself he didn't care, I desperately wanted him to."

"And what have you decided about that?"

A gull swooped low, landing on the beach and digging for a leftover treat. "Just that God longed to give me good gifts. What came before got me to right here, right now, and made me more thankful for them than I could have been before. After all, he gave me a family I never expected, Jack and Aretha, Caden, and . . ." Her voice trailed off as she suddenly recognized she'd been about to name him as her sweetest gift. At least he couldn't see the blush covering her face at that angle.

He cleared his throat. "I'm not a perfect man."

"Oh, really?" She laid the sarcasm on a little too thick.

"Hey, you didn't have to agree so quickly." He bobbed his shoulder, bouncing her head, but she found her spot again, safely tucked into his side.

"I was kidding. Go on. Tell me about your imperfections."

Now it was his turn for a bit of teasing. "Well, there are so few of them. And they're hardly noticeable. So you're a very lucky woman."

She wrapped her hands around his waist, pulling him close as his heart kicked into overdrive.

She'd done that. She'd made his pulse race like an express train. It stole her breath. Not a panic attack or anything resembling fear. Just shortened breaths caught up in the hope for what might lay ahead of them.

His hand moved in slow circles on her back, and she lifted her head to kiss the underside of his smooth jaw, the scent of aftershave still clinging to him.

"You shaved."

He nodded, catching her chin where it was tilted toward him. "I promised I would."

A roller coaster couldn't have made her insides fly apart faster. He'd made that promise after their first kiss. About their next kisses.

She'd hoped. She'd come to this spot hoping for at least one more kiss. And maybe more. She didn't know what the future would bring or what exactly she was ready for.

But she was definitely ready for one more kiss.

He was too. That simple fact sent her falling against him, knocking him into the sand, and half lying on top of him. "What were you expecting, Seth?"

His grin was slow and crooked, and he leaned up until only inches separated their lips. He cupped her cheeks with his hands, his breath fanning her face. "Nothing. I wasn't expecting anything. I was just praying you'd give me a second chance."

"I'm not going to lie." Her words were barely a whisper, and the way his gaze had zeroed onto her lips, he was probably reading them. "I was expecting ice cream."

He licked his lips. "I forgot my wallet." His words were serious, but she could see the humor flickering in his eyes.

"Never stopped you before."

"The kid at the ice cream shop refused me a second chance. You won't be as cruel, will you?"

She shook her head and touched her lips to his. Like lightning touching a pine tree, her world exploded, and she jolted back.

Seth's expression matched her own surprise. But he quickly recovered, tucking her hair behind her ear and smiling. "I guess that's a yes to the second chance?"

"I suppose." And just to make sure he didn't have to doubt it, she kissed him once more. The sand under her knees shifted as she lost herself to the tender touch of his hand on her back and the whispered brush of his knuckles along her jaw.

This was what it felt like to be cherished.

Heart swelling, she closed her eyes against the sweet torture of being so near to this man who made her lose her breath in the best possible way. When she finally pulled away and nestled into his neck, he smelled of salt and lumber and the inn they both loved.

"And just how many second chances do you think you're going to need, Seth Sloane?"

"I don't know, but I sure hope they all come with kisses like that."

She did too.

◆◆◆◆◆

Seth squeezed Marie's hand, tugging her closer to his side.

She shot him a look of frustration that made him laugh and reached with her free hand to snag another cream puff off of Caden's silver tray. "These are so good," she sighed, popping the whole thing into her mouth. She groaned in delight. "It's like she took cooking lessons in heaven."

He laughed again, bumping into Caden's mom and Aretha, who were appraising the antique furniture and decorations in the dining room. Aretha winked as though seeing them hold hands was something new.

"You've done an amazing job with this old place, Marie." Caden's mom—whose name he could not remember—nodded in appreciation at the framed seascapes along the walls.

"I wish I could take credit for it, but nearly everything in the Red Door is from Aretha's store. She's the one with excellent taste. I just borrowed from it."

Aretha glowed, pushing her hands out and passing the compliment on.

"I especially love the Montgomery Suite upstairs. The quilt with the quote about dreams is amazing."

His heart skittered, praying that during the endless tours no one had noticed what he'd left in that room.

"Thank you. That was a fun day—finding all those quilts." Marie tightened her grip on his hand, and he knew the memories she recalled. The auction. The time in his truck. The first time he'd ever opened up to her.

He'd been halfway in love with her even then but too inane to realize it.

As the women wandered off, Marie hooked her arm through his. They leaned against the wall, watching their friends mingle and mix. A large group, led by Father Chuck, lined the antique buffet, taking hearty helpings of Caden's treats.

Marie pushed to her tiptoes and leaned on his shoulder. "I knew that was going to be popular. Just wait until the guests arrive next week. It'll be perfect."

"Yes, it will." Just like her.

He smoothed her hair from the top of her head down to her cheek and leaned in to kiss her lips. At the last second, he decided their audience might not appreciate such a display, so he pressed his lips against her forehead, a promise of things to come.

Just as he pulled back, Jack stepped to the front of the room, raising his hands and calling for their attention. A hush fell across the crowd, smiling faces all turned to his uncle. By his side, Aretha buzzed with anticipation and excitement.

"You know I'm not a man of many words. So I'll keep this brief. Just want to thank you for coming out tonight and for what you all have done to make my Rose's dream a reality."

Marie slipped away, ducking into the kitchen and returning before Jack had even gotten to the next line of his speech.

"I know she'd be proud of this place and the people who work here. Caden, we're so happy to have you on board."

Her round face crinkled into a smile.

"And Seth and Marie, come on up here."

Marie led the winding way, never letting go of his hand. It was a mystery how someone so small could fill him with such joy, but he'd follow her until he figured it out.

"You know none of this would have happened without you two."

"I hope you mean that as a good thing." The room roared

at Marie's quip, and she grinned at them. "Seth and I wanted to give you something, Jack. The Red Door means so much to both of us, and we wanted to remember whose dream it was in the first place."

Jack's brows folded together as he accepted the paper-wrapped package she held out. With shaking hands, he pulled off the string and paper to reveal the photograph of the home three-quarters of a century before. The brass plaque ran along the bottom of the glass.

In a whisper, Jack read the inscription. "In memory of Rose, who prayed that hearts would find healing in this home. Rose's Red Door Inn."

Tears welled in Jack's eyes as he leaned over to show it to Aretha. She didn't try to contain her emotions, her hands covering her mouth as drops rolled down her cheeks.

"We thought the inn should be named after the woman who inspired it," Seth said.

"Thank you." The words weren't loud enough to hear, but Seth felt them as Jack slapped him on the back and pulled him into a hug. "I'd have wanted a son like you."

The back of his own throat suddenly felt scratchy, and he had to turn away to pull himself together. Rose's prayer had been answered. God had already healed at least three hearts here.

Much later, after the house was nearly empty and only the very best of friends still lingered, Seth whispered in Marie's ear, "I want to show you something."

Her eyebrows arched, but she didn't ask any questions, just followed him to the stairs that led to the back bedroom—the Montgomery Suite.

"Where are you kids off to?" Aretha's teasing voice caught

them just at the foot of the staircase. When they turned, Jack was hurrying to catch them.

"I've been meaning to ask what your plans are." Jack's voice was gruff, still plagued by the emotion of the night.

Seth shrugged and Marie shook her head. "We haven't had much time to talk about it yet," she said.

Jack held on to Aretha, looking down at her as she nodded her encouragement. "We've been talking." He lifted the back of Aretha's hand to his mouth, kissing it until she nearly glowed. "We love the Red Door—Rose's Red Door—but running an inn and an antique shop doesn't leave much time for newlyweds—"

Marie squealed, wrapping her arms around Aretha's neck and holding tight. "You're getting married? When?"

Aretha tittered with delight. "This summer."

Seth chuckled, pulling his uncle into a hug. "I should have guessed. You two have been thick as thieves lately. When did you decide?"

"Last night. When you're our age, there's no time to waste. Why put it off?" Once extracted from the embrace, Jack wrapped his arm back around Aretha's waist.

"I'm so happy for you." Marie sighed, holding her folded hands under her chin as her gaze traveled back and forth between them, pure joy in her smile. But it was the look in her eyes that made his stomach jump.

She wanted that for herself. She wasn't ready now. Maybe she wouldn't be ready very soon. But down the road. Someday.

Someday she'd wear white and walk down an aisle.

What nearly bowled him over was realizing how much he wanted to be the man waiting for her. And he *would* wait for her, right by her side. No matter how long it took.

Jack winked at Marie. "Since our sweet girl was hiding a Wharton MBA under a coat of paint—"

She covered her cheeks. "I tried to tell you. I tried to help."

"I know you did. I just wasn't ready to hear it. I knew there was more to you than you let on. You're one impressive young lady." With a wrinkled hand, he squeezed her elbow. "Since you both love this place as much as we do, and since you've got that fancy education . . . Well, your dad, he was wrong. This is the perfect place for you to use all that learning. And we couldn't be more proud of you."

Marie's eyes turned watery, her bottom lip trembling as she leaned into Seth's arm.

"That is, if you want to. We'd love for you and Seth to run the Red Door and take over all the day-to-day functions. It'll be Seth's inheritance someday anyway."

Marie bit her still quivering lip, hope flickering in her eyes like the sun reflecting on Rustico Harbor.

"We need to go to Boston at some point this summer." The grip on his arm tightened, and he patted Marie's hand. He wasn't going to let her face anything there alone. "But we'll talk about it."

"Of course," Aretha said. "You know where to find us when you decide."

The older couple wandered off, hand in hand, leaving him right where he wanted to be. Alone with Marie.

"I heard him bragging on your MBA to Father Chuck during the party. He couldn't be more proud if you were his blood."

Her cheeks turned pink, and she ducked her head. "The thing is, my dad was never really proud of me."

She hadn't said much more about her dad since that afternoon on the beach, and the tremor in her voice made him want to punch the man. Instead he slipped his arms around her waist and pulled her to his chest. "He wasn't?"

She shook her head until her ear settled in the center of his chest. "It was more about the prestige of having a Wharton graduate with the Carrington name. It was a status symbol among his friends, proof that his family was smarter and richer and . . . Well, I love Jack for caring like he does."

She stepped back, shaking her shoulders as though she could brush off every hurtful reminder of her dad. "So what is this thing you wanted to show me?"

He led her to the suite, around the foot of the bed, and to the antique writing table she'd made him carry from the auction. On top of the table sat her beloved typewriter. And in it a fresh sheet of paper.

"I left you a note."

She bent over to read the lines.

Dear M,
   I was afraid to love you. I'm not anymore.
   S

As she straightened up, a slow smile spread across her mouth. She wrapped her arms around his waist and licked her lips with the tip of her tongue. "I'm not afraid either."

He leaned forward until their foreheads pressed together and his breath stirred her hair. "What is it about this place?"

"I don't know, but there sure is something special beyond the red door."

Read an excerpt from
the next book in the

PRINCE
EDWARD
ISLAND
DREAMS

series.

Coming Fall 2016

1

There was only one thing better than the smell of freshly baked cinnamon rolls in the morning. The *taste* of freshly baked cinnamon rolls in the morning.

Caden Holt pulled a pan of piping hot sweet rolls from the bottom of her double oven, breathing in the intoxicating aroma and tapping the golden-crisp top of a roll to the rhythm of her favorite Broadway soundtrack. Her mouth watered and her toe tapped as she slathered a bun with her signature cream cheese icing. The white glaze oozed down the side of the treat, and she caught the errant drip with her knuckle. Closing her eyes, she licked her finger clean before tearing off a corner and popping it in her mouth.

A tremor swirled down her back as sweet, sweet sugar exploded in her mouth, everything good and right with the world.

It only took three more bites to finish off her usual morning treat—after all, she had to make sure breakfast for the guests was up to par—and she immediately regretted devouring it. All that was left was a drop of icing on the scalding pan. But a chef didn't fear heat. She'd gotten second-degree burns from less worthy causes.

After peeking over her shoulder to make sure she was still alone in her sanctuary, only the morning sun for company, she touched her finger to the tip of her tongue, scooped up the dribble, and licked it clean.

The sweets this morning would certainly pass muster, but she hadn't even started on the main dish. While breakfast desserts were her favorite part of a meal, she didn't work at a bed-and-breakfast pastry. As the executive chef of Rose's Red Door Inn, she was expected to make a full meal to start every guest's day off right.

Muted footfalls and hushed voices trickled from the floor above, promising that said guests would soon be poking their noses into the dining room, looking to fill their empty stomachs.

But for the next thirty minutes, she had the kitchen all to herself. Utterly, entirely, blissfully to herself. And the original London cast of *Mamma Mia!*

Lisa Stokke belted out her solo through the speakers tucked into the corner of the counter between a fully equipped stand mixer and canisters of the essentials. As Lisa's voice rose, Caden turned a wild pirouette that would have had her forever banned from the Great White Way—not that she'd ever been there, or on any stage for that matter. She slammed into the kitchen island and bounced off the refrigerator, grabbing the edge of the counter to keep from tumbling all the way to the floor.

Her foot caught on the corner of a cabinet, and she laughed out loud as Lisa hit her high note and Caden hit her low point. Arms flailing as she fell, Caden scrambled for anything that would help her stay upright. She managed to grab hold of a single sheet of white printer paper hanging from the silver clip on the refrigerator. As soon as she tugged it free, her rear end hit the floor and she lost her grip on the page, which—aided by the fan in the far corner—slithered between the fridge and the nearest cabinet.

"No. No. No." She shifted to her knees and crawled toward the black hole that had swallowed that morning's instructions.

Caden's boss, Marie, always left a list of special guest instructions on that clip. Food allergies. Gluten sensitivities. Young guests with picky palates. It all seemed innocent enough until one guest the previous summer had failed to mention his peanut allergy upon registration. Caden's famous peanut butter and jelly French toast had nearly sent him into anaphylactic shock. He was one forkful of deliciousness away from a serious emergency when his wife noticed his hives and rushed him to the hospital in Charlottetown. He'd made a full recovery and joked later that he'd married his wife for her observation skills.

But the memory still made Caden's insides squirm.

Food had such a strange and wonderful power. Wielding it made her feel simultaneously significant and vulnerable, fearsome and fragile.

To do her job well she needed the piece of paper glaring at her from the depths of the crack between wooden cabinet and stainless steel appliance. The unmoving refrigerator stood like a sentinel, refusing to budge from its guard. She tried to reach the page anyway, poking her chubby fingers into the crevice, but they didn't make it much beyond her fingernails. Maybe if she could just slide the fridge over.

She leaned her shoulder into its side, but it only groaned, taunting her to try again.

She did and got the same result.

Kneeling between the cabinets and island, she put her hands on her hips and huffed a sigh that sent a wisp of hair that had escaped her French braid floating up. And right back into her face.

She needed something long and narrow. With pinchers.

Tongs.

She pulled herself up on the edge of the alternating white and black counter tiles before rifling through the middle drawer next to the dishwasher. Spatulas and spoons tumbled about as she dug for the tongs she usually used to flip bacon. The tangled utensils scraped together, nearly falling onto the floor as she stretched her fingers to find what she was looking for.

Finally she hooked a handle with the crook of her finger and yanked it—and a deformed whisk—free.

Caden arched her wrist and sent the whisk toward the trash can, its wire loops swishing down the plastic liner.

She laughed to herself. "Two points."

Just as the cast of *Mamma Mia!* burst into the rousing show closer, she lowered herself back to the floor. The tip of her tongs clicked to the rhythm of the song as she hunched over her prey, eyeing it for the right angle. She moved in slowly, deliberately, trying not to disturb the sheet until it was safely in her grasp.

She just . . . had . . . to . . .

"Rats!"

Even as she bumped the corner of the paper, she recognized her mistake.

The paper fluttered, loosened by her miscalculation, and slid beneath the fridge, completely out of reach.

Just. Perfect.

She scrubbed her hand down her cheek and scratched behind her ear. Maybe if she glared at the spot where the paper had vanished, it would miraculously reappear. That was about as likely as a lobster crawling into her boiling pot.

Two loud footfalls right above her head make Caden jump, and she spun in the direction of the clock on the microwave. Thirty minutes until breakfast time. Fifteen until Marie came to check in and began serving the first course, a fresh fruit salad Caden had prepared the night before.

She'd run out of time to whip up the seafood quiche she'd written onto the large calendar hanging by the door to the dining room. At this point, scrambled eggs and roasted potatoes would have to do.

But first—the allergy list.

Marie sometimes left a copy of the manifest in her office, so Caden hurried down the hallway from the kitchen to the little room between the living quarters and the rest of the inn. Seth, Marie's husband, had built the nook into the restored home just so that his wife would have a place to manage the inn's daily goings-on.

Caden tried to step lightly—no easy feat—on the seventy-five-year-old wooden floors. They seemed to creak and moan even when she hadn't taken a step. It wasn't until she had almost reached the door that she realized it was partly open, and soft voices echoed within.

"It can't be as bad as that." The deep voice belonged to Seth Sloane, but it didn't sound much like the contractor turned innkeeper who had swept Marie off her feet. It was as thick as the red clay that gave Prince Edward Island its famous color. He cleared his throat, but it didn't help much when he continued. "There has to be something left. We had a good season last year."

"But we're only half booked for this summer." Marie sounded just as strained as her husband. "After this week, we have at least two empty rooms all season."

"Maybe they'll fill. Maybe we'll get another guest for all of June and July. Maybe that princess bride will decide to uncancel her wedding and the whole party will rebook and stay an extra week . . ."

"That's a lot of maybes."

Caden held her breath, wishing she could somehow sneak back to the kitchen and ignore the tremor in Marie's tone, but knowing she couldn't leave until she had her instructions. She raised her hand to knock just as Seth spoke.

"Maybe if we talk to your—"

"No." Marie lost all hint of uncertainty, her tone sharper than Caden had ever heard it before. "We're not—"

Caden spun at Marie's outburst, the floor shrieking like a never-ending fireworks display.

"Morning, Caden." Seth sounded both surprised and relieved to suddenly notice her presence.

She turned back, an apologetic smile slapped into place as she pushed the door open a few inches more. "I'm sorry to interrupt. It's just that the instructions fell under the refrigerator, and I need to get breakfast going."

The tightness in Marie's jaw didn't release, even as she shot a glare at her husband, who managed an unrepentant shrug. Then she turned to the computer and printed out another page with the guests' details. Her motions were sharp and controlled, her frown fixed in place.

"Here you go." Marie's voice held none of the tension that seemed to permeate the room, but there was a sadness in her eyes that sent Caden backpedaling as fast as she could.

Marie and Seth remained silent as she hurried down the hall, and when the door swung shut behind her, Caden let out a whoosh of air.

Whatever was going on in there, she didn't want any part of it.

Except that Marie was her best friend.

And what she'd heard sounded like the Red Door might be in trouble.

Which meant they were all in trouble.

A slamming door on the second floor jolted her into action. Scanning the page in her hand, she made note of two lactose sensitivities and one pineapple allergy. No cheese on the eggs for some of those guests. And the fruit salad was a simple apple, blueberry, and peach concoction. No problem there.

As she whisked a dozen eggs in a glass mixing bowl, she glanced out the kitchen window, enjoying the view of her herb garden and a corner of the bay beyond their neighbor's back porch and a narrow field of wildflowers.

She'd spent her whole life staring at that same patch of rippling blue. And though the kitchen had changed, the view from the window over the sink was always the same. The morning sun caught the tip of a wave, and it sparkled like a diamond.

Not that she'd ever owned one.

Caden glanced down at her empty ring finger and sighed as she covered the bottom of her skillet with a nonstick spray. It popped against the hot pan, and she poured the beaten eggs over it, bubbles immediately forming in the yellow mixture.

As she stirred the eggs, she risked another glance out the window.

A man stood between the inn and the water. He was far enough away that she couldn't make out his features or even tell if she recognized him. He certainly wasn't one of their neighbors, all of whom had a distinct stoop and slow stroll. But there was an appealing easiness to his gait, and she watched him walk the shoreline. As he bent to pick up a small duffel bag, his shoulders pushed at the fabric of his leather jacket. No one in this area wore that kind of coat. A gust of wind fluttered his dark hair, and he ran his fingers through the loose strands in an infinitely male move.

Nope. She didn't know him.

She'd have noticed a guy like that walking around town. North Rustico wasn't big enough to hide in.

After all, she'd been trying to hide here for years.

It never worked.

She stirred the fluffy eggs, giving them another dash of salt and pepper. And just a hint of garlic for good measure.

The door between the kitchen and dining room swung in, sweeping Marie's chipper greeting to the waiting guests with it. "Breakfast will be right out."

Caden turned and raised her eyebrows in question.

"Breakfast will be right out. Won't it?" Marie's brown curls had crossed the line from fun to frazzled, and the apron she looped over her head didn't help the situation. Whatever she and Seth had been talking about that morning had left her in a knot, so Caden squelched the urge to tease her boss.

"Fruit is in serving dishes in the fridge."

Marie already had half of them loaded on the silver tray, scooping them up and whisking back through the swinging door.

Oohs and aahs over the crystal goblets of mixed fruit carried in from the dining room, and Caden couldn't help the rush of pride through her middle as she plated scrambled eggs and roasted red potatoes, adding a cinnamon roll platter for each table.

With each swing of the door, Marie scooped up more plates, the lines around her mouth easing until an actual smile fell into place.

"This is so good," one guest mumbled around a mouthful of food. "What's in these eggs?"

Marie giggled, and Caden's heart gave a little leap of joy. She could easily imagine her boss sidling up to a table and giving everyone there a saucy wink. *Our chef only makes the best.*

Except Marie didn't say that. She didn't say anything about how Caden hunted out fresh eggs three times a week from the hens at Kane Dairy. She didn't say that Caden started her day at five each morning to make sure every guest was full and happy before leaving to explore the island. And she didn't say that Caden had a knack for serving up the best sweet rolls in town.

In fact, Marie didn't say a word about Caden at all.

"That's our little secret." And she left it at that.

A fist in her stomach sent Caden doubling over against the sink, head hanging low and heart even lower.

She loved this job. She loved this kitchen. She loved Marie. But lately it felt like they might not love her back.

"Excuse me."

Caden's head snapped up at the unfamiliar voice, but she had to duck into the laundry room to find the source.

Face-to-face with the man from the beach, she yanked on the strings of her apron as she stared into his unblinking gray eyes. But the bow at her waist caught in a knot. Her fingers suddenly forgetful, she fumbled with the fabric.

He had poked his head through the back door, holding the screen with one hand and his leather jacket in the other, one foot on the ground and the other on the outside step.

The planes of his face didn't shift, and the muscles at his throat stood in sharp relief to his otherwise relaxed pose. Which she only just realized blocked the bag she'd seen him carrying earlier. His deep brown hair was ruffled, standing on end above his right temple like he'd fallen asleep with his fingers combed through his hair and his head resting in his hand, and his jaw was darkened with at least a day's worth of beard.

"Are you Marie Carrington Sloane?"

Caden glanced over her shoulder, half expecting to see Marie materialize, but she remained alone. Alone with a man who knew Marie's maiden name. No one used her maiden name.

Especially not Marie.

"No." She dragged the word out, still jerking at the knot at the back of her waist, desperate to be free of her apron. "Can I help you with something?"

"This is Rose's Red Door Inn." And then, like he wasn't quite sure, "Isn't it? They said it was the big blue house between the boardwalk and the water."

She nodded slowly. "Yes. The one with the red front door. And a sign out front."

That earned a quarter smile as he let go of the door, holding it in place with his shoulder—a rather broad shoulder at that—and grabbed a brown leather journal from the back pocket of his jeans. It wasn't much bigger than his palm, but as he thumbed through several pages, she could see that tiny scribbles filled every crevice and corner. Folding the notebook at the spine, his finger ran the lines until he nodded and looked up. "Rose's Red Door Inn. North Rustico, Prince Edward Island. Marie Carrington Sloane, proprietor."

He offered only the facts and no commentary. Who talked like that?

"And Seth too." The words popped out before she'd really considered them, but something about the way he kept saying Marie's full name made her insides churn and the hair on the back of her neck jump to attention.

He wouldn't be a guest. They only arrived between three and seven. They never used the back door. And they most certainly never invaded her kitchen.

His forehead wrinkled as he gave his book another once-over, so she expounded. "Seth Sloane. Marie's husband. Co-owner."

Squinting harder at the page in his hand, he shook his head.

Well, he could shake it all he wanted. That didn't make Seth's presence any less real. Or Caden any more inclined to let this guy loiter on her back stoop. She pressed her hands to her waist and pulled herself up to her full height. Which wasn't considerable. But what she lacked in height, she made up for in breadth. And she used all the generous width of her hips as she marched toward him, praying that he would just back away.

Then she could go tell Marie about this strange visitor.

But he didn't budge. He just closed one eye in an almost wink and stared up at her. "Sorry. I didn't get that note. My editor—Garrett de Root—he made the arrangements."

"What arrangements?"

His gaze suddenly jumped over her shoulder, and she followed it.

"Caden? Is everything all right?" Marie's hands were full of empty breakfast dishes, which she carried like she'd spent her college years in the service industry. Although that was far from the truth.

"This guy—" She flung a hand at the mystery man, who promptly stepped inside and reached out his hand.

"Adam Jacobs."

Marie looked at the stacks in her arms and managed only a shrug. "Adam?"

"Yes, ma'am. I believe Garrett de Root contacted you about reserving a room for me."

Marie's half smile turned into a frown. "I wasn't expecting you until tomorrow. I don't have an open room tonight."

Acknowledgments

The characters on these pages aren't the only ones who helped get this book in your hands. Please let me thank just a few in real life.

Katie Schroder, Amy Haddock, Ashley Hendley, Kristi Smith, Ruth Anderson, and Kaye Dacus. Thank you for forgiving all the times I disappeared into my writing cave and failed to keep in touch. When I crawled out, you were always there cheering me on. True friends are hard to find, and I'm grateful for each of you.

Michelle Ule, early reader and red-pen wielder. Your feedback on the first draft of this book was invaluable. Thank you!

Todd and Mel Hirte. Thank you for your endless support and many prayers. You've waited for this book almost as long as I have, and now I'm so happy to share it with you.

Karmen Leggett, English and literature teacher extraordinaire. You selflessly poured into me during my school years, encouraging my love of literature and pushing me to truly grasp grammar. Thank you for your encouragement.

Vicki Crumpton, Jessica English, Michele Misiak, and the whole Revell team. What an honor it is to partner with you on this publishing adventure.

Rachel Kent, the best agent a gal could ask for. Thank you for never giving up on this project. Your prayers, advice, and support mean the world to me. I'm so glad you're in my corner.

Julia, Emily, Rachel, Jacob, and Caleb. I'm honored to be your aunt. You are my favorite characters!

Micah and Beth and John and Hannah. Thanks for cheering me on all these years. I'm lucky to be your sister.

Mom. Because of your love, I never feared taking a leap of faith. This book is evidence of that.

Dad. Thanks for being a shining reflection of our heavenly Father. It's hard to imagine God could love me any more than you do.

And, of course, the Great Storyteller. God, your story blows me away. I'm honored to be a tiny part of it. All to your glory.

Liz Johnson fell in love with Prince Edward Island the first time she set foot on it. When she's not plotting her next trip to the island, she works as a full-time marketing manager. She finds time to write late at night and is the author of nine novels, a *New York Times* bestselling novella, and a handful of short stories. She makes her home in Nashville, Tennessee, where she enjoys listening to local music, exploring the area's history, and making frequent trips to Arizona to dote on her five nieces and nephews.

Meet
LIZ JOHNSON

LizJohnsonBooks.com

| Read her BLOG | Follow her SPEAKING SCHEDULE | Connect with her on SOCIAL MEDIA |